BLOOD:
the Color of Cranberries

A NOVEL

PAMELIA BARRATT

Plowshare Media
LA JOLLA, CALIFORNIA

Library of Congress Control Number: 2008942424
Barratt, Pamelia
Blood: the Color of Cranberries

ISBN: 978-0-9821145-0-6 (paperback edition)

Published by:
Plowshare Media
P.O. Box 278
La Jolla, CA 92038

PUBLISHER'S NOTE

This is a work of fiction.
While, as in all fiction, the literary perceptions and insights are
based on experience, all names, characters, places and incidents either
are the products of the author's imagination or are used fictitiously,
and any resemblance to actual persons, living or dead,
business establishments, events, or locales, is entirely coincidental.
No reference to any real person is intended,
except for the obvious, recognizable, public figures.

For information about permission to
reproduce selections of this book, write to:
Permissions, Plowshare Media, P.O. Box 278, La Jolla, CA 92038
or visit PLOWSHAREMEDIA.COM

In memory of my parents, Kingsley and Dorothy Colton

Contents

PROLOGUE

The Totogatic is the smaller river of the two, wilder and less known. When it flows into the Namekagon, like a bride reaching the altar, she loses her name but not her influence. Rivers wed, mix until their currents are one. This process repeats itself at each confluence, when the Namekagon flows into the St Croix, and then again, when the St. Croix flows into the Mississippi.

People want to know the big story, that of the mighty Mississippi, but even the tales of its tiniest tributaries can be important.

This is a story from Spring Creek and Bean Brook.

I

RIVULETS FROM CHICAGO

CHAPTER 1

Preston stayed downstairs when his mother went up to bed. He told her he would soon follow but too much had happened that day to even try to sleep. He sat in Tim's rocker again watching the fire, savoring the memory of his presence. It still amazed Press that his brother had wanted to live up here in the North Woods. For six years he had lived in this small house. Press got up to stoke the fire, reverently repeating a ritual that Tim must have done a thousand times.

By midnight, the last log was in embers. Press put on his coat to go outside and fetch more wood. He heard the satisfying crunch his steps made breaking through frost, but when he looked ahead to the wood pile it seemed to go in and out of focus. Disoriented, he gazed upward and saw the northern lights for the first time ever. The shimmering colors in the sky were mesmerizing. If Tim were standing next to him, he would have explained their cause and called them "aurora borealis." Shortly, the ghostly fluctuations stirred up feelings of uncertainty in Press. He was confused about Tim's death and felt the need to decipher just what had happened.

With a fresh log on the fire, Press settled back in the rocker and began to review in earnest what he knew of Tim's life after he had moved to Wisconsin. His first recollection was in the early spring of 1913 when Press himself was still a junior at Amherst. A letter came from Tim. It began:

> *I finally found the piece of property suitable for growing cranberries, that is, one that is suitable that I can afford! It is a tract of 163 acres, located on the Namekagon River.*
>
> *I had to look up north in the so-called 'North Woods' because property in the middle of the state—the glacial lake*

area—was too dear....

This was the first time Press had heard about the Namekagon River. Before going to college, he had lived most of his life in central Illinois, so he could excuse himself for not knowing about a river in northwest Wisconsin. The letter went on:

...I had to dig into the peat in a variety of places, each time tasting the oozing liquid to be sure the soil was sufficiently acidic....

Wasn't that just like Tim? I'll bet he even smacked his lips, Preston thought.

Press had shared the letter with some of the others in his fraternity. Most remembered Tim because he had just graduated after the last school year. A fish out of water, more intellectual and focused than Press and his other, athletic frat brothers, Tim had never caught on to the subtleties that distinguish one fraternity from another. To him, the fraternity was just a place to sleep when he stopped studying plants.

Nonetheless, Preston was glad he had joined the same fraternity as his brother. He smiled thinking that they both probably would have chosen their father's fraternity (as well as his college) had there been fraternities back in the 1870s. Would they have gone to a different college if Dad hadn't suddenly died? Press doubted it. By that time, their Dad had already taught them Amherst's anthem, which Press started to sing softly while cleaning his room:

Oh, oh, oh...

Lord Jeffrey Amherst was the soldier of the king and he came from across the sea.

To the Frenchman and the Indians he didn't do a thing in the wilds of this wild country...

Singing made Press recall Tim's deep bass voice. It was always a pleasure to hear him sing. It amused Press to remember how his brother's personality seemed to change when he sang. 'In voice,' Tim opened up, became expressive, even charming!

Press smiled to think how different they were from each

other. After their dad died and their mom decided to move the family to the South Side of Chicago to be close to other relatives, Press found it pretty easy to adjust to the move. He made friends with some boys on the block who shared his interest in horseless buggies. They competed with one another to learn the most about automobiles.

Yes, we got into a bit of mischief, but no harm was intended. If only we could have restarted Mr. Perkins' car and driven it back to his house, no one would have ever known, he mused. Anyway, Press knew the move to Chicago had been a blessing for him. There were so many more horseless carriages there than in Princeton.

Tim's interests kept him at home, mostly, experimenting with the plants that he grew. When he went out, it was to the library or the botanical gardens. Press knew his mom approved of the direction in which Tim was going. She liked his orderliness and predictability. Press' main interest was automobiles and they frightened her. He would have to do something about that.

He was glad the royalties from all those textbooks his dad had written gave his mom a steady income, and he was grateful his dad had left money for both him and his brother. It wasn't a huge amount, but enough that Tim could venture into becoming a cranberry grower in Northern Wisconsin.

...It's a fine peat bog covered with brown brush which I'll have to scalp off. It's surrounded by a forest. The virgin trees are all gone, of course. The timbermen got to most of this area ten years ago, but jack pine, blue spruce, Norways, and white pine abound. Around water there are quaking aspen, poplars, and willows....

Tim's letter didn't mention a nearby town, but Press noticed the return address said "Springbrook, Wisconsin." It sounded so isolated.

When Preston graduated a year later, he looked forward to moving back to Chicago. He enjoyed the bustling city life, not to mention the numerous and increasing number of motorcars there. The town of Amherst was too slow-paced for his liking. He had made several good friends at the college. Many liked to ride in and drive automobiles, but few were very interested in their engines. Now that he had completed college, perhaps he could celebrate by spending a little of his inheritance. He would love to have his own motor to work on. A nice little runabout might be just the thing to help him meet girls.

So Preston moved back in with his mother who was eager for him to find employment. Her spacious apartment on Kenwood Avenue was well situated for his search, being just a few blocks from the horse-drawn tramway. Not really knowing what type of work he should look for, Preston spent most of the time visiting dealerships. He had no intention of buying a new car because he thought he should spend only a small fraction of his legacy. Even a used car with the new internal combustion engine would probably be too dear. He consoled himself with the thought that the efficiency of such motors still needed to be verified.

One day he walked into the Stanley Dealership on Halsted Street. The salesman pounced on him saying: "The steamers are very reliable motorcars—much safer than the hand-cranked petrol cars. A man I know had his arm broken on one of those when the crank shaft backfired on him."

Preston, not wanting to reveal how much he knew, remained quiet, but he was fully aware that the newly-invented electric starter motor had eliminated that problem.

"Can you show me your second-hand cars?" His eye had already caught sight of a cute little runabout in the back corner of the shop.

"The steam engine is so simple, less than 25 moveable parts! And you can burn anything to boil the water—very flexible. You don't need a multi-speed transmission. It reacts instantaneously if you want more power."

I guess I'm going to have to hear his whole spiel, before he'll answer my question, Press thought. I don't want to appear too eager. "Uh huh," he said to the salesman.

"There are just two levers—one here allows you to adjust the amount of steam sent to the engine. It acts with a hand-operated accelerator. Another lever controls the amount of fuel for the main burner."

"Uh huh."

An hour later, Preston had more information than he wanted and had bargained to buy the Model 62 Stanley Steamer runabout in the corner for $700, with its canvas top thrown into the deal. He picked up written material on the car and looked forward to explaining it all to his mother. He drove home in his new acquisition a happy man.

Press spent days learning how each part of his Stanley worked. He almost hoped to find a malfunction so that he would have an excuse to fix it. One day, he noticed a neighbor smirking at him. Then he remembered who he was—Mr. Perkins—the man who years ago owned the Rambler that he and his friends had "borrowed" one night for a little teenage fun.

Owning a Stanley had marvelous advantages. Now he could offer to take Marjorie Langtry for a spin up to Lincoln Park for a picnic. He tried to get his mother interested in the Stanley, explaining that the boiler was in front of the passengers.

"Yes, I've heard about that 'coffin-nose,'" his mother replied. Nonetheless, towards the end of the summer, Preston had successfully talked her into driving with him up north to visit Tim in Wisconsin.

By that time, Tim had built himself a small house adjacent to the peat bog. According to Preston's calculation, the distance between Chicago and Springbrook was about 430 miles—a calculation he didn't share with his mother. This estimate didn't include the extra miles required to search for water. Preston thought the trip would take a maximum of four days. It took six. Outside Chicago, the roads rapidly deteriorated.

CHAPTER 2

END OF SUMMER, 1914

Emily Milton, Preston's mother, had heard tales of people risking a car journey out in the countryside without a horse. She knew that the roads could be atrocious and that maps were mostly useless, lacking sufficient detail to be trusted. However, the possibility of having her family reunited, if only briefly, was enough to suppress her instinctive leeriness about the venture.

She thought Preston seemed so sure of himself—always confident of a positive outcome. He named his Stanley Steamer "El." Just starting El was no simple matter. Preston used a match to light his blow torch, and the blow torch to light the gasoline pilot burner. The pilot burner lit the main kerosene burner, which heated the water in the pressure tank to the boiling point, producing the steam which ran the engine. All of this was in the front of the car. She wished Preston hadn't told her that the kerosene was stored under her seat.

Emily understood that steam made "pistons" move, which somehow got the "crankshaft" to spin, causing the wheels to turn. She could parrot this explanation by the time they reached the Wisconsin border. A more thorough understanding was beyond her interest. What she wanted was to take better advantage of the time spent in the passenger seat. If only she could crochet or knit! The first day she repeatedly had to rip out her work. The jostling made stitches irregular. She finally resigned herself to just hanging on while she chatted with Preston. How she longed for the slower pace of a horse-drawn wagon.

Determined not to waste time, Emily took advantage of this long trip to tell her son old family stories.

"You know that you were born in your Grandfather Milton's house."

"Yes."

"Did you know it was one of three homes in Princeton which had served as a respite for runaway slaves before the Civil War?"

"Yes. Weren't Negroes snuck in so they could get some food and rest before moving on?"

"That's right. Did you hear about the time when a hostile neighbor made a surprise visit?"

"Oh, was that the time a man had to hide up the chimney?"

Preston instructed her to keep her eyes peeled for water. They found it necessary to refill the water tank about every 30 miles. To get the water into the tank they could use either the canvas bucket or hose, both of which were standard equipment with Stanleys.

The first day, they made the mistake of approaching a creek through mud and got hopelessly stuck. Emily knew Preston was humiliated to have to ask a man on horseback to pull them out. By the end of the second day, she had her own name for the car which she muttered under her breath. It was not "El" but "h-e-double toothpicks."

After awhile, Emily caught on to the fact that Preston's questions were designed to distract her from her discomfort.

"Tell me the story about you and grandma following granddad around during the Civil War."

"We only followed him when he went on that long march, the one people refer to as 'Sherman's march to the sea.' That was so difficult. I was just six at the time. Mother and I wanted to be with him, but all we had to eat was jerky and coffee. We slept in hotels where there was only one candle per floor...."

After the creek disaster, Preston and Emily preferred to drive up to a farm house to ask for water. Usually, the farmer and helpers would stop their chores to walk over and inspect the car. When possible, Preston positioned the car below a horse trough, hooked up the hose to the water tank and made jokes about El being thirsty while winking at one of the children.

"Elephant!" one squealed.

"Would you like to use the privy?"

"How's about a piece of pie?"

"Gladys, go get a clean glass of water for the gentleman and his mother."

Some farm people even offered to put them up for the night. In fact, it was hard to get away at times.

Later that same day, Preston said that he only knew grandfather Zearing as a blind man.

"That's true. His eyesight grew worse and worse during the war, but he didn't become totally blind until about six years after he came home."

"Do you know that Tim's and my favorite game was to go into the attic where Grandfather's black bag was kept? Tim and I secretly played with the surgical instruments in that bag. We took turns. Whoever played the doctor had to shut his eyes while the other of us laid down and played the screaming patient."

"Oh, you didn't...? Well, I'm glad I never knew."

Emily contemplated the differences in the two boys. In looks, she thought, Preston resembled Chauncey, her late husband. He had Chauncey's blond hair and handsome face. Emily recalled how troubled she had been during Preston's teenage years. He had such a rapid growth rate. He ended up three inches taller than Tim, who was older. Preston also seemed to have much more energy and enthusiasm than Tim. She had continually wished he would eat more and slow down. Of course, he did fill out eventually, she told herself, so I guess I shouldn't have worried so. Actually, it wasn't just his growth that was out of control. She remembered several incidents where he launched into new projects with too much eagerness, not thinking things through first. In so many respects he was unlike Tim.... Tim was meticulous about planning and analyzing. To Preston, it was the activity that was important.

The boys' aunts used to suggest to Emily that she needed to

take into account the fact that Preston was two years younger than Tim. Was she too hard on Preston? Tim's quieter demeanor was easier for her to cope with. He had her thin face and a long pointed nose, but his personality was more like Chauncey. Oh, how she missed Chauncey! A sudden bump lurched Emily out of reminiscing. The roads were terrible.

When they crossed the border from Illinois into the southern part of Wisconsin, they started to really enjoy the countryside. They found the rolling hills, scattered farms and deciduous woodlands a pleasant distraction from the unnerving jolts. Preston remarked on how productive the soils were there.

Once they passed into northern Wisconsin they noticed a dramatic change in the terrain. Ten thousand years before, glaciers had covered this part of the state, scraping off the good topsoil and grinding down bedrock to produce a sandy, less productive soil. There were fewer deciduous trees. In fact, this part of the state was known as the 'pinery' in the days of the lumberjacks. Water from the receding glaciers had collected in depressions, yielding numerous bogs, swamps and lakes. Preston no longer had to reach a farm to obtain water, as streams were abundant. Insects more than made up for the scarcity of people. The windscreen did not keep them from flying into their faces. Once they stopped El, the cacophony of their sounds smothered the quiet peace. Preston and his mother became targets for feasting deer and horse flies.

At least they never had trouble finding lodging. Even towns with fewer than a hundred residents would have a small hotel. Emily learned that these hotels had originally been built to accommodate loggers. According to Tim's letters, the search for virgin timber had started in the southern part of the state. The loggers had finished stripping the north ten years ago. Railroads followed the logging routes. Emily noticed that there were even some passenger trains heading north in their direction. This she would not forget!

The further north they went, the fewer the towns. Severe winters had stunted the growth of some trees. The deciduous trees seemed limited to black oaks, quaking aspen, cottonwood, and a few maples. Although the scenery was not especially attractive, there were compensations. At night they heard the eerie calls of loons. Whip-poor-wills and crickets kept them awake. Deer were plentiful, of course, but they also saw an occasional black bear or moose. Emily had the distinct feeling that she and Press were intruders in a land that belonged to other creatures. Swarms of mosquitoes and gnats reminded them of their lowly status.

Emily remembered hearing about the difficulties her father had on his travels during the Civil War. Now, sixty years later, she doubted the roads were any better. They still had to negotiate bridgeless river crossings. She was thankful for the pneumatic tires, but they were little help on these cart tracks. Three days into the trip she was sick to death of the tire punctures and breakdowns, but not Preston. So far, every time they had a flat, he seemed eager to take out his repair kit to make a patch. She began to dread the return trip to Chicago. By the time they reached Springbrook even Preston had lost some of his enthusiasm. They still had two-and-a-half miles to go over roads deep with sand. Twice Emily had to get out and push.

On the rise of a hill they spotted a small wooden sign nailed to a tree with 'Milton' chiseled into it. The sign marked an entrance through the woods. Not really a road at all, thought Emily, so she asked: "Shall we get out and walk in?"

"Not on your life! We can get through this." Preston drove El down the lane barely missing stumps and rocks. Once they saw light at the end of the woods, Press used the klaxon liberally to announce their arrival. A little frame house came into view.

Tim must have heard the horn from the other side of the bog. He came running, arriving out of breath but with a grin that would melt snow. Although Emily and Preston were covered in dust, Tim didn't hesitate to give them big hugs. Emily laughed along with her sons. How good it was to be together.

CHAPTER 3

Pleased to have his family with him at last, Tim wasted no time in explaining how he had become interested in cranberries. Although they already knew some parts of his story, he felt that they wouldn't truly understand unless he started from the beginning. Allowing them just a few minutes to freshen up, he led his mother and Press outside his house while telling them: "When I entered Amherst, my first botany professor was Augustus Hall...." He expected a reaction but got none, so he continued. "The Halls have been cranberry growers for close to a hundred years in Massachusetts. Professor Hall started telling me about the marvels of the cranberry—*Vaccinium macrocarpon*. Later, he said he was impressed with my seriousness and strong interest in science."

"Ha, you were hoodwinked!" Preston interjected.

Tim ignored his brother's teasing. "By the end of my first year at the college, I had started a three-year investigation of cranberries under Hall's guidance. He arranged for me to visit several cranberry bogs in Massachusetts. I was able to question each of the growers about pest management, harvesting and marketing while we walked around their marshes.

"By the time I graduated, I had every intention of becoming a cranberry grower, but where? Massachusetts was too far." Tim didn't say "too far from Mom," but that is what he meant. He was thinking he should be closer to her in case she needed his help. "Sadly, Illinois didn't have the right terrain. In fact, the suitable land closest to Chicago was well up north into Wisconsin. Widespread peat marshes are usually found in areas that were once covered by glaciers. Growing cranberries requires water and a good supply of sand. There were several successful cranberry bogs in the middle of the state, but that land was far too pricy.

I had to save most of my money to pay for developing whatever property I purchased. So I pushed my search further north than I originally intended, into Indianhead country, also known as the North Woods.

"I had to spend months in county offices looking at maps and more months trudging to inaccessible swamplands. Finally, I discovered this fine peat bog adjacent to the Namekagon River."

"What does 'Namekagon' mean in Indian language?" his mother asked.

"'Waters of the Leaping Sturgeon' in Chippewa. This area and much of the north Midwest had belonged to the Chippewa Indians. Actually, I shouldn't use the word 'Chippewa.' The correct name for the people and language is Ojibwe. Evidently, white settlers had corrupted the pronunciation of Ojibwe to Chippewa."

"Are there Ojibwe people around here still?" Preston asked.

"Yes, but most live on reservations now. They still gather cranberries and wild rice from bogs and lake shores all over northern Wisconsin. I was told by one of the men working for me that in Ojibwe culture, the cranberry is more than a red berry. It is a symbol of peace and friendship, to be eaten at feasts of peace."

Tim went on to explain that once he found this property, he walked to the nearest farm to borrow a shovel so he could sample the soil. "The sampling went on for three days until I was satisfied that it was sufficiently acidic."

Preston put on a grimace of disgust while their mother briefly laughed.

"What a job it was to find the owner of the bog. It took weeks. I finally had to pay an agent to help me. When I returned to the same farmer to hire his team of horses, I showed him my deed to the property, and he said: 'Sure enough, so Jimmy Johnson sold you that brown brush swamp and timberlands, did he? He lives down Earl-way now. How did you find him? He's an old friend of mine.' It appears that all I had to do was ask this farmer where Mr. Johnson was." Tim stopped when he noticed his mother and brother exchange glances. "I know what you're thinking: 'I'm too close-mouthed for my own good.'" Tim saw Press smirk again. Just like old times, he thought.

"Let's go inside and I'll make us some tea," Emily suggested. "I'm still a little weary from our journey. I better sit down."

Once they were settled at the table in the sitting room with cups of tea, Tim eagerly continued telling them of his accomplishments. "So, in 1913, I cleared this part so I could build this two-story house. I scalped the brown brush off a small section of the bog and began digging ditches. Then, in the late fall, before winter set in, I built that small barn to house the horse and wagon that I needed to buy.

"Of course, I couldn't do all this work myself. I think I already told you in one letter that I had hired three Ojibwe Indians from the Lac Courte Oreilles Reservation. One of them is particularly fine, a hard-working young man named John Pete Kingfisher. Maybe you'll meet him tomorrow when we go walking on the bog. I love John Pete. The other workers are his friends, Sam Frog and Willy Wolf."

"Are those their real names?" asked Preston.

"Sure. Anyway, they built a small bunkhouse in the woods near the bog to sleep in when they're working here. In fact, once we start harvesting the berries—in about 5 years—I anticipate hiring more Ojibwe. So the men dug two wells—one for my house and one for the bunk house. This was not as difficult as it sounds because the soil is sandy and the water table is high. We only had to dig down 15 feet or so. If you're not too tired, I can show you the maps of the property and tell you my plans for the cranberry bog."

The next day, Tim walked them over his land. There were few roads cleared enough for his wagon to pass so they simply walked, pushing their way through tall grass or sinking into soggy peat. Grasshoppers flew off in all directions with each step. Tim was amused watching his mother being startled by frogs, stepping gingerly so as not to trample any.

"How is your money holding out, Dear?"

The truth was that Tim was concerned that he wouldn't have enough to get all the work done in the five years before a crop could be harvested. To avoid answering his mother's question, he pointed out the workers digging ditches across the bog. He suggested that they go meet them. One worker started walking toward them. It was John Pete Kingfisher. Later, his mother commented on how clear John Pete's English was. Tim told them that John Pete was unusual. Most Indians didn't speak much English at all.

One day, Tim walked them down to the Namekagon River, a half-mile from his house. On the way, they passed the small reservoir he had started to construct. It was now dry, but once the first beds were planted, he told them, he would buy a pump to fill it with river water. He explained that the vines needed to be protected from frost by flooding the beds. To use a minimum amount of water, the beds would have to be very level before planting them with cranberry vines.

When Sunday came, Tim wanted to take his mother and Press into the town of Springbrook so they could attend the service at the Congregational Church.

"I've been going there each Sunday for a couple of months now."

"That's wonderful. Is this something you got interested in at Amherst?" his mother asked.

Tim and Press exchanged glances.

"No. It gives me something to do here and a chance to meet people, and sing, too. I enjoy it."

They drove into Springbrook with Tim seated rather precariously on the large, black box mounted over the differential gear on the rear axle.

"You can see Springbrook's a small town." Tim had to almost shout to be heard by those fortunate enough to have a proper seat up front. "Although, I heard in the logging days it used to be bigger. It has about 80 residents now, maybe 20 homes. I'm estimating of course."

"More like 19, I would say," Press said.

Tim realized Press liked to make fun of his concern for precision. He needs to be ignored, Tim thought.

Emily commented that the town appeared to be a complete community. "Here's a general store. There's a tavern, a railroad depot, and the Town Hall."

"Yes, and there's a school, a small hotel and two churches: one Catholic and the other Congregational—where we're going. All of them serve not just the people living in town, but also those in the outskirts within a five mile radius of town, like me."

Driving up to the church in the Stanley Steamer caused quite a stir. Tim had reason to be concerned that Press would become the center of attention. Maybe it wasn't such a good idea to drive it here. Although motorcars occasionally had passed through Springbrook, few people had ever had the opportunity to really look one over close at hand, let alone talk to the owners. Tim could see that Press was relishing the attention given to their arrival.

CHAPTER 4

Preston was somewhat puzzled by Tim's suggestion that they go to church. He had never known him to want to go to church before. Maybe this is what happens when you're alone and isolated? Mom seemed pleased at the suggestion even though it was not a Christian Science Church. On the drive into town, Tim had said that he liked hearing Biblical stories—my brother the scientist! Press was amazed.

Before they left Tim's homestead, Press had taken some water from the well to clean up El. She was covered with dust and mud that had accumulated during the six-day journey. He dried off the water and tried to polish the metal body. When they drove up to the little fieldstone church in Springbrook, the people who had congregated outside the entrance stopped their chatting and turned to watch. Press expertly brought the Stanley to a gentle stop right at the edge of the board walk. Tim hopped off the rear gear box and opened the door for his mother. Several people gathered around them. Some even touched the car as though they were petting a horse.

One girl came right up to Tim and asked to be introduced to his family. Press couldn't help but notice how good-looking she was. Her light brown hair glistened. Her eyes were large with long eyelashes and perfectly formed brows. Press was surprised that her creamy, smooth skin didn't show the effects of country living. Her cheeks had a faint blush. She seemed to have known that they were coming this morning.

When they were settled in their pew before the service, Preston looked around at the other people. They appeared pleasant enough. He noticed the pretty girl again—Sarah, Tim had said her name was. She was sitting in the first pew. He was about to nudge Tim and make some remark about her to him when he saw Tim's gaze was already fixed on her. Ah ha, Press said to himself, so that's the reason we came—Bible stories my eye!

During the service, Preston became fascinated with the pastor, not by his sermon but by his appearance and manner. Tim said he was Reverend Clarence Ellsworth, a tall, lanky man with piercing, deep-set eyes and thin lips. The sermon was not memorable but it was delivered in a loud, firm voice that came close to being threatening. He discussed a Biblical story and ended by summarizing the moral that the story illustrated. At first Press was impressed with the confidence of the Reverend, but after a few minutes of careful listening, his confidence began to grate and seem more like rigidity. Press would have welcomed an occasional expression of doubt.

Press had no guilt about letting his mind wander. He considered the role religion played in his own family. The only one who is religious is Mom, he thought, and I wouldn't call her a devout Christian. She's more a devout Christian Scientist. In fact, as far as Preston could recall, he had never heard her say anything about theology. Yet she read every day from Mary Baker Eddy's *Science and Health*. That book meant much more to her than the Bible. What she cared about was achieving inner peace. She worked hard at it. Does that make her devout, Preston wondered?

Whenever the congregation sang, Preston became embarrassed by Tim's performance. No question about it, he had a powerful voice, but Press felt Tim was showing off—singing louder than necessary. Then it occurred to Press that standing next to Tim during the hymn singing made their difference in height obvious. No doubt, Tim was just trying to compensate.

After the service, they were introduced to Reverend Ellsworth. Press soon realized that the Reverend was the father of the pretty girl, Sarah. They also met Sarah's younger sister Meg. She was chubby and rather plain like her mother. Press chuckled to himself when he noticed Tim constantly looking at Sarah.

Some people had brought food to share, extending the time

people chatted. Without appearing obvious, Preston tried to watch Tim and Sarah talking to each other. She had an almost perfectly proportioned face. Her hair was loosely gathered in back. Preston never spoke to Meg, who was busy serving food.

That night, Tim told them that about a month ago, Reverend Ellsworth had asked Tim about his plans for his property. "Having learned my lesson about being close-mouthed, I told Sarah's, I mean, Reverend Ellsworth, all my plans for developing a cranberry bog, whereupon he offered to introduce me to some of his friends and acquaintances—a banker for example, who might be able to be of some help."

"That's very nice, Dear. Has Mr. Ellsworth been out here to your bog?"

"No. Actually, the only person who has come here from town is Meg, you know, Sarah's sister."

"Not Sarah?" Preston asked.

"No, Sarah tells me that Meg loves to wander around riding her horse. I have hardly spoken to her—been too busy."

"Why doesn't Sarah ride here with her? Then, I bet you wouldn't be too busy." Preston was enjoying teasing Tim.

"I don't think Sarah likes to ride much."

～

The trip back to Chicago was arduous but Preston and his mother were buoyed up by good feelings toward Tim.

"He seems to know what he's doing," Emily commented.

"Yes, and he certainly relishes the prospect of becoming a cranberry grower. He doesn't seem to mind the years of work ahead of him."

"Wasn't it nice to see people make a fuss over him? You know how reserved and quiet he is. Now it seems he's been accepted in this rural community and wants to be a part of it. Do you think he's interested in that Sarah Ellsworth?" his mother asked.

"Come on, Mom, you must have seen how he couldn't take his eyes off her."

"What I liked about her was that she dressed in the current

fashion without bothering with expensive fabrics. I believe that many fashionable young women in Chicago now wear the empire waist and a hemline just above the ankle. You probably don't notice such things."

Ha! If only Mom knew that I notice little else—just women and cars, Press said to himself.

"Did you see that cameo broach she wore at her throat? It was of no value, but her overall appearance gave the impression of someone with taste, if little money. I thoroughly approved." A few sudden jolts must have interrupted his mother's thoughts for when the road became relatively smooth again her line discussion took another direction. "I wonder if Tim is close to having spent all of his inheritance from your father? I now understand that growing cranberries requires a considerable investment before it can be a money earner."

"Yes. He has certainly undertaken something big." Big was the only word Preston could say to be tactful. So as not to worry his mother, he didn't express the degree to which he felt Tim was probably overextended.

"Didn't Tim say that it took five years before a newly-planted bed could be harvested, and no bed has even been planted yet? I suppose like any pioneer, Tim has to take chances," Emily said.

Preston just nodded in agreement. He felt sure his mother was also wishing that Tim had been less ambitious in his choice of livelihood.

"I'm glad Tim seems fulfilled, but it's not the life for me," Preston confessed. "I couldn't take the isolation. Tim, though, never mentioned being lonely."

The trip back gave them many hours to talk. Slowly, Preston told his mom about his own ambition. Of course, there were numerous interruptions—sudden events that required repairing El. The six days they had together gave Preston the time to refine his plans and his mother the time to assimilate them. What he wanted was to open up a shop to repair motorcars.

"More and more people are buying cars," he explained. "I'd

like to get into the repair business early so I can establish a reputation."

His mother thought carefully before she responded. She didn't want to squelch his enthusiasm. A sudden bump from a rough spot in the road made Preston start to laugh. He glanced over at his mother to see if she was alright, and noticed the look of resignation on her face.

"I know you like fixing El, Dear, but would your knowledge of the Stanley Steamer help you fix other types of cars?"

Preston noticed the mildly smug expression on his mother's face when he explained that the Stanley Steamer had passed its peak in popularity.

"Oh, really," she said.

"Now everyone is excited about the internal combustion engine. I don't think people will be buying Stanleys much longer, but I have read up on combustion engines. I had the chance to work on one at Amherst. I think I could learn as I go and keep one step ahead of my customers."

A month later, back in Chicago, Preston overheard his mother saying to his aunt in the front room, "I always knew Preston would choose to do something with mechanics, but what I can't fathom is where both boys got their courage. Their father, bless his soul, only wrote books that taught teachers how to teach; so different from growing cranberries and fixing cars."

Preston was lucky because his mother's sister, Aunt Luelja, was somewhat deaf and carried her ear trumpet with her at all times. It never really helped her to hear, but it had the advantage of reminding the speaker to talk louder. And so, his mother almost shouted, "Yes, Preston has always been fascinated with automobiles. Remember the time he and a couple of his friends 'borrowed' a car and rode it down the street? They couldn't get it started to return it. The boys hoped everyone would think that it just rolled downhill, but our neighbors suspected otherwise. So embarrassing! He was sixteen then…. Yes, if his enthusiasm has lasted six years, it's not going away."

Months later, Preston bought a small building on East 57th Street in the Hyde Park region of Chicago's South Side. It was a convenient location for his new business and only three blocks away from where he and his mother lived on South Kenwood Avenue. He hung a black lacquer sign over the door with 'Milton's Motorcar Repairs' written in gold lettering. Slowly, Preston began to acquire the necessary equipment to help him repair cars. Over the next eighteen months he built up his business so he had a steady source of income. Even his neighbor, Mr. Perkins, came in to have Press work on his old Rambler. He had forgiven Preston's teenage prank, paid handsomely for the work Press did, then spread the word among neighbors of how good Press was with engines.

Meanwhile, Preston and his mother received letters from Tim recounting his progress with the bog. In the fall of 1915, a short letter had arrived on a new topic. Tim wrote that he was engaged to be married to Miss Sarah Ellsworth! Lucky man, Preston thought. He remembered how pretty Sarah was. The letter didn't elaborate much, but Tim did urge them to plan to come up north for their wedding, which would be in a year's time. Letters that followed said little of Sarah, but that didn't surprise Preston. Tim had always been reserved in personal matters, yet Press had a nagging feeling that he didn't really know much about Sarah.

Preston's car repair business gradually improved. By the time Tim's wedding approached, he realized that he could not afford to be away for a long time, so he told his mother that this time, sadly, they would have to take the train to Springbrook. Emily tactfully said nothing, but Preston knew what she was thinking because a while ago he had overheard her tell Aunt Luelja that she would never again ride in El beyond the Field Museum.

Tim met them at the Springbrook depot. After the flurry of greetings and hugs, Tim pointed out Sarah's house across the road from the depot. It was next door to the Congregational Church. It seemed a little odd that neither Sarah nor her parents were there to greet them and that Tim didn't offer any excuse as to their absence. Preston joked around with Tim which helped to put his mother at ease. He knew she was disappointed. They both wanted to get to know Sarah as much as possible before the wedding. Tim drove them in his horse-drawn wagon out of town, to his home on the bog.

In the days leading up to the wedding, Preston became increasingly uneasy. It disturbed him that Tim and Sarah didn't seem very close. Other people might have thought Tim so shy or inexperienced with women that he couldn't charm his own fiancée, but Preston knew better. That is to say, Tim was inexperienced with women, Preston was sure of that, but he wasn't shy. He just didn't know how to be charming because he was a serious person. Ideas, theories, or observations were the things he liked to talk about. If others around him were engaged in small talk, Tim just became silent. He knew Tim couldn't chat easily, but what bothered him was that Tim rarely looked at Sarah. It was almost as if Tim wasn't really interested in her.

By the time Preston was absolutely convinced that something wasn't right, the wedding was the next day. He needed some time alone with Tim before he could tactfully begin to question him about his feelings for Sarah. With all the commotion surrounding the nuptials, they never had the opportunity to talk in private. After the wedding, Tim and Sarah left for their honeymoon in Minneapolis. Preston and his mother returned to Chicago.

~

Just when things were going well for Preston, he shocked his mother by deciding to enlist in the Navy. Her first reaction was amazement. Why would her placid, non-aggressive son be interested in fighting in a war? After a while, she began to openly express her disappointment in him. "I thought you had grown up, that you had finally overcome your restlessness. I was so proud of you starting your own business, but now I see you haven't changed at all. You still switch from one project to another. You're making a rash decision."

Preston, however, had his reasons. One of his best friends

at Amherst had been a lad from Liverpool. In May of 1915, Mel Corkran was sailing home on the Lusitania when the passenger liner was torpedoed by a German submarine off the coast of Ireland. Mel was one of the many passengers who drowned. From that moment on, the war was not just a European conflict to Preston. He followed it closely in the newspapers. When the Navy began training volunteers, Preston signed up. His decision was not rash. Years later, however Preston would realize that he had been naïve about the complicated machinations that precede war. He, like others, had been too willing to believe the propaganda.

Several years after the war ended, Preston learned that there were munitions and contraband hidden onboard the Lusitania, unbeknownst to its passengers. In fact, to compensate for this additional weight, the ship carried only half of its capacity of passengers. The Germans found out, and although they had previously agreed not to attack passenger liners, they felt the duplicity of the British Admiralty gave them the right to do so. Preston, along with many Americans, was ignorant of these facts. When the Lusitania was torpedoed, the American public became incensed, and when the U.S. declared war on Germany in April 1917, Preston was already being trained by the Navy. He told his mother: "I am not abandoning my business. I have an able assistant who can run Milton's Motorcar Repairs while I'm gone."

The discipline that the Navy gave Press about personal habits stuck with him. However, these traits were minor compensations. Near the end of the war, Preston was wounded by a piece of shrapnel, which lodged in his neck. The wound eventually healed, but he lost most of the hearing in his left ear. He was still a fine-looking man but he had an ugly scar down the side of his neck. Preston left the Navy at age 27, returning home to live with his mother and to resume running his motor repair business on the South Side of Chicago. He refused to talk about the war. He was no longer innocent.

CHAPTER 5

1920

Emily Milton felt some warmth from the April sun as she stood next to the mound of earth that covered Tim. The ground on which they all stood was spongy and wet from the April snow melt. Preston was standing beside her, thank God. His hand gently cradled her elbow, steadying her. The first telegram came after Christmas, notifying them of Tim's sudden death. The burial had to await the spring thaw, so she and Preston had spent four months preparing for this day, but now, in this setting that Tim helped to create, she felt losing him was unbearable.

Sarah and her mother, Rose, were standing opposite them on the other side of the grave. At the head, the Reverend Clarence Ellsworth conducted the simple memorial service. There was little eye contact between the two families. In fact, Emily thought, the Ellsworths had not said much to them since yesterday, when she and Preston got off the train in Springbrook.

Emily noticed that when Clarence wasn't reading from the Bible, he looked out over the cranberry bog. Emily followed his gaze and noticed that a section was covered by water. Only dikes protruded above the glazed surface.

Yesterday, the Ellsworths met them at the train station in Springbrook and drove them out of town to Tim and Sarah's house. They were courteous but not markedly warm, Emily thought. Oh well, it's a difficult time for all of us. She took a deep breath of the cool, clean, pine-scented air that Tim loved. There was quite a breeze pushing through the scraggly jack pines, but if she listened carefully, she could just hear the reedy whispers of cedar waxwings. Tim loved the North Woods. Emily was glad he was buried here next to his cranberry bog and in front of the small house that he built. It was a more appropriate resting place for him than a gravesite next to her husband, Chauncey, in their Chicago cemetery. He belongs here, she thought. This was where Tim put his stamp on life.

Emily couldn't help but feel that the surroundings were giving her messages. Mosquitoes and grasshoppers were demanding her attention. They were important witnesses of Tim's life. Yes, it was appropriate that Tim's grave was situated between his little house and the cranberry marsh. Tim had built the home and had spent his last six years trying to transform this remote bog in the North Woods so it would one day produce cranberries. He was so ambitious and hard working. His vibrant spirit will always be here in this bog.

Four months ago, just a few days before the New Year, Emily and Preston received the telegram stating that Tim had hit his head in a fall down the stairs and was instantly killed. Letters soon followed.

… Tim's body will be kept in the icehouse until we can bury him in the spring when the ground has thawed enough to dig his grave. In the meantime, Sarah will move back home with us. We are closing up their house and will let you know when it is warm enough to proceed with the burial. We think it best to delay the memorial service until then, and that would also be the reasonable time for you and Preston to make the long trip to Springbrook from Chicago…

The suggestion seemed reasonable, since in winter months, Springbrook was always covered in snow and ice. Tim's Christmas letter had mentioned that the temperature had dipped down to 35° below.

…With a fire in the kitchen's wood stove and one in the fireplace in the sitting room we are quite cozy downstairs. Upstairs is not so pleasant but bearable. We have enough wood chopped to last the winter…

Tim did not say much about Sarah, nor did Sarah add anything to his letter. She did write one letter to Emily, after Tim died. All other communications were from her father.

Standing next to Tim's grave, Emily was overcome with grief, realizing she would never see her son again.

The Ellsworths had thoughtfully opened up Tim and Sarah's house, stocked it with some basic food, and laid a fire in the fireplace. Considerate as this was, Emily felt annoyed and disappointed to learn that Tim had already been buried. Not that she had to view his body, but she did want to help lay her son to rest. After all, she and Preston had arrived precisely according to Clarence's schedule. Perhaps, as Reverend of the Springbrook Congregational Church, he felt he knew best about these things and was not accustomed to seeking approval from others.

Emily forced herself to listen to Clarence. He was reading from the Bible again.

...Blessed is the man that walketh not in the counsel of the ungodly, nor standeth in the way of sinners, nor sitteth in the seat of the scornful....

He has probably given memorial services many times before, thought Emily, which would explain why he performed his present task so perfunctorily. Emily looked at Sarah. She seemed so remote. She and Tim had been married for three years, yet she was not tearful. With her hands clasped in front she kept her gaze rigidly fixed on the ground. Maybe she is just too sad to look at us or express herself with tenderness.

Tim was no more than 30 when he died! Now she would never see his smile again. I don't know if I can get through this, Emily thought, but I must try to rally for Preston's sake. Reverend Ellsworth continued:

...For the Lord knoweth the way of the righteous: but the way of the ungodly shall perish....

At this same moment, Preston registered his own impressions. He was focused on Reverend Ellsworth's biblical quote.

Not being religious, he certainly could not recognize from what section of the Bible it came, but the tone and message itself did not seem appropriate for Tim. An unusual passage to choose for any memorial service, he thought.

Preston had not been home long from the Navy and memories of burying men at sea were fresh in his mind. Indeed, they always would be. Those men had to die and be buried without members of their family present. No matter his rank, every sailor's burial was taken seriously. The danger was constant and each man knew he might be the next to die. Dissatisfied by what he was hearing Reverend Ellsworth say, Preston thought he would pay his own tribute. He began with singing in his mind the first verse of the *Navy Hymn*. He could picture and almost hear Tim himself singing it:

> *Eternal Father, strong to save,*
> *Whose arm hath bound the restless wave,*
> *Who bidd'st the mighty ocean deep*
> *Its own appointed limits keep;*
> *Oh, hear us when we cry to Thee,*
> *For those in peril on the sea!*

Preston felt the tears coming. I should distract myself, he thought. He looked at Sarah. Her eyes were downcast, so he could spend some time looking at her. He thought it somewhat odd that she had hardly said anything to them since they arrived. She was still just as pretty as she was when he first saw her years ago. Was she sad, Preston asked himself? No, not exactly, yet there was tension in her clasped hands. She seemed more uneasy. Maybe she's annoyed with her father's ministry, too.

That Holy Commander there—he isn't going to give any of us a chance to express our grief. He's going to do all the talking. He is in control. Preston knew the type.

After the ceremony, Emily asked them if they would like to come inside and have some tea. Clarence said that they had no more time today, but they would like to come over to discuss some matters tomorrow.

"Yes, and we will be bringing a small lunch," Rose added in a pleasant tone.

~

Tim's small house had four rooms. The kitchen and sitting room were downstairs. They were connected to the two bedrooms upstairs by a steep stairway. The steps were narrow and slippery. Upon descending, Preston always found it necessary to duck his head to avoid hitting the overhang. Too little head clearance there even for Tim, who was shorter. He could understand how Tim could have slipped and fallen to his death.

Preston had tried to come up north to visit Tim as soon as the war was over, but Tim suggested that they put it off to a later time. So, Preston had not seen Tim since his wedding.

During the war, Tim had written him several letters, but one was special. So special, he had brought it with him from Chicago. In that letter, Tim had asked Preston to attend to a matter at a suitable time.

After being mesmerized by the northern lights and restocking the supply of wood by the hearth, it was after 1:00 A.M. His mother had gone up to bed hours before and must be asleep by now. He couldn't run the risk of her knowing about this. It was time to reread the letter. He turned up the kerosene lamp and sat again in Tim's rocker.

February 6, 1918

Dear Preston,

I think mother has written you to tell you that a poem was discovered in a pocket of father's hunting jacket. I'm sure she sent you a copy of the poem as she did to me. Mother thinks he wrote it just before he died. Now it has been published in several newspapers. What we discover after someone dies is so important. Dad's poem suggests that he knew he was going to die and that he wanted us to know how much his family and home meant to him. I worry about you daily. Please write me things that you hope I will never forget.

   I have something to tell you that I don't want you to know until after I die, but I do want you to know then. I have hidden something behind a stone in the fireplace in our house here. This stone looks like a belly. I don't want mother or Sarah to find out for reasons that will be obvious. It will appear that I have made a terrible mistake. Yet I will always be grateful for that mistake and the little time we had. I had better not say more. Please don't write to me about this.

   My dear Preston, please take care of yourself,

   Tim

Preston took the lamp in hand to carefully scrutinize the fireplace's stonework. One of the center stones looked round and protruded a little beyond the others. In the center was a hollow the size of a pea. A belly button, thought Preston! He tried to get the stone out, but found its spherical shape difficult to grasp. He took his jackknife from his pocket and leaned over, ready to chisel the stone out from underneath, when he saw a small slot that couldn't be seen standing up. By inserting his jackknife in the slot and lifting up, he was able to dislodge the stone.

Once removed, he could see inside the hole that remained. There he found a paper wedged at the back. It turned out to be a photograph—a photograph of a little baby, on the back of which was written, "Emma, born April 15, 1917."

Preston sat at the table for a long time trying to imagine what had happened. Was it possible that Tim had had an affair? How could he do that? His wife was so beautiful! Upon further thought, when he recalled their wedding, he remembered that Tim never appeared to be in love with Sarah, nor she with him. Then it hit him—the absurdity of Tim behaving so. Tim, who couldn't even chat with girls! What on earth happened? Who is the other woman? This would explain the Ellsworth's coolness towards them. Mom must never know. It would break her heart. He quickly replaced the photo and then the stone. He went to bed but hardly slept the rest of the night.

The next day, Preston noticed that Sarah stood around while Rose and his mother set the table for lunch. It's her house, he thought, yet she doesn't take charge. Trying to break the ice he asked her directly: "Have you been back here since Tim died?"

"No," she answered hesitantly.

"It's a sweet little house, don't you think?" Preston noticed a faint shudder on her part. She had no time to respond before her father said, "It makes her sad to be here, so it's best she stay away."

The five of them sat around the table in the sitting room sharing the light meal. Preston's sadness was made more acute by the lack of warmth from both Sarah and her father. Her mother was fairly friendly, but none of them seemed to care about what his mother was going through. She had suffered so many losses. Tim was her third child to die and Dad passed away only ten years ago. Mom had been so proud of Tim.

Preston worried that he would not be able to follow the conversation. His loss of hearing caused him to miss things that were said in social situations. Fortunately, however, Reverend Ellsworth spoke loud and clear, perhaps because he was used to addressing whole congregations, Preston thought.

He wasted no time getting to the point. "Sarah does not want to live here anymore and she wants none of the household possessions that we have left here. It would be unfair to saddle Sarah with Tim's debts. After all, she has no knowledge of the cranberry business."

Although they were taken aback by this abruptness, Preston and Emily understood that what Reverend Ellsworth suggested was the only fair way to proceed. The Reverend handed Preston an envelope that contained two identical lists of all of Tim's debts:

> 1. *$1,000 to the Bank of Hayward at 3% interest,*
>   *to be repaid in 1927.*
> 2. *$20,000 to Harold Morris at 0.5% interest,*

to be repaid in 1929.

*3. $25 to neighbor Guy Wade: feed & board
for Tim's horse over this winter.*

4. $100 for casket and digging Tim's grave.

Preston blanched. Oh my God! Is this going to be blackmail? If I don't agree to take on Tim's debts, maybe they'll tell Mom what he has done and try to ruin his reputation. I cannot make this more painful than it already is for Mom, he thought. So Preston agreed to sign and date both copies which stated that he "was thereby assuming all of the above-mentioned debts." Then, Mr. Ellsworth presented them with another document also prepared in duplicate for both Sarah and Preston to sign. You'd think he might have written to us about all this, Preston thought. This document stated that all the possessions and property formerly owned by Timothy and Sarah Milton would now belong to Preston Milton, Timothy's brother.

"Shouldn't we register this change in ownership with the proper department of Washburn County?" Preston asked.

"That's impossible to do without a death certificate," Clarence explained. "Tim's death was not registered, but my lawyer friend says if you pay the taxes on this place for five years, you will automatically become the owner. If anyone questions you before that time is up, you'll have this document as proof that you are the owner."

The Ellsworths drove off in their horse drawn wagon soon after lunch, leaving Preston in a daze. By that evening, he felt the full impact of what he had signed. He knew nothing about cranberries except the little Tim had told him. He remembered from Tim's letters that there was not much to do during the winter months. Perhaps it won't be so bad, Preston thought. I can at least spend the winter months in Chicago helping to run the repair business. Maybe after a couple of years getting the bog to the productive stage, I could start to pay back Tim's debts. In five years, I might be able to sell the place and return to motorcars. In his mind he tried to go over what Tim had explained about the business years ago.

That night, Preston and his mother sat down at the table in Tim's sitting room, both deep in thought. Preston broke the silence first to ask his mother about her impressions. He didn't want to add to her sadness but he just had to know what she thought of the Ellsworths.

"I mean, it's not that they weren't proper, but they were so cold, even worse than the way they had been when we were here for the wedding. Why were they so distant and businesslike? Were they worried about Tim's debts?"

"If that were the case, wouldn't they have relaxed and been more cordial once you said you would pay them? I can't help but think, Press, that the Ellsworths don't like us."

"Yes, I have to agree."

The next morning, Preston and his mother again began talking about Tim. Being in his house and knowing he would never be there again added to their sadness. They felt a tender respect for the cozy home.

"Do you think it is strange that Sarah doesn't want to live here?" his mother asked.

"Not really, it would be lonely for her to be here all on her own."

"She seemed despondent, don't you think?"

"Yes," Press answered. "I didn't like the way Clarence always tried to talk for her."

"Perhaps I can't warm to her because she didn't show much feeling for Tim."

"None of them did," Press commented.

After some thought, his mother went on to say: "I wondered if they're just strange people or did something happen to which we are not privy. Probably just as well that we don't know."

Press couldn't help but be in awe of his mother's perceptive powers. He warned himself that he would have to be very careful to keep her from knowing about Tim's illegitimate child. Was it that "mind-over-matter" stuff that she practices? I'd better stop thinking about this. She'll probably read my thoughts.

Press considered how best to proceed. He had only $10,000, a large part he had inherited from his father, the rest he had saved. He certainly didn't have enough to pay off Tim's debts. If he sold the place now, he would not be able to recover the money that Tim had put into it, and selling an undeveloped cranberry bog wouldn't be easy.

As if on cue his mother said: "To sell this place wouldn't show much respect for Tim's dreams."

I might as well do my thinking out loud, Press thought. "I will spend a few years bringing the bog up to production level and then sell it."

They agreed that Press needed to assess the state of the marsh and Tim's cranberry business right now. After that, he thought, he and his mother could return to Chicago. It would take him a week or two there to get his affairs in order before he returned to Springbrook alone. Once back here in Springbrook, he figured, he would have to stay through the end of October just to get the work on the bog done.

After some toast and a cup of tea, Preston and his mother put on their coats and went outside to look over the bog. It was a chilly morning and the grass was heavy with dew. They walked around the house and down to the bog. In no time, Emily's skirt became so wet it began to weigh her down. The bog itself was flooded. Only the crisscrossing tops of the dikes protruded above the water's surface.

"Of course, Tim always said, didn't he, that the bog had to be flooded over the winter?"

"Yes, and as I recall he said something about a layer of sand. When did he put that on? Do you know?"

"No. When should the water be drained off? I would think pretty soon. The growing season could be starting now. Oh hell, I don't know anything about this." Preston began to realize that inaction or wrong timing could be disastrous for the crop.

"I wonder if any of these beds have been harvested yet?"

Preston said to his mother. "I remember Tim saying that it took five years for the vines to become embedded enough to withstand a harvest."

"Yes, I remember that."

"Tim started planting some beds the summer after our first visit, if I remember correctly. That would mean that some beds will need to be harvested this fall. Dear God, how do I harvest them? And how do I get people to buy them?"

"You'll figure it out," his mother said.

His mother's confidence helped to calm him down. As they walked out on a large dike, they could see the bog as a whole. It was irregularly shaped and flanked by aspen, poplars, and birch trees. They walked across it to the far side, where they came across a deep ditch.

"I'm betting that this is the drainage ditch. Tim would have to have some way of draining water off the bog when it was no longer needed for flooding. Doesn't this ditch seem much deeper than those around the beds?"

"Yes, it does."

"By opening some gates, the water would flow into this ditch and be taken to what? The reservoir? No…, more likely to the river itself. Maybe we can tell if we follow this dike. It seems to run parallel to this deep ditch."

In following the dike, they saw the reservoir off to their left. The dike and drainage ditch bypassed it by fifty yards and headed for the river.

"It seems that Tim made several changes since we were here last."

"As I remember this reservoir, it was quite a bit smaller. Isn't it beautiful filled with water? This is really something. … Are those blue-winged teals out there?"

"They are indeed!"

The teals didn't fly off as expected, as they were somewhat hidden behind the cattails and rushes at the shoreline. Hazelnut bushes at the edge of the woods obscured part of the marsh from view. At the far end of the reservoir, they found the sluiceway and a short path that led to the Namekagon River, where there stood a building little bigger than a shed.

"This must be the pumphouse. I remember Tim writing about it. My, he has put a lot of work into this place! I don't remember that nice sluiceway."

"There is supposed to be a diesel engine inside," Emily added.

"Yes, that's right—to pump the water from the river into the reservoir. Let's take a look at that pump." Preston's eyes brightened. They went inside. He examined the pump. At last, he had come across something that he understood. "Looks like it runs on vegetable oil," he commented. His spirits were improving—machinery always did that for him.

"You see, the river water can be pumped up to the sluiceway which is higher than the reservoir. Once water is in the sluiceway, gravity carries it to the reservoir," he explained.

They walked back to the bog and looked over the gates that controlled the flow of water. They consisted of cement slots into which wooden planks could be slipped to stop the flow of water. Preston noticed that the system enabled a small number of beds to be flooded independently of the others. Each bed was surrounded by ditches, which could carry water either to flood or drain the bed. On the other side of the ditches were dikes. All dikes were connected. Some were merely footpaths whereas others could carry a horse-drawn wagon.

They went back in the house to eat a bite of lunch. Preston found Tim's charts of the bog in a cabinet drawer in the sitting room. Spreading them out on the round table they found a small-scale map of the entire bog. Each bed marked off, dated as to when it was planted, and with what type of cultivar. It appeared that starting in 1915, Tim had planted three 2-acre beds a year, so that now there were altogether fifteen beds covered in cranberry vines.

Preston found notes in the drawer that explained the differences in the three varieties of vines that had been planted. Two were native to Wisconsin: Searles and Ben Lear. The third type, Stevens, was a hybrid. They were likely to be quite large. All three types of cultivars promised to be deep red in color. What Preston found most reassuring was that Tim kept records of everything: the work, the cost of specific jobs and the workers who had been hired. They also found drawings of the warehouse that Tim had constructed near the bog.

"This is so like Chauncey. Tim definitely had his scientific bent," his mother said.

"I think that Tim wrote in a letter that when the berries are picked, they have to be dried before they are sorted."

"Yes, he said something about the sides of the warehouse.... Oh yes, they could be propped open so a breeze could go through." After lunch they set off to inspect the warehouse.

The temperature had not warmed up much. Preston wondered if it might freeze that night. He laughed. Was he thinking like a cranberry grower already? They walked down a very sandy road that led to the warehouse. It was a large wooden building that must have been unfinished because it had only two floors. The plan back at the house showed three floors. Once inside, they noticed that Tim had been in the process of building what appeared to be drying crates. There was a large pile of laths on the floor.

"Fortunately, he has finished making five of these crates. He must have needed many more, because there are so many laths here. Well, at least I have a model to go by." It helped Preston to do his reasoning out loud. "Hmm, they are about 2' square and about 6" deep, very light weight, designed to be stacked. Two sides and the bottom are made of laths spaced about 3/8" apart— enough to let air in without having the berries fall through the slats. The other two sides are of solid wood, probably to help keep the crate rigid and give it strength so it won't collapse when stacked. This would work for cranberries, I guess, because they weigh so little. Yes, that's right. They are so light that they float."

His mother said: "Preston, you're beginning to sound like you're enjoying this. Maybe you have a scientific bent, too. You always did like to figure out how things work. Perhaps this can become just as interesting to you as machinery and cars."

Preston wanted to remind her that he had only committed himself for 3–5 years, but to keep her in a positive mood, he agreed.

Emily was looking up at a beam supporting the floor joists for the second story and commented, "That's a strange place to keep a metal box, way up there on a beam."

Preston couldn't quite hear her—something about a "metal box"—but before he could ask her to repeat herself, he spotted a stack of boxes in the corner. "Oh, dear God, here is another type of crate, heavier and smaller. What is it used for? Look he already has about forty of these made."

Emily surmised that since those crates were built first, maybe they were the first ones used in the harvesting process.

"Yes, good thinking, Mom. Tim wouldn't start making a second type of crate if he hadn't made enough of the first kind, so I'm hoping that I don't have to make any more of these." After several minutes of quiet thinking, Press asked: "Mother, do you remember the name of the Indian man, Chippewa I should say, that Tim introduced us to? Remember? He spoke English quite well."

"Yes. Tim always spoke so highly of him—hard working, enthusiastic. Um, John Paul Pintail?" she giggled.

Press liked to hear her giggle. He felt that she was often too serious. "No, it was John Pete," Preston corrected with a smile. "What was his last name? A bird, as I remember."

"Kingfisher, wasn't it? John Pete Kingfisher. That's it," Emily exclaimed.

"I'm thinking, Mother, he could be helpful to us. I would guess he knows much of what Tim planned."

"Yes, he's worked for Tim for at least five years."

After the warehouse, they went to look at the Indian cabin

in the woods. The wooden door creaked when they pushed it open. Sufficient daylight came through the two windows to see two wide bunk beds lining one wall. They were handmade from roughsawn planks. Some old-looking straw was atop of each, serving as mattresses, Press thought. There was a crude table and three chairs, but no fireplace. Preston saw something scurry across the floor. He knew this wouldn't scare his mother as she had lived in the country herself as a child. Nothing hung from the row of pegs on the wall. Outside there was a stone circle where there had been fires. A few logs were placed around it to sit on. Twenty-five yards away was a well.

Preston turned to Emily, "I think I should make a trip to the Indian reservation. It's about thirty miles away. I would like to try to find this John Pete Kingfisher, if possible. Would you like to come with me? We'll have to take Tim's horse which is being boarded at the neighboring farm. Yesterday, I noticed the harness and wagon in the barn."

Preston thought it would be best to continue employing someone who may already know what Tim's plans were. Would they be able to find John Pete?

"I want to go with you. I've always wanted to see an Indian reservation," his mother said.

The next morning, they rode off in Tim's horse-drawn wagon, leaving the bog around 8:00 A.M. They thought it likely that they would have to stay the night somewhere, but they hoped they could do the trip in one day. Everything depended on whether they could find John Pete. After 14 miles, they arrived at Hayward, a town with a population of around 1,000. With half their trip behind them, they talked about stopping to rest the horse if they found an appropriate spot.

"Do you hear drums?" Emily asked. Listening carefully, Preston did hear them. His hearing was better at lower frequencies.

With their curiosity aroused, they drove their wagon toward the drumming and found themselves in front of the Town Hall, where a crowd of about sixty people were gathered. Half appeared to be Indian. A few of the younger Indians were dressed in brightly beaded buckskin, while the older men and women were wrapped in blankets over their plain clothes. Indian speakers were addressing the mixed crowd, while some Indian men were beating drums.

Emily and Preston stood watching in fascination. Finally, Preston thought to ask one of the Indians if they knew a man from the reservation whose name was John Pete Kingfisher. The man pointed to one of the speakers. Preston had no memory of what John Pete looked like. From the edge of the crowd he could scrutinize his features unobtrusively. He was a nice looking man of medium height and darkish skin. He wore trousers that were too big for him, held up by suspenders. His long-sleeved, off-white shirt was buttoned up to the neck, showing off a necklace of feathers and beads. On his head he wore a fedora, which shaded his face.

John Pete wasn't at the reservation that day because he and several other Ojibwe men and women had come into Hayward from their village of Pahquahwong on Lac Courte Oreilles (LCO) Reservation. Their village, Pahquahwong, was often called just "Post," as it had been formed originally as a trading post over a century before. It was fortunate that the Miltons had stopped in Hayward and not pushed on to the reservation looking for him.

Preston and his mother waited patiently until the crowd finally dispersed, before going up to speak to John Pete. At close range, they could see more clearly his chiseled cheekbones and broad nose. John Pete remembered meeting them five years ago. He said that he and his wife were planning to go to the bog in a few days to start working for Tim, as he usually did at this time of year. It was evident that he didn't know that Tim was dead, so Preston had to tell him that he had died last December. John Pete drew back and became very quiet. Finally he spoke, saying he couldn't believe it.

"He was such a young man, not much older than me!" he

exclaimed.

"Yes, it is a terrible tragedy."

John Pete's eyes narrowed looking at the ground and remained deep in thought.

Preston explained that they had been on their way to the reservation to see him.

"Do you want me to work?"

"Yes, we sure do."

"I will. Can I get my wife, Ziigwan? We just got married and we have a baby boy. She is at the reservation."

John Pete talked repeatedly about Tim, saying what a good man he was, asking many questions. Where was his wife? Where was he buried? Finally Emily felt compelled to ask John Pete how he had come to speak English so well.

"My mother died when I was two, and my dad and I went to live with his brother, whose wife was a white woman. She taught at the reservation school and that's how I learned English. I'm not that much of an Indian activist, but there are times, like today, that they ask me to speak for them."

"What was the protest about?" Preston asked. "Something about a dam on the Chippewa River, I gathered."

Preston's simple question could have unleashed a lengthy dialogue from John Pete, who loved to talk, but instead he said, "It's a long story. Perhaps it would be best if I give you this pamphlet that we prepared. It explains the history fairly well."

Before they arrived at Post, both Emily and Preston had taken the time to read the pamphlet:

> Long ago, when white settlers were moving west to the Mississippi River, your government wanted to help them get wood to build their homes, yet the pine forests were on our land. They belonged to the Ojibwe people.
>
> The government first tried to move us off of our land and have us settle west of the Mississippi. We wouldn't move. Next, the government started 'negotiating' treaties with us Ojibwe. There were, altogether, three treaties in the years

1837, 1842, and 1854. We know now that the government never intended to follow through with what the treaties promised. The last one established reservations where Indians in Wisconsin could live under tribal law. We were promised to never have to move from these reservation lands.

Our people have a different pattern of living. In fall, winter and spring we like to hunt and trap. During those times we separate from each other and spread out far and wide over our lands so as not to compete with one another. When spring comes, we gather to make maple syrup. In summer, we pick blueberries. In fall, we harvest wild rice and cranberries. All year round, we fish. In winter, we cut holes in the ice to spear fish, but when the ice has melted, we fish from our birchbark canoes.

It is a different pattern from the way white folks live. We prefer it, but today it is nearly impossible to live this way. The government doesn't want us to move around. It wants us to own private property and to farm. We like to garden in the summer. Then we grow squash and some other vegetables, but we don't want to farm. Today, we have had to change the way we live. Furthermore, white people live and farm throughout our reservation. The government forced us to send our children to boarding schools which are off the reservation. There, our children are not allowed to speak Ojibwe. The government continually tries to keep us from being Indians. They can't change the color of our skin but they want us to act and live like white settlers and to lose our attachment to our tribes.

"You mean you're not Chippewa Indians?" asked Emily.

"Yes we are, but we prefer to be called Ojibwe."

Emily remembered Tim telling her that six years ago. "Did you have to go to a boarding school?"

"No, those of us who went to the Post school were not sent away, probably because we already had a white school teacher—

my aunt. I think of her as my mother."

In 1887, the government initiated the allotment policy. Ojibwe families on our reservation were allotted a maximum of 160 acres each, while the government sold off the remaining reservation land (56%) to the public, starting the "Great Indian Land Grab." The purpose of the policy was to encourage us to assimilate and become farmers on privately owned property. It has had the effect of impoverishing us and repressing our tribal, communal living. Today the Lac Courte Oreilles Reservation is a checkerboard of white-owned property.

Emily thought that this might be the reason so many Indians had trouble managing alcohol, observing that people often drink excessively when they give up hope and become spiritually lost.

"My village is called Post," said John Pete. "Things have changed so much on the reservation, just in my lifetime. Now, most of us live in frame houses, whereas we used to live in wigwams. You'll see some wigwams still, but nowadays, those that have them just live in them during the summer."

"If you don't mind my asking, how old are you, John Pete?" Emily asked.

"Twenty-one. I first came to work for Tim when I was fifteen. So much has changed. Many of my people served on logging crews at one time or another. You know, we used to own all the pine forests. Now, all the large tracts of pine that are left are owned by corporations. Both our white and red pine trees float so logging companies used rivers to get their logs to sawmills. The upper Chippewa River has more than 150 dams built to carry the logs smoothly down river. We Ojibwe worked alongside white settlers in logging camps and on the log drives down rivers. Now most of the timber is gone, so they're looking for ways that the water can be used to produce electricity."

The power company wants to produce a series of storage reservoirs on the headwaters of the Chippewa River and

*its tributaries. About 6,000 acres of reservation land
would be flooded, including our village of Post. Our maple
groves, wild rice and cranberry beds, hunting lands and
our village will all be underwater. It would produce a
massive flowage that would become the third largest lake
in Wisconsin. Everything that our people at Lac Courte
Oreilles hold sacred, from the natural resources to the
graves of our ancestors, would be underwater. No amount
of money can compensate us for this loss.*

When they arrived at Post, Emily estimated the village to
have two dozen homes. Amongst them was a larger building that
turned out to be the schoolhouse. It was a two-story structure
made out of logs with dovetail joints. It had three windows on
the side facing the road.

"This is where my aunt taught us," John Pete explained.

"How old is the school house?" Emily asked.

"I don't know for sure, but it must be over a hundred years
old."

Further on, they stopped in front of a log cabin long enough
for John Pete to pick up his wife and baby. Within a few minutes,
a pretty young girl with glistening black hair, holding a swaddled baby, climbed into the back of the wagon. Her name was
Ziigwan. John Pete threw in some blankets and some bundles of
clothes before handing his wife some pans, a coffee pot and a few
other household utensils. They were ready to go in ten minutes.
John Pete had changed into overalls and a shirt more suitable for
work.

There seemed to be others who lived in the cabin with them,
because after they pulled away, a boy came running out after
them waving a brown floppy hat. Preston stopped the wagon.
Laughing, John Pete gave the boy the fedora he was still wearing
in exchange for the floppy hat, saying something in Ojibwe. It
seemed to Press that John Pete had borrowed another man's hat
for the protest and now was reunited with his own. They waved
goodbye again and Preston drove off.

A few days later, Press asked John Pete if he knew of any place in the warehouse where Tim might have kept business records. John Pete said that he thought Tim kept those papers up in the house. Press mentioned this to Emily, wondering if she had seen any such things, when she recalled the metal box she had noticed up on a beam in the warehouse. The following day she went with Press down to the warehouse to look for it. "Let's see it was on a beam in the ceiling. I don't see it now. Hmm, I was standing about here when I said something to you, but then we got distracted."

"How big was it?" Preston asked.

"I'd say about the size of a cigar box.... Oh well, I can't see it now."

Preston wanted to return to Chicago to get his affairs there straightened out before he launched into the cranberry business full time, but after talking to John Pete, he realized that the winter flood had to be taken off so the vines could begin their seasonal growth. Going home now was impossible. His mother would have to go back on the train alone. John Pete had said that throughout the spring, there would be nights requiring flooding. According to Tim, he said, you could only stop worrying about frost around the first of July. Preston's heart sank when he realized it would be mid-summer before he could even visit Chicago.

That night he wrote some long letters to various people in Chicago to explain his predicament. The most important one was written to his assistant:

...The shop will not be able to take on any major work until next December. From now until December, only accept repair jobs that you yourself can handle. I'll be back in December to continue my usual work, but then only through the winter months...

Preston was heartbroken. His career of choice, motorcar repair, was in real jeopardy. Two years after the war ended, the country's spirits were high and the economy was booming. There were parties to go to and pretty girls to meet, and here he was, spending the prime of his life in the back woods of Wisconsin. He anticipated loneliness. He dreaded being a failure as a cranberry grower, but he had no choice. He had to do right by his brother Tim, and maybe by staying in Springbrook, he could resolve some of the questions he had about Tim which troubled him.

CHAPTER 6

By 1925, after devoting five years to growing cranberries, Preston was beginning to feel comfortable with the bog and the North Woods. Each harvest was bigger than the last. Now, there were 15 beds in production. Three years prior, he began planting new beds, figuring that would help him sell the place when he was ready to do so. He also built another Indian cabin for John Pete and his family that had three rooms. John Pete was very dependable and was a good leader for the other men who worked on the bog. The original cabin was used as a bunkhouse at harvest time when many more hands were needed. Sometimes, additional Indians would walk all the way from the reservation in hopes that Preston would hire them. When they couldn't be hired, they would stay with the other men in the bunkhouse for a few days before walking back.

Some years, Indians brought a large teepee to accommodate friends and relatives, a practice which did not benefit the actual wage earner. Paychecks quickly disappeared, but sharing food and drink was a deep-seated Ojibwe tradition, and one which Preston admired, as long as the drinking didn't become excessive and lead to fights. If someone was killed, Preston thought, I would probably never know it. The body could be buried deep in the woods without a trace. During harvest, I have too much on my mind. John Pete manages the Indians. He speaks their language, and after the harvest, the problem ends because the Indians return to the reservation.

Preston's berries were pooled with those from other growers in various parts of the country. The American Cranberry Exchange distributed them to Midwest markets under the brand name of Eatmor. After harvest, the beds had to be prepared for winter. A winter flood was put on. Preston hoped that the ice layer built up in two weeks would be thick enough to allow sand to be easily spread on top. After sanding, the water under the ice layer was drawn off so the vines could breathe. At that point, the ice layer could collapse from its own weight in the spring, when temperatures rose. When the ice melted, the sand would permeate down and layer the vines to stimulate new root growth.

During winter there was little that could be done on the bog itself. Finally, time could be devoted to things like fixing machinery, making changes within the warehouse, and improving the sorting system.

Two years before, Preston had faced the fact that he couldn't run the motorcar repair business, so he sold out to his assistant. He continued to go down to Chicago each winter for 2–4 months because by the end of harvest, he was tired of living like a bachelor and needed more companionship. While living on the bog, he always had so much to do that he rarely met people other than those who worked for him. He tried each year to go to the Congregational Church on a couple of Sundays. He hoped to learn more about Tim. He also had the feeling that John Pete knew something, but would not share it with him.

Early on, Press heard that Sarah had moved to Minneapolis. Later, Rose, her mother, told him that she had married a man from Minneapolis. He noticed that the church had fewer people attending and that the Ellsworth's house next door was looking run-down. Louise, who tended the general store in town with her husband Harry, was very friendly and inquisitive. One day, Preston asked her if she remembered his brother.

"Of course, I am so sorry. He was killed falling down stairs, I heard."

"Yes, that's right."

It occurred to Preston that Louise might be the woman with whom Tim had had an affair.

"Did he come in here often to buy some food?"

"Yes, about once a week. Your brother was quiet. I didn't talk to him much. He was very careful about what he purchased."

Preston laughed. "That sounds like him." He had a sudden flash of longing to be with Tim. After a pause, he went on to ask, "And of course you knew Sarah."

"Oh yes, I went to school with her for years. It was her sister Meg that I was close to though."

"Oh, now I remember, there was a sister. I haven't seen her the few times I've gone to the Congregational Church though."

"No, she moved away several years ago."

"Does she ever come back?"

"No, but I would love to see her if she did."

"I suppose she married someone and is busy with a family."

"Nobody knows, she kind of disappeared suddenly and the Ellsworths never mention her."

"How long has she been gone?"

"A long time, let's see, she left about two or three months after Tim and Sarah got married."

Preston wanted to look nonchalant so as to make Louise think his inquiry was merely casual. "Oh, I also need five pounds of flour. I almost forgot."

Once out of the store, Preston thought hard about the time Meg left. The baby was born April 15. Nine months before would be mid-July. Sarah and Tim got married in August. The timing was right. That could explain why Tim seemed little interested in Sarah at the time of the wedding. But Meg was plain. Why would Tim be interested in her? Maybe that was all just coincidental and Louise was really Tim's lover. She is very attractive and sharp, he thought. So, Press went out of the store with two new questions: Where is Meg and when did Louise and Harry get married? He would have to seek those answers another time. It was important, Preston knew, not to appear too inquisitive.

~

By the fourth winter in Chicago, Preston started receiving invitations from people he didn't know. He asked his mother, "Christiana Bartholomew? Who is she? I'm invited to a reception for her. And here's another, 'A tea dance to honor Olivia

Peacock'—where are these people coming from?"

His mother then admitted that she had been afraid that Preston would never meet anyone, because he was in town for only a few months of the year, so she saw to it that his name was put on the list of eligible bachelors that debutantes invite to their parties.

"Trying to hitch me up, are you Mom?"

"I just want you to have more fun, Dear. You work so hard and are so isolated up there."

"Yes, some Cornelia Winston Gilbert will want to lure me into marriage so she can come up to the North Woods to be my wife."

"You've almost paid off all of Tim's debts. Pretty soon you'll probably want to sell the bog, won't you?"

Preston was surprised at his own feelings. He could not see himself giving up the bog now. When Tim died, it had been a tremendous burden, but after a few years, he had actually started to enjoy being part of the bog life, being outdoors, working with the land and other elements of nature, building machinery and devising new mechanisms for the work that went on in the warehouse. There were so many variables that always had to be taken into account. The bog was a community that he belonged to. He didn't dominate it. That would have been impossible. He merely influenced its direction.

He tried to share these thoughts with his mother.

"Well that may be," she said, "but it's time you went to some parties like other young people, and possibly meet a girl you could marry."

"So you aren't a social climber, just a social engineer?" he teased. Preston did look forward to going to parties and talking to people his age, but often he found socializing in groups difficult. With many conversations going on, he was rarely sure he had heard everything needed to join in with an intelligent remark.

His mother's strategy worked and backfired at the same time.

After a couple of winters as an eligible bachelor, a girl did take Preston's fancy. Her name was Josephine Haylock, of Haylock Jewelers. The Haylocks were an old Chicago family, well connected and wealthy, typical of the debutante crowd. Preston didn't care about that, but he saw Josie as someone who had lots of spunk.

Her debut was given at the Blackstone Hotel. While Preston worked his way to the front of the reception line—a process that took 30 minutes—he had ample time to look at Josephine. She was tall like the man standing next to her, who Press assumed was her father. Even from a distance he could see she had a bubbly personality. She had something to say to each guest. A young man about four ahead of Press in line said something that made her throw her head back and laugh. In so doing, she displayed a full set of rather large teeth, which she immediately tried to conceal by raising her elegantly gloved hand to her mouth. Preston thought he heard "Humpafine." Later he learned it was her younger brother's name for her ever since he was a child, when he had trouble saying "Josephine."

Witnessing this familial scene put Press at ease. When it was his turn to shake hands with her, he was surprised when she squeezed his hand quite firmly. "I haven't seen you before," she said bluntly.

"Well, I spend a good part of the year up in Wisconsin."

"Really, how's that?"

"I'm a cranberry grower."

"Well, I'd like to hear more about that. I hope you'll ask me to dance."

Press was aware that her mother, the next person he had to shake hands with, gave Josie a nudge. Press felt she either disapproved of Josie's forwardness or of her wasting time on a mere cranberry grower from Wisconsin. Nonetheless, Preston was determined to dance with Josie when the chance came, but first he'd have to get through the sit-down dinner in the adjacent room. There must be 500 guests, she's never going to remember me, he thought. An hour or so later he got his chance. Holding her close to him so that she spoke into his good ear, he could hear everything she said and was able to give quick and witty replies. They asked each other questions and laughed between answers. She had a whimsical *joie de vivre* that was both entertaining and refreshing. He was more than ready to be carried away by her light-hearted free spirit. Perhaps it was her youth that charmed him. She was thirteen years younger than he, not very serious about anything and excited by everything. It felt good to laugh again. For five years he had been quiet and burdened with responsibilities.

Once Mrs. Haylock heard that Preston was an Amherst graduate she said, "Well our Josephine was also schooled on the East Coast. After which she pursued dramatic and musical studies in Chicago. She has always been serious about the piano, you know. As a teenager she practiced 5 hours a day."

"Really!"

"Yes, she's given several concerts."

"For friends and relatives," Josie was quick to add.

Preston had heard Josie tell stories. Her flare for drama and exaggeration amused people.

"What's my favorite type of party? I don't have to think long to answer that one. It's a costume ball."

"What have you gone as?" Preston asked, ready to be amused.

"Queen Elizabeth. Daddy provided me with both a scepter and crown."

"Good God!" Preston imagined Josie as Queen Elizabeth in his house back on the bog, eating boiled potatoes and sausage, and burst out laughing.

So Preston met Josie at her debut in January at the Blackstone Hotel and began seeing her again at other parties. One night she said to him:

"You seem so quiet."

"Lets dance and I'll explain." Press was pleased with himself for coming up with this clever ploy to have a chance to hold Josie close. Preston explained his trouble hearing, due to his injury.

"I'm very sorry about that." After an appropriate pause, and with a twinkle in her eye, she added: "I guess we'll have to keep dancing so we can communicate easily."

Preston gave her an affirming squeeze and thought she quivered with delight.

For his part, Preston couldn't get her out of his mind. They agreed to write to each other when he had to return to Wisconsin. In her first letter she wrote:

February 20, 1925

Dear Press,

I did so enjoy meeting your mother before you left. I just realized she lives near my grandmother.

I never told you that three weeks before the ball at the Blackstone where we met, Mother and Dad had also arranged a tea to celebrate my "coming out." This was just for Mother's friends. Even though we have a large apartment, we had to have three sets of guests at different hours. The flowers were banked to the ceilings. Mother's only fear was that the front elevator would give out. It had never broken down in all the five years that we had lived in the building, but Mother was obsessed with this idea for weeks ahead of the date. Press, just like your mother's quote of Mary Baker Eddy's, "If you think of error, error comes," and it did! Just at the very end of the reception, when the last dwindling guests of the third batch were about to go, the front elevator could not move above the first floor. Our guests had to use the service elevator!

I am so looking forward to hearing about the cranberry farm and the Indians. How cold is it up there now? Can you hear wolves at night? Do you know you are the first farmer I've ever befriended?

Yours truly,
Josie

CHAPTER 7

FALL OF 1926

It started to concern Emily that Josie and Press were falling in love. Josephine was quite tall, too tall for Preston, Emily thought, but she had to admit that she was lovely to look at. She had a long Roman nose and fair complexion. Her dark wavy hair was cut short in the new bob. Emily was intrigued with Josephine's mouth. If she closed her lips, she could barely cover her large white teeth. This was somewhat unattractive, she thought.

What concerned Emily more was the Haylock family. It wasn't that she didn't like the Haylocks as individuals, but she thought that there should be more to one's life than just laughing and having fun. Nothing seemed very worthy about any of their endeavors. The older generation of Haylocks went on hunting parties and bragged about the hundreds of birds they shot. The next generation, Josie's, was outrageously extravagant both with money and alcohol.

Emily compared this with her formative years during the Civil War. She remembered its deprivations, how cold and hungry they were, living for days on hard-tack. The accomplishments of her family, Chauncey's and hers, led to substantial improvements of social well-being. Their close relatives had been doctors, teachers, clergymen, and college presidents. There was even a governor. We tend to be fair-minded people, content with quiet pursuits, respectable, and faithful, she thought. All the Haylocks accomplished was to accumulate money and have a good time.

Emily was sure the Haylocks also had misgivings about Josie's and Press' relationship but for different reasons. They probably wished Preston had ten times more money, and so he should, with the way their girl spent it.

In spite of these misgivings, the engagement was announced in March of 1927, and the wedding was scheduled for the following November. The parties all had to fit into the two days here and the weekend there that Preston could afford to leave the cranberry bog and return to Chicago. They're going to kill him, thought Emily. What was it Josephine said—sixty-six parties were to be given in their honor?

The bridal dinner was at the Opera Club. When Emily arrived she was greatly disappointed to see so much alcohol being served. She overheard some guest say that Mr. Haylock was renowned for his martinis. Tonight the guests were just served his "sociables" and "talkatives." In deference to the seriousness of the occasion, his "knock-outs" were not offered. Later, Emily heard Mrs. Haylock brag to some guests that there were two restaurants in Havana which carried the "Haylock" on their cocktail list. As if this were not enough, after dinner the guests were served champagne!

The wedding was held in the St. Chrysostom Episcopal Church, named for the saint who launched a crusade against excessiveness and extreme wealth. The irony was not lost on Emily. The day before, when the bridal party arrived at the church for the rehearsal, they found the whole rear end of the church interior in scaffolding. The church was waiting for a new stained glass window, which had been donated and ordered years ago. It finally arrived a few days before the wedding and had to be placed and set before the cold weather descended upon Chicago. This discovery caused a great to-do, the upshot of which was that Mr. Haylock had to pay $150 to have the scaffolding taken down and another $150 to have it re-erected after the wedding.

According to the society pages of Chicago's papers, "The wedding was smashing! Together with its lavish reception at the Drake Hotel, it was the social highlight of the year."

Emily had learned over the last year that it was Josie's grandfather who was responsible for making the Haylock fortune. He had six children, one of whom was "Aunt Marie." It was well known that Marie had guarded her share of the inheritance carefully and invested it wisely. She had a husband but no children, so by the time she was elderly, she was very wealthy indeed. Aunt Marie was always the one to whom the younger generation went when they had a financial problem. She had a reputation of being an astute judge of character—every family needs a person like Marie, thought Emily.

Instead of a wedding present, Aunt Marie gave Preston and Josie cash to make improvements on the little house in the North Woods. Marie foresaw Preston's problem of carrying Josie over the threshold of a dwelling incredibly beneath her current standard of living. Emily had foreseen the same problem but didn't have the means to do anything about it.

CHAPTER 8

For the seven years since Tim's death, Preston had put all his money into the bog and lived by himself in Tim's little house. To stretch Aunt Marie's gift as far as possible, he and John Pete did much of the renovation work themselves. The former sitting room was reclassified as a hall/dining room because it opened onto a new large living room, off of which was built a bedroom and bathroom. Not one for understatement, Josie told Chicago friends, "It was the first bathroom in a private home for 100 miles."

Preston and John Pete put in a basement with a furnace that had ducts leading to all the rooms. They added another bedroom upstairs, which became known as the "sun porch" because three of its walls were screened windows. Each window was hinged at its top so it could be held open by hooks from the ceiling. Preston imagined he and Josie loving to sleep up there on a hot summer night. Off the new living room, they built a large porch, which overlooked the bog.

One day, John Pete asked Preston where Tim was buried. This took Preston by surprise, because they had just finished building a porch off the new living room. The porch faced the bog and from it you could see the headstone for Tim's grave that Emily had bought years ago. She and Preston placed it so that it faced the bog.

"Why, there," said Preston pointing toward the grave, "Tim is buried there."

John Pete had a slight frown on his face and asked: "Did you bury him there?"

"Well, no, mother and I came up from Chicago just after he was buried."

"I see."

It was intended that the new porch would be the front entrance to the house, but old habits were difficult to break. Most people entered through the creaky "back door" into the small scruffy kitchen with its wood stove and icebox.

Now there was running water to the bathroom and kitchen sink. The house was wired for electricity. A generator was installed in the wellhouse and an electric hot water heater in the bathroom. However, Press did not intend to use the generator more than once a week, unless they had company. All the rooms had brackets for kerosene lamps.

They arrived home from their European honeymoon in the spring of 1928. Preston went straight up to Springbrook to take the winter flood off the cranberries. Josephine remained in Chicago for a week to buy lamps, china, upholstery material, paints and wallpaper for their new little home in Wisconsin. Fortunately, she could have most of those things shipped ahead.

Press was pleased to be picking up his new wife at the Springbrook depot driving his emerald green Franklin. Although second hand, it was the Victory Model and it was in mint condition. He had to pick Josie up in a late afternoon snow storm that bordered on being a blizzard. "It handles beautifully in the snow," he reassured her. "This is a good test of my Frankie." He loaded all the pieces of Josie's luggage in the back seat and then placed the snowshoes he had brought from home at the very top of the pile..."So they are easily accessible in case we can't make it all the way to the bog," he explained to Josie. He realized he was a bit too eager perhaps, even cocky, so he added, "Don't worry, the house is snug and warm, and I've engaged a maid, Ethel."

This first exposure to life in the North Woods prompted Josie to write her cousin MaryAnn some detailed descriptions of her impressions:

> *...Ethel was so shy she could not look me in the eye. Preston had disconnected the plumbing in case the pipes froze. There came a time when it was necessary to go outside, whether one wanted to or not. Press turned to Ethel and said, "Mrs. Milton*

is a stranger around here. Will you kindly show her around and escort her outside?"

Ethel took me out to the little house, flung open the door and said: "Here you are Mrs. Milton."

As soon as I crossed the threshold, Ethel stepped inside too, and took possession of one hole for herself, indicating with a gesture that the other hole was for me. We sat in communion together and she began asking me several questions about our honeymoon. Once outside of the little house, Ethel reverted to her shy self and hardly looked at or talked to me.

Josie was a mere 22 years old when she became a cranberry wife. Preston knew she was unaccustomed to country living, a farming lifestyle, and hardship in general. Even though he never read her letters to her cousin MaryAnn, he could tell she needed that outlet for her frustrations:

The honeymoon is by no means over except from one angle, and that is the schedule. Preston is of course a Navy man. In no small or hesitant voice he told me that strict hours must be kept. With a few fumbles I finally got it right. I now have breakfast on the table at 6:30 A.M., at noon I dish up a hot dinner, then I prepare supper to tempt my man when he comes off the marsh at 6:00 P.M. The crew is working a 10-hour day now and, of course, Preston's hours are longer still....

In another letter she wrote:

One noon, after I had labored the better part of the morning over a delectable dinner, I was surprised not to have Preston come to the house promptly. I knew he had driven into Springbrook, two-and-a-half miles from the marsh, but I was still ignorant enough of husbands in general, and farmer husbands in particular, to believe that when they insisted upon a schedule that they intended to keep it as well.

Twelve-thirty came and went—one o'clock passed me by waiting alone. One-thirty was approaching and my dinner had sagged unmercifully when in chugged Preston. Before I had a chance to pout or look abused he came into the kitchen all smiles and said, "Hello, Josie. Is dinner ready?"

"It has been for some time," was my restrained reply.

"I'm sorry to be late, Doll. What are we having for dinner?" he cheerfully inquired.

I enumerated the various items, including the curdled corn pudding, the biscuits hard as rocks, and the limp salad, all of which information he took in with his customary grin and said, "Wait a minute; I want to wash up. I'll be right back." A few minutes later when he returned to the kitchen, he announced, "I'm starved. Bring on the chow. I'll bet it's good!"

"Not so good. But what took you so long?"

"Well, it's quite a story," he said, between mouthfuls. "You know I've wanted to have that pump fixed. It hasn't worked right for some time and I'm sick of fussing with it. Well, I took it in to old Burt and we decided to weld…and then I thought, while I was at it, I might just as well have that shaft ground which I had in the car. He did a good job.… I ran into Tony Speiler and he and I spoke about the road.… Well, after I left Tony, I got some tobacco at the store and headed for home. I had plenty of time and so when I was passing Hamilton's place, I saw him out front and thought I would speak to him about buying that trailer, so I drove into the yard. And what do you think? Do you know just as I got there—right before me in front of the house—George murdered his brother, shot him dead as a doornail! It all happened just like that. Rudy was chasing him with a pitchfork—George says he has been making a lot of trouble lately—and George managed to get to the house and get his gun and he let go just as I drove in. Of course, there was nothing for me to do but stay with George and his mother, Bertha, until the sheriff came, and that's the reason I'm late."

Press loved having Josie with him. The meals she cooked were delicious—a little on the fancy side, but delicious. Would he ever be able to go back to boiled potatoes and sausage? He realized that her responsibilities now were not those for which her upbringing had prepared her. Yes, she had been spoiled. She could no longer have whatever she wanted, but he could tell she was trying to adjust to his budget.

In a later letter to MaryAnn, Josie wrote:

Press often hired some young girl to help me with the household chores. We can't understand why one maid after another quits. There was Ethel, Olive, and Katherine, etc. They did not like eating separately from Press and me. One gave birth to a child soon after leaving. We hadn't realized that she was pregnant. Several were homesick. How could they be homesick? Press explains that these girls are used to work, hard work, in fact, but employment as a maid was new to them. In Springbrook, class distinctions are subtle and not of much consequence. Most people feel quite at home with each other, he says....

Press was also pleased that Josie enjoyed decorating their house. One day she said she was tired of calling the place "the marsh" or "the bog," so she started calling it "Miltonberry." Preston liked the name and thought Tim would have approved. She informed her friends and relatives to address their letters to "The Miltons, Miltonberry, Springbrook, Wisconsin."

Josie hired help to wallpaper the dining room and bedrooms. The floral designs gave a warm feel of country living. For each bedroom she had a dressing table and stool made, which she had covered in material that matched the wallpaper. Preston took Josie to Spooner—the largest nearby town—so she could buy material for quilts. She wrote her cousin:

...The selection was limited, of course, but it would do. We commissioned Ma Speiler and her daughter, Sophie, to make quilts for each bed. The two original bedrooms that Tim built I've called the 'pink room' and the 'blue room.' I ordered an upright piano to be placed in the dining room. I have plenty of time to play since Preston is usually out on the bog all day.

Press gave Josie the task of taking the big iron hoop down from where it hung outside the back door, carrying it down to the edge of the bog, and clanging it several times to announce that it was time for lunch. He loved hearing the clang, not only knowing he would soon be able to eat a delicious meal, but feeling Josie was a part of the working day on the marsh. He noticed with mild regret that to the bog's edge was as far as she ever ventured. She was comfortable in the house, gardening or driving in their Franklin. He could understand that being raised in the city, she could not get herself to walk out on the dikes or through the woods on a logging road. She had nothing to wear that was appropriate and just couldn't get herself to buy rugged, utilitarian clothes.

At the sound of the gong, the workers walked to the shady side of the warehouse and sat on logs to eat what was in their lunch pails. The Indians retired to their cabins in the woods where they hoped there would be something to eat. Preston and Josephine ate at the round walnut table in the dining room while the maid of the day ate in the kitchen.

One afternoon, when Josephine went down to the edge of the bog to ring the gong at lunchtime, she noticed a dead bird on top of Tim's grave. She told Preston about it. He immediately left the luncheon table and returned a few minutes later. "It's another red-winged blackbird.... Mother and I found one, years ago, exactly in the same position, same type of bird. Quite a coincidence, because redwings hang around water, so you always see them at the reservoir, where there are reeds, but never up here."

That night, Preston suggested that they sleep in the sun porch upstairs. It was a hot evening. They barely needed a sheet. He opened all the windows. They usually read before going to sleep, but in this room there was no place to put a kerosene lamp next to the bed. Preston had something else in mind. Josie had on his favorite nightie. The cotton was sheer and soft. She appeared both embarrassed and thrilled that he was looking at her.

He told her how when he made this room, he had looked

forward to such a night as this. At the first climatic moment, with perfect timing, a family of whip-poor-wills outside their windows began calling.

"I guess we have their approval," Josie said. She was ready to fall asleep, but then the screech owl started going, to say nothing of the crickets and frogs.

"We're never going to be able to sleep."

"Isn't that a shame?!"

One day, Press came home with a pair of socks and sneakers that he thought would fit Josie.

"I wish you would wear these tomorrow so I can take you on a tour of the warehouse. There is a lot I would like to show you."

The next day, as they walked down to the warehouse, Josie mentioned to Press, "It seems every time someone from Chicago finds out that you are a cranberry grower they say: 'I thought all the cranberries were grown in Massachusetts.'"

"It did start out that way, back in the 1870s. Even then, almost as many were grown on Long Island and in New Jersey. Since 1920, Wisconsin has become a significant producer. Most of Wisconsin's cranberries are grown on reclaimed wetlands in the central part of the state. Tim was one of the few growers who chose an area so far north. This bog is pristine, it has never been drained or used for producing any other agricultural crop."

"Thanks for these gym shoes. It would have been hard going in all this sand without them. Oh, look at that. What are they?"

"Goldeneyes—a type of duck," he answered. "They're here all year long. Do you hear that whistling noise their wings make?"

"Yes," said Josie. Then she added: "I hope Dad doesn't see them when he comes up to visit."

"I wouldn't allow any to be shot. He will have to behave while he's here." This rekindled Press' worry about Mr. Haylock's influence on their lives. For example, he was already paying the rent on a small house in Kenilworth, a suburb of Chicago, so Josie and Press could easily come down to the city anytime. It was wonderful that they had a place to live in the winter months, when it was bitterly cold in the North Woods, but Press didn't want to be indebted to Mr. Haylock.

Kenilworth was on the North Shore of Chicago. There, they could entertain friends and see the Haylocks frequently. His mother could also come up from the South Side to visit them, although she much preferred coming to stay with them in Springbrook. She was attuned to country living. This brought his mind back to Josie and how she needed some educating, so he said, "Cranberry bogs and their reservoirs are havens for birds and other wildlife, since most people try to avoid bogs because of their harsh conditions."

"It does seem alive with critters here both day and night."

"Cranberries are actually hearty. Most plants couldn't survive this acidic soil. Peat has few nutrients, so it doesn't lend itself to other types of farming. The difficult aspect of growing cranberries is frost."

"Will you have to flood tonight?"

"No, it won't be cold enough. When we harvest the berries we'll flood the bog, though. Let me show you why." Press went out on a dike, bent over and picked a green berry then sliced it in half with his pocket knife and held it for Josie to inspect. "See these cavities inside the berry? They're filled with air and that keeps the berry buoyant. When the berries redden up, they're ripe enough to harvest. It's then that we'll flood beds, one or two at a time, so the water just covers the vines. The berries want to float, so they pull on the vines and hold them upright. That makes them easier to rake, and the flood water lessens the impact when the men step on the vines."

They were approaching the warehouse now and walked into it on the ground level. Josie turned to the wall and said: "So those are the rubber boots I've heard about. They're so tall."

"Yes, the crew wears these hip boots because they have to wade through the flooded beds."

"Wouldn't the berry become soggy with so much water?"

"No, they're covered with a waxy coating called a cuticle that keeps them from becoming waterlogged when they're in the water, and from drying up when they're out. That coating is also important because it gives cranberries a shelf life of three months, which is really long compared to other fresh fruit." Preston was enjoying this. He realized how much he had learned since Tim died. They walked further into the warehouse. "Those are the rakes hanging up there on the wall. Rakes were first used for harvesting in 1920. Cranberries can now be gathered ten times faster than picking them by hand. They have revolutionized the harvest. See these tines on the side of the scoop?" Press took a rake down from the wall and held it by its two looping handles. "On the downward swing the tines enter the water and comb through the vines. On the upward swing the berries are pulled off the vines and they roll into the scoop. The process is gentle enough that the vines are not pulled out of the ground."

Josie had to give it a try herself. Swinging the rake in her frilly dress and sneakers was pleasantly ludicrous. "This is heavy," she said as she tried to swing it again.

"Yes, and that's why the rakers are paid the most money. The work is very hard on the back. Did you know that the rakers synchronize their strokes? They walk the bed in parallel lines but in staggered positions, so they don't hit each other with their rakes." He was pleased she was so interested. He led her further inside and pointed to the boxes stacked in the corner.

"When a rake is full of cranberries, it's emptied into one of those boxes. They float on the bed. When they're full, someone picks them up and puts them on the wagon that takes them to the warehouse."

"I know harvest comes in late September through October. Who can you hire at that time to do all this work?"

"Actually the timing is good. We start harvesting after the local farmers have brought in their crops. I don't think I've told you that Indians make the best rakers. Their backs don't seem to bother them as much."

"Do you think that they need to earn money more than the

farmers, so they ignore their back pains?"

"No doubt. I remember one year a farmer, Lawrence Neste he was, tried raking and quickly gave it up. He claimed it was the hardest work he'd ever done.

"Indians like to participate in the harvest because they have the chance to earn money while still being able to live together in the bunkhouse. Some bring tepees so their families can come with them."

"I really would like to see a harvest. Do you hire women?"

"Yes, they usually sit at conveyor belts and sort through the berries, throwing out those that are spoiled."

Josie looked around. "Oh, is that the box you ship them out in?" She pointed at a small crate under the stairway leading to the second floor.

"What is that doing there? I've never seen a crate here before." Preston didn't like to have things out of order, and he was sure the crate hadn't been there earlier. "It should never have been put here." He retrieved the crate and opened it up. Josie came right to his side so she could peer inside. She reached down and pulled out a piece of paper.

"Look at this drawing. How cute! It looks like a child might have done it." She withdrew several more sheets. Press recognized Tim's writing on the papers. The text was neat, as Tim's handwriting always was, but the drawings were quite crude.

"Whoever did these drawings certainly was no artist, but listen to this story."

Preston's heart sank. He had a feeling of what was to come, and it was something he dreaded.

Josie read aloud from the first paper:

Tales of Elm Grove

Emma Cranberry lived in Elm Grove, next to a cranberry bog with her faithful companion, Blackie the black-backed woodpecker. Blackie had chipped out a hole in the biggest elm tree for Emma to live in…

Josie continued reading the story in silence for a moment, then looked at the next sheet of paper. "This next tale is about Emma's adventure with her friend Frankie Frog…. These are so sweet! I wonder who wrote them?"

Josie said nothing more but looked up at Press. He knew she had sensed that he was upset.

"OK, Josie, I guess I must explain, but you must promise not to tell anyone else what I'm going to tell you, and that means even your cousin MaryAnn."

They returned to the house and Preston told Josie all he knew about Tim having an illegitimate child. In a way, he was relieved to be able to share all of this with her. He had kept it to himself for eight years.

After a half-hour's discussion, Josie asked, "What does the red-winged blackbird we found on Tim's grave the other day have to do with it?"

"Oh, I forgot to explain that John Pete is convinced that Tim isn't buried in his grave." Preston told her that John Pete tested the grave with a dead red-winged blackbird. "He says if the bird doesn't fly off within a day, then the dead person's soul is in trouble. According to John Pete, if the soul were at peace then it would be able to revive the bird and let it fly off."

"Really!"

"A bunch of hooey if you ask me, but he says it's based on an old Ojibwe story."

"Why didn't you just dig up the grave?"

"I'm sorry, as much as I like John Pete, a dead blackbird remaining dead is not enough to make me believe that something is fishy about Tim's grave."

"I wonder why John Pete is suspicious? I mean, he must suspect something or he wouldn't have bothered with the red-winged blackbird test. Twice! You did say that you found another dead bird on Tim's grave some time ago, didn't you?"

"Yes, when Mom and I were up here right after Tim was buried." Preston didn't want to tell Josie, because she was far too inquisitive as it was, but he had wondered if John Pete didn't make up the red-winged blackbird story just to get him to...to do what? To dig up Tim's grave, just as Josie suggested? Press preferred that Josie would lose interest in all this, and right away. She could be impetuous and determined. Thank God she didn't have the strength to dig up the grave herself or she would probably try!

Press explained to Josie that he was still an outsider in this community and that he needed the good opinion of the people with whom he had to work. "It did cross my mind that Clarence might not have been totally honest with us, but after all, he's a clergyman. That's the type of person you would be least likely to suspect of anything malicious."

"Hmm, the black collar effect!" They remained silent for a while before she continued, "Wouldn't your mother be horrified, if she knew about the child?"

"Exactly, and I'm horrified too. I can't imagine how it happened. Mom wouldn't recover from the humiliation if she knew. You know what pride she has in our family."

"Oh yes, I certainly do!"

Preston tried to ignore the tone of Josie's remark.

Josie pursued her curiosity with relish. "Why did the Ellsworths bury the body before you and your Mom arrived, if there wasn't something to cover up?"

"Oh yes, I forgot to mention that Clarence did say something about the body thawing faster than he expected. Evidently, its odor was horrific. They wanted to spare us from that by burying it before we came."

"Another thing that I can't figure out is why Tim didn't just marry that other woman, whoever she was? It appears from the letter he wrote you when you were in the Navy that he really loved her, and from the date of Emma's birth their relationship must have started before he married Sarah. Didn't you say neither Tim nor Sarah seemed excited about their marriage?"

"Yes, that's what Mom and I both thought."

"Well, one thing is certain—we have to dig up Tim's body. Do you think it will have completely decomposed by now? Even if it has, we may find something that would help clarify all this."

Josie is trying to take charge, Press thought. I have to slow her down. "I don't know, but I would imagine that after eight years it would have decomposed completely. And another thing, Mother is coming next week. She'll probably stay a month, and the first thing she will do is visit Tim's grave."

"Can we plant new sod, so we can tell her that the grass on the front lawn needed to be re-established?"

"That's expensive," answered Press.

"Well, maybe we could plant flowers there instead of grass and pretend we wanted to make the gravesite fancy."

Preston didn't say so, but he thought his mother would like things to be kept as natural as possible. He dreaded opening the grave. "People will get suspicious if they see we're digging up the grave."

"Who will know? Let's see. Oh dear, Gladys is supposed to come tomorrow to help out in the kitchen. We'll have to send her home, or maybe she has a telephone so we could tell her not to come?"

Preston suggested that, with all these complications, they should put off opening the grave at least until after his mother's visit. For one thing, if they did find something wrong with Tim's corpse, they would have to call in the sheriff. Then his mother and the whole town would find out everything.

After his mother's visit, Preston kept putting off opening Tim's grave. Finally, Josie stopped asking him about it. She had the distraction of preparing for a visit from her parents, thankfully.

By 1929, Preston was harvesting 27 acres. This brought in about $7,000. Clearly, this was not enough to live in the way Josie was accustomed. Josie contributed money that went to pay for niceties like the piano, and occasionally for a more utilitarian need, such as a truck for use on the bog. In 1930, Josie paid for a third floor to be added to the warehouse. During harvest, the berries could be dried in crates on the upper two floors, with the side panels propped open to let in air. She made sure the entire warehouse was painted white with green trim to match the main house.

The milling process began on the top floor. Dried berries would be poured into a funnel which allowed the chaff to pass through a screen while the berries continued along, falling onto a series of boards and conveyer belts. The boards caused good berries to bounce and be directed to a conveyor belt. The system eventually brought the good berries down to the bottom floor and into the sorting room, where women sitting on stools weaned out any remaining bad berries. Over the years, the same sorters came back to work. These were women of all ages. While sorting, they chatted amicably and became good friends.

The final job was to put the berries into pine, quarter-barrel boxes. The top was nailed down and on the sides was stenciled *Eatmor Cranberries*. Truckloads were driven to the depot in Springbrook for shipping to markets around the country.

~

Over the years, Preston occasionally had long conversations with John Pete when they were out on the bog together.

"My people covered much of Minnesota, Wisconsin and Michigan, as well as the Southern Canadian lands of Ontario, Manitoba and Saskatchewan. We were spread out like cirrus clouds, making it difficult for the white man's diseases to kill us off. They wanted our land. First they wanted all of us to move to Kansas and Oklahoma. 'How can wispy clouds be a threat?' we asked. It was our land they wanted. We were 'unsettled weather' to them, so they collected us on small reservations. At least we are on lands that we know, unlike other Indian nations. This bog is our land. Our burial grounds are throughout these woods.

"We were a great nation. We extended from the northern shores of Lake Huron as far west as the Turtle Mountains of North Dakota. My dad always said: 'Our greatness is of a form that the white man has trouble understanding."'

These talks with John Pete increased Preston's reverence for the land, and instilled new notions in him regarding the importance of the native Indians. He remembered them most when he was walking alone on the bog. He felt a presence of all the people that walked the bog before him. It was both humbling and spiritually satisfying to feel those connections.

Preston shared some of this with Josie at night, when they had time to relax and talk. She remembered when she studied Longfellow's poem, *The Song of Hiawatha*, in school. Her teacher had said that only the name Hiawatha came from the Iroquois— that the actual stories were Chippewa. "The next time we go into Spooner I will try to take out a copy of *The Song of Hiawatha* from the library, and we can read it together."

By 1930, they both felt that Press needed the help of a foreman—someone who would live year-round at Miltonberry, as well as relieve Preston during the wee hours of the night when the bog had to be flooded.

John Pete was fine at what he did. When he was at Miltonberry, he worked hard and did well at directing the other Indians. He set a good example for them. But John Pete and his wife, Ziigwan, wanted to live on the reservation during the winter months, so they could be with their people when there was no work on the bog. Press worried that if John Pete were the foreman, some of the other hired hands might balk at taking orders from an Indian. Also, as foreman, John Pete would have to purchase things for the bog. John Pete had lived much of his life bartering. He did not have much experience with money. After several interviews, Preston hired a carpenter, who agreed to be the foreman and build a house for himself across from theirs.

For the first few years of their marriage, Josephine's parents visited Miltonberry each summer, but after a while, they came up only every other year. Mr. Haylock liked the outdoors if it involved duck hunting or drinking cocktails on the terrace, but walking through tall grass or watching men dig ditches and fix machinery were not things he cared about. He often praised Press for his diligence to his cranberry "business." It irked Press that the man seemed incapable of saying the word "bog."

As for Mrs. Haylock, she wore long underwear while at Miltonberry even though her visits were during the hottest part of summer. She didn't like to expose her skin to direct sunlight. This meant she rarely went outdoors. "She's like a hothouse plant," Preston muttered under his breath. Neither of the Haylocks experienced (or were even remotely aware of) the very aspects of Miltonberry that Preston loved the most.

With a mother like that, no wonder Josie doesn't take more interest in the bog, thought Preston. Her excursions from the patio were merely to plant a row of dahlias. To Preston, the bog was beautiful—a flat expanse of 30 or more acres, surrounded by woods. It was teeming with life. Looking down as you walked along its dikes, you would always be startled by grasshoppers and frogs that waited until the last second to hop out of your way. The sheer variety of insects was astounding. How could anyone not be intrigued by praying mantises, walking sticks, and daddy-long-legs? On the patio Josie worried about mosquitoes, deer flies and gnats. Ticks were added to that list, if he could get her to walk in the woods. The threat of bloodsuckers kept her from swimming in the river. She did relish the frequent breezes, which brought her a cornucopia of pine fragrances, but to her, much of the North Woods was not the magical experience that it had become for him.

What Josie did take an interest in was Tim's death. She couldn't leave the topic alone. Just the other day, she had asked to re-read the letter Tim had sent him during the war, the one about hiding something behind a stone in the fireplace. After she read it, she said, "You know, Press, there are other possible explanations for Tim's death that we haven't considered."

"What do you mean?"

"Tim's letter is awfully gloomy, don't you think?"

"Well, yes. I suppose, but he was afraid, perhaps, that I would be killed. It was written during the war."

"Have you ever thought that he might have been thinking that he would die soon?"

"Don't tell me you're suggesting he thought someone was going to bump him off?" Josie had a great imagination. She had trouble accepting the plain truth. She tended to want to make every event into something dramatic and complicated.

"Well, that is a possibility," Josie continued. "In fact, there are several possibilities. It's also possible that he may have been thinking of taking his own life."

"No, I doubt very much that Tim would have ever considered suicide. He was the type of person who was happy in his own head. I mean, his pleasures came from calculating, reading, theorizing, experimenting—that sort of thing."

"If he had committed suicide, do you think Clarence would want people to know?"

"No, he probably would have considered it a disgrace."

"…enough of a disgrace to cover it up?"

"Yes, I suppose that is possible."

"So he might have wanted to bury the body without your seeing it?"

"Yes, that would fit, except Tim would never have committed suicide."

"OK, I will lay that aside for the moment, do you want to hear another possibility?"

"Sure." Press tried hard not to crack a smile.

"Maybe Tim struck a deal with Sarah. He would disappear while she faked his death. Then he would be free to go off and marry the woman he loved, leaving Sarah a widow, who would be free to remarry. The only trouble with this theory is that Sarah would probably need help in making a coffin and having Tim buried, so her father would have to be in on it."

"No. That's no good. Tim would never leave his cranberries, and he would have to lose all contact with Mom and me for the rest of his life if he ran away. He just wasn't that type of person. Besides, if he took on another name and married the other woman, he would be committing bigamy, and he would be leaving Sarah all his debts."

"Not if they figured that you would be willing to take them on."

"Josie, sometimes you make my head spin! My brother would never have purposefully left me all his debts. He was far too responsible for that. The simplest explanation is usually the best, in a situation like this, in accordance with the law of parsimony. Tim simply slipped and fell down the stairs."

But Josie wouldn't be convinced without more evidence, or some final proof. She was not going to stop trying to figure out just what happened to Tim.

II

THE MAIN STREAM

CHAPTER 9

In 1889, Clarence Ellsworth and Harold Morris started their studies at Rice Lake Seminary School. They had been randomly selected to be roommates. Many late night stories back and forth eventually turned their relationship into more a pledge to secrecy than a friendship. Harold knew he could trust Clarence.

If it weren't for the pledge, their lives after graduation would probably never have crossed again. Over time, Harold noticed that Clarence became focused on the little community around Springbrook. Although his ministry work seemed to keep his family out of poverty, Harold could tell it was not very satisfying to him. He seemed most happy talking about his beautiful daughter Sarah.

For his part, Harold never became a minister. He was the son of a well-known, rags-to-riches lumber magnate who owned sawmills and lumber camps all over northern Wisconsin. His father wanted Harold to follow in his footsteps and take over his business, the Morris Lumber Company. Harold knew his father was afraid that he wouldn't have the toughness to run the business.

"You have to be shrewd," his father told him. "Your agents have to be instructed to buy good timberland any way they can. You may have to dupe Indians into thinking they are getting a good price when, in fact, their timber is being grossly undervalued. Although peavies and pike poles were designed to help free up log jams, they may have to be used as weapons in order to get your logs to the dam before those of another company."

When Harold said he wanted to go to seminary, his father proposed: "First spend a year or more working as a lumberjack and log running. When you're finished, if you still want to go to seminary school, fine, you can go." Harold overheard his father say to his mother, "I'm fairly sure our bright boy won't fall for that religious nonsense once he's exposed to the excitement of the lumber world."

Before Harold left to begin his logging experience, his father cautioned, "You can't get caught up on the small stuff in this business. Don't become overly concerned with ethical principles and the morality of little acts. You've got to see the big picture. Watch out, Harold, you've never had to fight for anything. You've only lived an easy life. The opportunity to get something of value only comes once. You have to be ready to grab it when it comes. Yes, your life has been too easy. You have to be toughened up. Also, it will be good for you to know the logging business from the bottom up, to understand first-hand each stage of the process."

Being a young man of eighteen years, Harold looked forward to the adventure his father proposed. In the summer of 1888, he got to accompany a headman whose job it was to plan how a new area was to be logged. The territory was around Lake Gilmore. The headman planned the location of the bunkhouse, cook shanty and logging roads. Only after these structures were built and the roads were cleared, did the lumberjacks start to arrive.

From the headman, Harold learned the order of operations. The first trees to be felled were those on the edge of the lake. Oxen pulled the logs on skids down the relatively short distance to the water's edge. The logs would be left there on the banks until spring. When the cold weather set in, these logs froze together, and as the snow deepened the men switched to using sleighs. Four-to-six-horse teams would pull a 16-foot wide sleigh, on top of which the logs would be stacked to a height of at least 12 feet.

From October through March, Harold worked as a lumberjack in the woods around Gilmore Lake. Snowshoe rabbits frolicked about as the men and horses worked all the daylight hours. Harold was one of 43 men in the crew. He wore the same clothes all winter long, boiling them once a month in an attempt to get them clean. No one shaved. Beards helped keep them warm. By

November, they all had lice. At night, with wet woolens hung up on the rafters to dry, the odor inside the bunkhouse was almost overpowering.

By 1888, the crosscut saw was being used to fell trees rather than the ax, although a notch was axed in the trunk so the saw could get started. The men always worked on the edge of the woods and made sure the trees fell in the area already cleared. Harold learned that "swampers" were men who cleaned up the ruts so a team of horses or oxen could get in with a scoot. That was one of the lowest paid jobs because it took no skill.

For one week, Harold was allowed to try to ax the 'bark mark' on logs so they could be identified as belonging to Morris Lumber Company. Once logs were mixed up in the water it was important to have a way of identifying their ownership. The mark 'ML' was too tricky for Harold to master, so the foreman politely suggested that he get experience being a loader. This was the best paying job of all because it took great skill. Loaders stacked the logs on the sleighs. Some of the logs were five feet in diameter. "I never got the knack of that either," Harold told Clarence. "Oh well, I thought, there were plenty of other tasks for me to experience. The foreman was always polite to me, but I could tell he thought I botched up most jobs."

As they got deeper into the winter, the wages increased from $16 a month to $2 a day. Eventually, the logs would be moved by water to the sawmill in Stillwater, Minnesota, on the Saint Croix River. Their operations were so remote that nobody knew how much the lumberjacks left to rot. Clear wood (without knots) brought the highest price—$6 for 1,000 board-feet—so the lumberjacks left behind all of the tree above the first branch.

Each day began before dawn, with the men being fed a hearty breakfast in the cook shanty. During the day, the cooks prepared three meals to be carried to wherever the men were working. Then at night, well after dark, they were served a huge meal back at camp in the cook shanty. The wonderful food kept the men going with something to look forward to.

"All would have been well, if I had only tried to learn the lumberjack trade. Unfortunately, being the owner's son, I was not disciplined whether I performed badly on or off the job."

Most cook shanties in lumber camps had no female workers, but in this camp, the head cook was Ojibwe and he insisted on having his very capable daughter as a helper. The other lumberjacks were quite aware that the pretty Lily Pine was off-limits, but Harold gradually realized that he could get away with becoming her friend. Nobody reprimanded him. The lumberjacks, foremen, and cooks just looked the other way. Lily and Harold talked and walked together. Harold even managed to take time off to be with her. All the cooks slept in the cook's shanty. At night, Harold found he could creep in the dining room to meet Lily.

"When spring came our 'friendship' had to stop, because sleeping arrangements completely changed." Harold had to move on to his next experience: driving the logs to the sawmill in Stillwater. The creek running out of Gilmore Lake was dammed up so that by spring, the lake level rose. The melting of snow and ice inundated the logs waiting on its banks. "As the logs began to float we gathered them in a bundle (boom) of 1,000 and lashed them together with hooks and chains."

The lumbermen of this era constantly demonstrated their ingenuity. Without the availability of steam power, they devised a method of moving the boom across the lake to the dam. This was not easy, because the lake had no current and they couldn't pull the boom from the shore. The system involved two boats and anchors, with a windlass wound by two horses, using thick ropes for towing.

When the boom reached the dam, the chains were removed and the logs were free to be sluiced through the dam, six at a time. "They floated on that creek for only a half-mile before it flowed into the Totogatic River. Then things got tricky. The Totogatic is a small river with a fast current. For 12 miles or so, we as 'runners' had to prevent logs from jamming." Eventually, the Totogatic flowed into the slower moving Namekagon River.

Five miles further down stream, the Namekagon joined the Saint Croix River. This river would carry them directly to the Morris sawmill at Stillwater, just east of Minneapolis and St. Paul.

"I used to think of us runners as fresh-water cowboys— rounding up our logs, corralling them into booms, directing them through sluices, and shepherding them downstream."

The more dams there were, the easier the passage. Logs often got caught up in rapids and at bends in the river. Then runners jumped from log to log using their peavies and pike poles to free up the jam. When the jam broke, the foreman would shout: "Greenhorns ashore! Married men up trees!"

"I never figured out what that meant exactly, but I think I correctly assumed that I belonged in the greenhorn category. I tried to always stay close to the shore. Some of the runners were daredevils who defied orders to come ashore. They rode the logs through any rapid. If one fell in the water, there was no chance of swimming to shore, as the entire river had logs bobbing in it. Those of us who were river runners wore caulks on our boots to help us 'stay on the sunny side.'"

All logging companies provided a wanigan between dams. A wanigan was a boat about 18 feet wide and 60 feet long. It carried supplies, the cook shanty and 'beds' only for the cooks. Once Harold became a runner, there was no opportunity to be with Lily. The runners, like the lumberjacks, were served five meals a day. At night, Harold joined the other runners to sleep in tents on shore. Each tent held four men and two "beds" consisting of two blankets on the ground and two blankets for cover.

At times, the foreman would have to send a runner back to the previous dam with the message to let out more water. The runners had to work continually during daylight to take advantage of the flow. The run took two-and-a-half months and the men had no time off. "I resisted smoking or chewing tobacco, but when we reached Stillwater, where we were paid, I joined some of the men for drinking in the saloons. The smart ones avoided temptations by cashing their checks and buying money orders to mail home. I got very drunk. One night a horrific fight broke out and parts of that saloon we were in got smashed to smithereens. By the time these men returned home, there was little money left for their families."

In the early days—the days of Harold's father—the logs were moved only by water. Without machinery, technical assistance, roads or maps, the men had to resort to brute strength and ingenuity. These were the conquistadors of the North Woods. Greedy and aggressive, they grabbed whatever they could. By the late1880s, railroads helped tame their pursuits. Railroad companies profited from the logging business and willingly built spur lines to get as close as possible to the lumber camps. It was due to logging that small towns like Springbrook now had access to a passenger train.

Although Harold found his logging experience exhilarating, he realized he was more suited for an administrative job, and he still wanted to go to seminary school before working for Morris Lumber Company.

It was during seminary school that Harold confessed to Clarence that he had fathered a boy with Lily Pine, who lived on the Lac Courte Oreilles Reservation. He felt very guilty about it because he realized he had been reckless with Lily's future. "I decided not to tell my father. He would have been furious, but not for the right reason. He would be disappointed in me for being a softy, for caring about the future of a girl whom I used."

After graduating, Harold found that certain skills he had picked up in seminary school helped him run his father's business. For example, no matter what the subject of a business deal, Harold could dig out of his memory an appropriate quote from the Bible. This helped to sanctify the negotiation and put it on a higher plane than just wheeling and dealing. He learned the art of oration and could stir people with his speech. These techniques could obscure his maneuvering while turning a financial deal to his advantage.

In 20 years, Harold had more than tripled his father's business.

He had timber concerns in three states: Michigan, Wisconsin and Minnesota.

Each year, Harold took money to Lily and little Sammy. Lily soon married a reservation man, Mike Cloud, who was pleased to adopt Sammy and give him his last name. Harold began to think that the relaxed attitude of Ojibwe people about bastard children was more ethical than that in his culture, but he kept this thought to himself.

A few years later, Harold married Mamie Johnson from Minneapolis, daughter of the owner of the Soo Railroad. After Harold and Mamie had their own baby—"darling little Richard"— Harold broke down and told Mamie that little Richard had a half-brother living on the reservation. Mamie was offended and saddened. From then on, she kept a close eye on Harold.

Although Mamie refused to let Harold officially recognize Sammy as his son, Harold was determined to continue with his annual child support, but he had to be sure Mamie didn't find out. It was then that he thought of Clarence Ellsworth. So, several years after leaving seminary, Harold suddenly invited Clarence to join him and his other cronies at his private hunting lodge in the woods on the Totogatic River for deer season. During the week at the lodge, Harold found a moment to take Clarence aside to ask him privately to deliver what was in the envelope to Lily Pine on the reservation.

By 1912, Harold began to reflect upon his accomplishments and found another source of guilt. Lumbering had made him wealthy, but left the land scarred. Due in part to his greed, much of the beauty of three states—states that he considered home— had been destroyed. True, cutover lands encouraged settlers to move up north to farm the land that had been cleared by lumbermen, but the beauty of dense woodland was gone and would take at least 200 years to recover. He was losing interest in the lumber business and was more than ready to turn it over to his son. Harold began grooming Richard to expand the business in the Pacific Northwest.

How could he make amends for stripping the beauty from the north? The answer came when he considered the middle of Wisconsin, where there had been a great glacial lake, which had receded to produce cropland. Harold saw that cranberries—a native food crop—did well in the middle of the state and hit upon the idea that its production should be promoted in the north as well. Cranberries were not only compatible with wetlands, they helped to preserve them. Cranberries became the answer. He decided to offer financial incentives to cranberry pioneers.

Harold smiled to himself when he realized that he had become the very "softy" that his father had warned him about. Seminary had taught Harold that "you cannot serve both God and Mammon." By encouraging cultivation of cranberries, marshlands would be developed, providing habitats ideal for birds. On the uplands surrounding marshes would grow pink lady slippers, blue flag irises, and black-eyed susans. He envisioned ruffed grouse, badgers, raccoons and river otters returning to northern Wisconsin.

~

Whatsoever a man soweth, that shall he also reap.
—Galatians 6:7

CHAPTER 10

WINTER OF 1915

Using Mr. Ellsworth's directions, Tim had no difficulty finding the Morris Lumber Company building. Fortunately, it wasn't far from the Minneapolis train station. As a structure, the building stood out from those around it. Like them, it was constructed of wood but with much more attention to design and detail. One large turret ran up beyond its three stories anchoring it to the corner of two busy streets. On the top floor of the turret was Harold Morris' office. Tim entered the outer office clutching his drawings and maps. On the facing wall hung a huge painting of a great blue heron standing motionless in a wooded stream—alert, and ready to stab a fish. Tim was very nervous, but Mr. Morris seemed pleased to meet him and was eager to hear about Tim's cranberry bog. He inquired about several details when Tim showed him his drawings of the bog and property. They discussed at length Tim's plans and schedule for the bog's development.

"What diseases and pests are you anticipating having to deal with?"

Tim had no difficulty answering such questions. He had read everything he could find about cotton ball disease, fire and fruit worm, etc.

Mr. Morris probed further; "How would you treat for fruit worm?"

Again Tim was ready. He had even studied some of these topics at Amherst.

"As Clarence has told you, I like to help promote cranberry cultivation in the northern part of Wisconsin. I might be interested in helping you, but I would like first to understand your exact financial situation." Mr. Morris took notes as Tim explained how he had spent his inheritance so far, what was left still to spend and the fact that a $1,000 loan from the Bank of Hayward was outstanding.

"I see. OK. I want to suggest that you join the American Cranberry Exchange. It's a cooperative for the purposes of marketing cranberries. This will give you access to a marketing cartel. I also want you to know about some other cranberry growers that may be able to give you advice from time to time." He wrote down some names and addresses and handed the paper to Tim.

Tim's heart was beginning to sink. It looks like I'm not going to get the loan, he thought.

"Well, you appear to be a practical man and you seem to know quite a bit about cranberries. Yes, you are exactly the type of grower whom I would like to support."

Tim tried not to show his relief.

"But because you are an outsider, that is, from Chicago, I would feel more comfortable about loaning you the $20,000 if I was sure you were more attached to the community. I wouldn't like to loan you the money only to see you sell out in three or four years and move back to Chicago."

"I do intend this as my life's work."

"Good. Come back in a year's time and give me some evidence that you are part of the Springbrook community and I will loan you $20,000."

Tim was thrilled. He boarded the train back to Springbrook thinking that now he definitely would have enough money to get his cranberry business up and running. He was sincerely grateful to Mr. Ellsworth for connecting him with Mr. Morris. What kind of proof could he offer Mr. Morris that he was in the cranberry business for the long run?

Both Mr. Ellsworth and Sarah met him at the depot.

Chapter 11

Meg was seated in front of the sewing machine working on a dress for Sarah's honeymoon. It was a new pattern so there were some tricky parts. "No ruffles," Sarah insisted. "Ruffles are out. Just loose folds starting under the breast."

Meg asked her where she found this pattern.

"It was advertized in a magazine that I saw in Walgreen's."

It had always struck Meg as odd that her sister could be so focused on the way her clothes looked, when her pretty face was by far sufficient to impress people.

"Do you like this brocade ribbon? Of course it isn't true brocade but I think it will do nicely at the top of the folds, don't you?"

"Yes, sure."

"Would you mind sewing that in by hand so the stitches won't show?"

"Really, Sarah, you could do that yourself." For at least three years now, Meg had been doing all the sewing for the family. Usually she didn't mind, because she was a much better seamstress than either her mother or sister, but it annoyed her that Sarah, who did so little work of any kind, could so easily ask her to do more.

Sarah went off in a huff, irritating Meg even more. All Sarah ever seems to do is to arrange the flowers in Church, Meg thought. A minute later, Sarah came back into the room: "Look Meg, I know that my getting married is hard for you. You'll be left with a lot of work to do, but you too will be able to leave someday. You'll meet some nice young farmer."

Meg thought she could read Sarah's mind: she's thinking

"pig farmer!" It was time that she tell Sarah directly what she was thinking. "I worry about you, Sarah. How are you going to cope as a wife if you don't make yourself do the everyday chores around here? I know you think that once you marry Tim Milton, you'll get to go to Chicago all the time, ride the El or streetcars, and shop in department stores."

"Well, we should be spending the winters there when there isn't much to do on the bog."

"Did Tim tell you that?" Meg kept looking at her sewing but couldn't help adding: "Does he know you don't like to cook, weed the vegetable garden, keep the… "

"Shut up, Meg. I know you're jealous. We are different. I don't like living in Springbrook. I like cities, people, a more sophisticated way of life. "

Before Sarah could leave the room again, Meg quickly said: "Exactly, but by marrying Tim you are going to spend your time on a cranberry bog." Sarah remained silent, not because she was reflecting on what Meg had just said. No, she has just run out of other displays of her bad temper. Now she was ready to sulk. She has the emotional maturity of a six-year-old, Meg thought.

Meg asked herself, was she jealous of Sarah? She didn't want to be jealous. She wanted Sarah to be happy. Meg wasn't sure that Tim Milton made Sarah happy. Here they were engaged and yet they didn't often talk to each other. The only time she went out to Tim's place was with Mom and Dad.

Several times after church, Meg had tried to talk with Tim, but he wasn't very sociable. He seemed quiet and stiff. She wanted to get to know him to be sure Sarah was doing the right thing. Two weeks ago, she had finally made some headway when she questioned Tim about his cranberry marsh. He finally took his eyes off of Sarah and looked at her for some time, smiling, speaking freely about the bog and the improvements he was making to it. I think that made him happy.

What really worried Meg was that she didn't know why Tim and Sarah were getting married. Had Dad instigated this she wondered? Over the last few years, there had been several trips to the Twin Cities, supposedly for the purpose of going shopping or visiting her Mom's relatives. Somehow, once in Minneapolis, Dad always tried to contact Harold Morris to suggest that the two families meet. That was never possible, however, for one reason or another. Recently Meg stayed home from these trips. Her mother pleaded with her to come, but Meg said someone had to stay home to take care of the animals.

Meg knew that her father's friendship with Harold Morris meant a lot to him. Was he now encouraging Sarah to marry Tim because he was trying to become a cranberry grower? Is this another effort on her dad's part to curry favor with Mr. Morris? No, it is more likely that dad thinks Tim would be a good match for Sarah. She overheard her dad tell her mother, "He is educated, hard working and ambitious. Did I tell you that Harold says cranberry growers can become wealthy men?"

A few weeks later, Meg rode her horse over much of Tim's property, as she had done occasionally in the past. Now, more than ever, she was convinced that Sarah would not enjoy living there. Sarah was not the outdoor type. What a shame. Meg herself would love to live there. Ever since she was in her teens she enjoyed taking long walks through the woods. Her family was used to seeing her return windblown and muddy. Recently, Meg realized her advantage over her sister. No one expected Meg to look nice. Her hair was too curly to ever appear neat. She was short and slightly overweight. But these very features, perhaps, ensured her the liberty to explore the outdoors. Meg had long since given up trying to explain to her family the thrill of watching wrens go from hatchlings to fledglings or discovering wolf tracks on a trail.

Some time later, her family went to Minneapolis for a week. Meg had an additional reason for staying home this time. It gave her a chance to make the curtains she had promised for Sarah and Tim's wedding present. Sarah had already selected the material for each of the five windows.

"Can you imagine," Sarah told Meg a few days before, "Tim asked me, 'Why do we need curtains? There's no one around to look in.'" She laughed, "I think he understands now. Anyway, he has already put the curtain rods up."

Before sewing, Meg had to take measurements. This meant a trip to Tim's house. After seeing her family off at the depot, Meg saddled up Maple. Two weeks ago she had found a path in the woods that she thought might lead close to the cranberry bog. Now she had the time to investigate, so she guided Maple over what she imagined to be an old Indian trail. She knew the Namekagon River would always be on her left. All she would have to do is keep a half-mile southeast of it and she should run into the cranberry bog. Meg imagined herself to be on an old tote path that trappers had used to bring their furs to the trading post, now called "Springbrook." According to some old timers, it was first known as the "Namekagon Trading Post." When it grew to be a town, it was called simply, "Namekagon." Then, about fifteen years ago, the new Postmistress, who couldn't cope with spelling "Namekagon," changed the town's name to Springbrook, a name she thought would imply its location between Spring Creek and Bean Brook.

The path led Meg near a lovely elm grove. She dismounted Maple to explore the grove by foot before riding on to the bog. At the spot where the path petered out completely, she saw the Indian cabin on Tim's property. It was noon when she arrived at Tim's house, a good time to catch him in. She knocked and called out his name several times, but he didn't seem to be there, so she rode down to the bog to look for him. There she found some Indians working who said that they hadn't seen Tim all morning, so Meg went back to the house, called out again and got no reply. She thought it would be all right to enter.

With her tape measure, pencil and paper, Meg recorded the size of the window in the sitting room when she thought she heard something up stairs. She listened carefully. It sounded like a weak voice saying, "Who's there?" she thought.

Timid and somewhat frightened, Meg forced herself to climb the stairs and was distressed to find Tim in bed with a raging fever and barely aware of her. Noticing the thermometer by his bed, she shook it down and took his temperature—104.2°. Trying to remove the sound of alarm in her voice she asked, "Tim, do you have any willow bark?

"No," he said weakly.

"I'll get some and be back soon."

Meg found an extra cover to put on him. Before leaving the house, she took a quick look at what Tim had in his icebox and cupboards. She and her mother had experience responding to emergencies like this in their church community. This time, she took the road home so she could ride Maple at a fast pace. She found the willow bark and put it in her saddlebag along with a ham hock, a few carrots, potatoes and onions. She knew Tim had flour but forgot to look for yeast, so she brought some anyway. On her saddle she tied an old blue comforter that her family rarely used. Without putting too much of a strain on Maple, Meg returned as fast as she could while thinking how she could quickly make an infusion of willow bark for Tim. Outside his kitchen door she had noticed a kerosene stove. She would use that instead of the wood burning stove in the kitchen, which would take too long to fire up and make it unbearably hot on this mid-June day. Ten minutes after arriving, Meg ascended the steep steps to Tim's bedroom with a cup of tea. She thought he looked better before he even took a sip—white as paste, still, yet he was able to muster a smile. Such gratitude warmed Meg, and she was determined to keep on nursing him.

Meg returned to the kitchen to make soup. There was no bread so she prepared dough and set it to rise. This was typical work for Meg. If anyone later thought she was being brazen, she would remind them that pastoral care was one of the things she often did for the church.

It wasn't safe to leave him alone, so Meg spent the night in the other bedroom. His fever was going down, but she wanted to be sure he kept drinking willow bark infusion. By morning his tem-perature was only 100.2°. She had done all the measuring needed to sew the curtains, so she decided to go home after serving Tim a light breakfast, promising to return later in the afternoon to check on him and bring him some dinner.

Over the course of the next few days, Meg sewed the curtains using her family's Singer. Not knowing what she was missing, she was perfectly comfortable pumping the foot treadle. Meg scoffed when she recalled Sarah saying, "As soon as electricity comes to Springbrook, I will learn to sew." For herself, Meg knew that when it did come, she would miss the soft glow of kerosene lamps.

Each day, Meg went to the bog to check up on Tim. When she had finished making the curtains, she used his flat iron to get out the wrinkles before hanging them.

"Sarah is right, don't you think? Curtains give the rooms a finished look."

"Yes," said Tim smiling. "It is definitely cozier."

Meg noticed that Tim kept watching her. This both thrilled her and scared her. Occasionally she felt herself blushing.

Over the days that Meg's family was away, she and Tim had many long conversations. She had the crazy thought that he was pretending to be sicker than he was, just so she would stay. Tim showed her maps and explained his plans for the cranberry bog. He had scheduled the work right from the onset so the bog would begin producing cranberries three years from now. Meg took it all in and asked many questions. She learned about the ware-house that he wanted to build in a few years and how it would be used during the harvest. She asked what had to be done to the bog over the winter and how the vines would be protected from the cold.

CHAPTER 12

Love is a feeling that has no boundaries.
Give it. Accept it and feel its power. — Ojibwe Proverb

~

Tim realized that he had hardly discussed these things with Sarah and wondered why. He recalled having started several times to explain the workings of the bog to her, but he felt he was boring her, so he never continued. The only time she was interested in what he talked about was when he described Chicago. Did his mother's apartment have a telephone, she would ask? Had he ridden the streetcars, gone to the Field Museum? Would they be able to go down to the Windy City over the winter to visit his mother?

Being ill gave Tim the rare opportunity to think of things other than cranberries. Sarah's questions surfaced to his consciousness. He wondered what they implied. Would she be content married to a backwoods cranberry grower? What really started bothering him was that he realized he enjoyed being with Meg more than Sarah, in fact, much more.

After Tim's temperature had been normal for a full day, Meg "allowed" him to go out on a walk.

"Please come with me. I must go down to the bog and check up on the work being done, but I may not be able to make it on my own. Can you come with me?"

They strolled leisurely to the edge of the marsh where they could see men digging ditches in the distance. Tim recognized the brown, floppy hat of John Pete. Slowly they wove their way over dikes to get to him. Tim introduced Meg to John Pete and continued speaking to him while he looked over the work the men had done in the last few days. "You've made a lot of progress while I've been ill."

"Oh, I'm sorry you've been sick. We wondered why we hadn't seen you." John Pete looked at Meg.

Tim explained that his fever had kept him indoors for the last three days.

"Now, you really are a paleface!" John Pete said smiling.

"I am hoping his fever doesn't return. I've been nursing him with willow bark tea and ham hock soup these last few days," Meg explained. Tim tried not to smile. "If Tim doesn't appear for a day or two," Meg continued, "would you mind going to his house to see if he's all right?"

"Of course, I will. Do not worry," John Pete said with a grin on his face. "I always have willow bark and can make more if you need it again."

Meg and Tim continued their walk. When out of ear shot, Meg asked Tim if John Pete usually smiles a lot.

"No, he is usually quite serious."

"Well, it's good to see you smiling. You must be getting better."

The refreshing aroma from pine needles was invigorating. There was always a breeze on the bog. When they approached the reservoir, Meg said she wanted to stop to see the red-winged blackbirds.

"I hope you don't mind that I asked John Pete to keep an eye on you?"

"No, that's a good idea. I think I'm going to need a lot of looking after, I'm still not as strong as I should be." Tim couldn't stop himself from smiling.

"Seriously, does John Pete know where we live in town so he could come fetch us, I mean Sarah, if you need help?"

Once spoken, Tim noticed that Meg immediately looked down as though she was flustered. He became very serious as he realized that Sarah had never shown herself to care for him like this. He was touched. He couldn't look at Meg until he had his emotions under control. Fortunately, he spotted a beaver to distract himself. It was working hard at building a dam in the reservoir.

"Look at that little guy, trying as hard as he can to undo my work."

"At least he seems to be building his lodge in the middle where it isn't blocking anything.… I love it here. Look at how the aspen leaves glitter," she commented, "as though the reservoir is wearing a jeweled necklace."

Tim felt increasingly anguished over his impending marriage to Sarah. Each day with Meg he had become more doubtful. Now he knew for certain it was a mistake. He could no longer deny he was falling in love with Meg. She was more his size and had his energy, enthusiasm and values. He liked her outrageously curly hair that refused to be tamed by barrettes. Curls crept out from anywhere and started bouncing as she walked. Even though she was slightly over-weight, she was anything but lazy. Sarah didn't seem very lively, probably because he didn't bring that out in her. She seemed a little glum, in fact, more like her father in spirit. I have chosen the wrong Ellsworth girl to marry. Would his feelings for Sarah come back when she returned? No…he never had feelings for Sarah as he has for Meg. If only they weren't sisters. If only Sarah wouldn't come back.

They decided to walk all the way down to the Namekagon.

"Why is the river's water so dark brown?"

"I think it is the tannin from the leaves that fall in. John Pete says that people from the reservation have always added a little of their maple syrup to make it more palatable to drink."

Tim showed Meg the pump house and explained how the beds planted with cranberry vines could be flooded whenever there was a threat of frost. She examined the sluice and commented how smooth and uniform it was. "Did you make this?"

"John Pete and I made it."

"Laying the cement in a curved channel must have been difficult. I can't wait to see water being pumped into this…this sluice… and flow to the reservoir."

She made Tim feel proud. They walked to the river bank. He pointed out that the Namekagon flowed at about four miles an hour here. He showed her the nine-foot deep pool by the pump house. She asked if he ever fished here.

"Sure, but I usually just catch catfish…occasionally a small mouth bass…and sometimes a northern. You'll have to come fishing with us someday," he said looking her straight in the eye.

"Oh I didn't know you and Sarah had gone fishing."

"I meant with me and John Pete." Tim looked across the river and said quietly, almost to himself, "I can't imagine Sarah likes fishing very much, does she?"

"No, she doesn't…. We had better go back to the house before you get exhausted."

They walked back in silence. There was so much Tim wanted to say.

As they neared the house, Meg couldn't help but tell him of the marvelous trail she had discovered in the woods.

"It comes out at the Indian cabin."

"Oh, the bunkhouse! I would love to know that trail. Would you show it to me tomorrow? I would like to learn how to use it."

Meg hesitated for a short time. "OK, I'll come by at noon with a picnic lunch and I'll bring you all—you and John Pete—some vegetables. Our garden has started to take off."

Tomorrow would be their last day together before the Ellsworths returned from Minneapolis. Tim thought he had better reach a decision by then.

The next day, they rode through the woods, Meg on Maple and Tim on his horse, Winnie. Winnie was on the old side and didn't have the energy that Maple had. This didn't bother Tim, who felt completely recovered from his illness.

"She's very reliable as a draft horse," Tim said laughingly, "never moody, but she isn't a very exciting ride."

"I'm glad Winnie isn't so demanding. You probably still need to take it easy."

"I wish I always had a nurse at my side." He noticed that she was out of breath. He couldn't take his eyes off of her.

"I brought a light picnic lunch".

Now she is blushing! "Thank you. I brought a thermos of tea which I hope you'll like." She won't look at me, Tim thought. Does this mean she cares for me? Tim felt in high spirits.

They rode on in silence for ten minutes or so, before Meg said, "I have no idea who owns this land. Do you?"

"No. I hope they're friendly."

They both laughed and agreed that most people around there were very friendly.

"I want to show you a lovely grove of elm trees. It's to the left, after that big boulder."

"I'd like to see it. Elm's one of my favorite trees."

"Mine too."

Meg led the way as they navigated around some hazelnut bushes. After 50 yards or so, they came across a beautiful stand of elm, six or seven trees in all, each with a trunk two feet or more thick. The area had little underbrush. They dismounted. Both of them were taken aback by the sense of strength that the trees exuded.

"It's amazing that timber men haven't found these," Tim said. "I think we should definitely keep this a secret."

"Yes, probably so.... Dad, says that the whole northwest of Wisconsin was covered with trees as big as these. He told me that after the Menomine were forced to turn over their land to the U.S. government, white settlers began to lumber it. In the 1840s, I think he said."

"How does your father know so much about the timber business in these parts?"

"He has an old friend he went to seminary with, Harold Morris. Mr. Morris made a fortune from lumbering. Have you heard of him?"

"Yes, I certainly have.... He's the man your dad helped me get a loan from—a huge loan that will start a few weeks after Sarah

and I have married…" His voice trailed off to be almost inaudible.
"Do you know Mr. Morris is a patron of cranberry growers?"

"Really! Yes, I think dad has said that."

"Well, Harold Morris seems like a man of conscience. He has certainly been generous to me. He is only going to charge me a half-point of interest on the loan." Tim noticed that the color had drained from Meg's face.

"I see. Well, he can afford it from what I hear. I think he owes dad a favor, but I don't know why."

Really, Tim thought, then is my loan the payback? He had his eyes fixed on hers. Meg looked uncomfortable. She seemed to be trying to avoid his gaze. Now she was blushing again, yet she wouldn't look at him. Then she launched into a discussion of the history of lumbering as though she was forcing herself to be distracted, "Dad said that white folks first lumbered the southern and eastern parts before they moved into our part of the state. Dad says the Indians were to blame, too, because they stayed in the logging camps all winter, earning money by cutting up the logs and sending them down rivers. But the way I see it, what were they supposed to do? Their land had been taken from them."

"What does your father say to that?"

"Oh, I don't discuss things with him that we differ on. It's better that way."

"Does Sarah?" Tim asked, knowing the answer.

"Well, that's not the sort of thing that interests her."

They were both caught in their own thoughts. So as not to leave her hanging, Tim pursued the discussion by adding: "Railroads also had a share in promoting logging. They made it possible for the lumber camps to move deeper into forests." He didn't think that she was any more interested in this conversation than he was, but they both were scared to go where their real interests lie.

"Dad says that things have slowed down here now because timber barons like Mr. Morris have become more interested in the forests in the Pacific Northwest."

"Yes, the virgin forests there."

They sat on a log and ate their lunch. Tim noticed that Meg had on the same dress she wore the day before. She seemed very practical and down to earth. Today, however, she wore her hair up, gathered in a bun at the back of her neck. Of course, it was unruly and tightly curled strands dangled about, giving her a carefree look that he liked.

"In addition to this trail I have another surprise for you," she said to Tim. "But we'll have to be quiet for a bit. At least I saw them the other day." They waited, then heard the tapping of a woodpecker. They stood up to look for the tree where the drumming came from.

"There it is," said Tim. "It's almost completely black."

"Yes, I see it. I think it's actually called a black-backed woodpecker.… The next time we go into Spooner, I hope to check on its name in the library."

"There is a blue tinge to the black, don't you think?" asked Tim.

"Well, I thought so the other day, but now I only see it as black."

"Come over here. If you look into the sun, you will only see the silhouette, so it appears black, but come here where I'm standing, with the sun behind us."

Meg went over to stand beside him. "Oh, I've lost it now. Where is it?"

Tim moved behind her and put his hands on her shoulders to guide her line of sight. This happened so fast she had no time to react. Then he gently put his hands on her head to guide her more exactly.

"I see it," she said out of breath. He bent down and kissed the back of her neck. She froze—was she mad, indecisive or scared, Tim wondered? The back of her neck reddened.

"I'm sorry," he said. "I don't know what came over me." Meg was still motionless.

"I am going to break off my engagement with Sarah," he said quickly.

"Oh no.... Why?"

"You must know why. There are so many reasons, but you are the main one." Meg was breathless again.

She still couldn't look him in the eye but her gaze had worked its way up from the ground to his shoulder. "I didn't intend this to happen. I was only trying to help you get well," she said.

"Thank you. You have been very successful. I have never felt healthier in my life." She smiled and took a little peek at him.

"I don't want to hurt Sarah," she said in a meek voice.

"Are you sure she would be hurt?"

"I think she isn't suited to be your wife, but that doesn't mean that she wouldn't be hurt if your engagement were broken off."

"Meg, I'm sorry. I realize now that I don't love her and never did. What a fool I've been."

"Maybe you'll think otherwise tomorrow, when you see her again."

Tim rode back to town with Meg. He gave the excuse that he wanted to learn the trail, but truthfully he didn't want her to go. "I'm sorry that I've put you in such an awkward position. Please forgive me." He thought he could read her mind, so he said, "My problem with Sarah is something I have to deal with. You are in no way responsible. Thank God I realized this before we got married."

Tim did turn Winnie around when they reached the edge of town. Now he would know how to use the trail in both directions. He called after Meg saying, "That was a wonderful picnic, the best I have ever had."

"I thought so too," she said with a beaming smile.

$\sim$

CHAPTER 13

1939

Harold Morris pulled into the back lot of the Bank of Hayward. He turned the engine off and tried to calm himself. This is it, he thought nervously. He had had plenty of time to think while driving the 120 miles from Minneapolis to Hayward, but he still was unsure how he should broach the topic with his son, Sam Cloud, whom he had never seen. He was worried about how Sam would react. Sam was fifty, a grown man, with a family of his own and president of a bank—an amazing accomplishment for an Ojibwe. At this point, would Sam even care if Harold confessed to being his father?

Harold longed for a son, not that he didn't have one, but Richard was distant and unloving. Richard was so much like his own father, Harold thought. Those traits skipped his generation. Maybe Harold wouldn't have bothered trying to contact Sam had only Richard and Sarah had children, but it seems that they not only didn't want children, they didn't seem to want parents as well.

At rational moments, Harold even understood why they didn't want children. Sarah was self-absorbed, perhaps incapable of devoting herself to the sacrifices that motherhood requires. Richard, for his part, was indifferent to people who didn't have something that he wanted. Harold could easily see Richard ignoring his own children. Maybe they both knew that they wouldn't be good parents. Richard and Sarah had reduced their visits to twice a year, even though they lived in the Lowry Hill area of Minneapolis, which was less than a half-hour's drive to Howard's home on East Lake of the Isles Boulevard. To be fair, a contributing factor was that Richard often had to travel out to the northwest coast to manage the lumbering of that forestland and Sarah enjoyed accompanying him. She loved to sample the life in Seattle and Vancouver.

Richard and Sarah did not know about Sam Cloud. The few times Harold talked about Sam to his wife she became defensive. She saw herself as competing with "that Indian woman." Thank God I never told her about the money I've been giving them, Harold thought. Clarence delivered the sum to Lily each year after hunting season. In 1908, when Sam had reached the age of 18, Lily told Clarence that Sam had his own bank account, and that if Harold still wanted to give money, he could send it directly to Sam's account. Harold looked into this and discovered that Sam was going to college at the same time that he worked part-time for the Bank of Hayward, where he had the account. All reports indicated that he was a fine young man. By 1929, Howard learned that Sam was married and had three children, and then four years ago, Harold was told that Sam was president of the Bank of Hayward. Harold struggled with the frustration of not being able to tell Sam how proud he was of him.

All through those years Lily had never asked Harold for anything. Since the time he was a lumberjack, he had never had any direct contact with Lily. Harold wondered what Sam knew. He had no idea whether Lily had ever told her son who his real father was. The yearly deposits into Sam's account could not be traced to Harold, so Mamie wouldn't find out. When Mamie passed away, Harold began to think that maybe he didn't have to die a lonely old man. There was nothing holding him back now from seeing Sam and his family. He was prepared to be rejected and could certainly understand if they wanted nothing to do with him. His chances were best, he thought, if he approached Sam at the bank and not at his home, so Harold made the long drive from Minneapolis to Hayward, arriving there purposely at ten minutes before closing time.

Harold took a quick look at himself in the mirror. He was 69, and aside from a few wrinkles, a receding hair line and being out of breath a lot, he thought he was physically in good shape, just lonely.

"Mr. Cloud has gone home for the day," the bank clerk told him.

Harold's heart sank.

"Would you like to make an appointment to see him for another day?" The clerk kept staring at Harold.

"Yes, I'll do that…. I'll call up and make an appointment."

"Should I mention your name to Mr. Cloud?"

Such an innocent question, but to Harold it was like crossing the Rubicon.

"Yes, tell him Harold Morris came by, and I'll call to make an appointment. Thank you." He fumbled opening the door to the bank and walked out hesitantly to his car, looking back at the bank. His mind was in a whirl. He stumbled on a crack in the sidewalk, but was able to recover his balance. A man dressed in a suit was at his side in no time.

"Is there something you need?"

"Oh, no thank you, I was looking for someone." Harold looked down at the man and was utterly amazed. He was looking at a younger, shorter, fatter version of himself but with darker skin. "I…was looking…for Sam Cloud, the president of the bank."

"Well, I'm Sam Cloud," he said with a hesitant smile on his face. "Can I do something for you?"

"I'm Harold Morris. I've wanted to meet you for a very long time." Harold was out of breath. His eyes started filling up.

Sam gave Harold a gentle smile. From the look on his face, Harold thought Sam knew what was coming. Before Harold could stumble out with what he wanted to say, Sam asked him directly, "Are you my blood father?"

"Yes, I am…. I'm sorry I didn't come to you long ago. I am so sorry…."

After a long pause Sam said, "Well I'm glad you have now," and after another long pause, "I always felt your spirit was with me."

"I should have come long ago."

"Fifty years ago."

"Yes, fifty years ago." By this time, tears were pouring out of Harold's eyes. Harold knew how it felt to be rejected. Sam gave Harold a hug. The top of Sam's head came to Harold's chin. They stepped back just to look at each other. The joy they both felt seeped out in the form of grins and then soft laughter.

"Why did you wait so long?" Sam asked.

"I felt I needed my wife to agree, and she didn't want me to admit to being your father, but now she has passed."

"I felt the rejection. There are several of us on the reservation that have felt that rejection…but I have a lot to be grateful for too. The money you sent me helped to put me and my brothers and sisters through college."

"You didn't need all of it for yourself?"

"We don't do things that way."

"Yes, of course."

"Would you be able to come home with me and meet my family, or come another time?"

"I'd love to…now…or anytime that's convenient."

"Let's do it now, you never know what will come up between now and later."

Harold followed Sam's seven-year-old Chevy. They turned on to Chief Lake Road and finally into a driveway that came to a dead end at the back of Sam's small two-story house. Laundry was on the line, but none for little children. Then Harold reminded himself that his grandchildren wouldn't be small. In fact, they would soon be old enough to live on their own. Sam himself was five years older than Richard. Did they look alike, he asked himself? Yes, a little. Harold thought further of the grandchildren—he had never seen them crawl, take their first steps, lose their baby teeth. Did they get visits from the tooth fairy? Ojibwe people probably didn't have that custom. What customs do they have, he wondered?

The house sat at the top of a gentle slope down to the lake's shore. There was a porch on the lakeside where Sam was leading him. They passed a rusty old car that looked like it was ready for the junkyard. In the distance Harold could see quite a large vegetable garden. A swing hung from an oak tree on the left side of the porch and on the right side was a wigwam, of all things! Why? Two canoes were turned over resting on the shore. There was no more time to look around because a friendly looking woman came out on the porch to greet them.

Harold drove out of the Indian reservation absolutely thrilled with the reception Sam and his family had given him. The two hours they spent talking was not enough. The Clouds asked Harold to go fishing the next night on the lake, if he was still in town. Harold stayed another two nights in Hayward just so he could go fishing with them. He would drive back to Minneapolis in two days. No one would miss him there.

He had a lot of thinking to do. For one thing, he had to decide whether or not now was the time to tell Richard about Sam. He was afraid of Richard's reaction, not because he might be upset at discovering he had a brother who was Ojibwe. He actually didn't think that would bother Richard very much. What he was more worried about was that Richard would immediately realize that he would have to share some of his inheritance with Sam. Harold had heard some rumors about Richard not being very nice to people who stood in his way. Would Richard do something to Sam?

Sadly, Harold began to fear for Sam and decided to keep their relationship a secret from Richard as long as he could. In the meantime, he vowed he was no longer going to neglect this other son of his. He would go see Sam as much as he could. It just might turn out that Richard would never know about Sam. Harold could leave Sam money without Richard finding out, by setting up a secret trust for him. As soon as he got back to Minneapolis, he would see a lawyer about that—not Melvin Howe, the family lawyer, but a different lawyer, one no one knew.

III

CONFLUENCE

CHAPTER 14

EARLY SUMMER 1939

Josie was disheveled. She had not gotten dressed for the morning when Louise arrived to help out in the kitchen. Louise was on time and Josie was expecting her, but not her young companion. So as not to be seen, Josie quickly retreated to the other end of the house and proceeded to get dressed. In the process, she managed to get the attention of her oldest daughter, Marie. Josie didn't like having local visitors. They could stay for hours. Preston could neatly escape to the bog, whereas she was left to make conversation with someone with whom she had nothing in common. "Marie dear, go see who has come with Louise. Be discreet."

Marie ran off in her overalls, her long brown braids swinging back and forth as she ran. Josie's curiosity was aroused enough to take a quick peek out of the bathroom window, watching them enter the house. In short order, Marie came back to report: "Mom, she's not from Springbrook. She's from Massachu… Massacset…"

"Massachusetts?"

"Yes, Massachusetts. That is really far away isn't it?"

"Yes," Josie rushed to the mirror to powder her nose and put on lipstick.

"Why is she here? Do you know?"

"She would like to see the bog and have permission to walk around it. Something about bird watching… I think."

Josie looked at herself in the mirror. She practiced her smile, parting her lips ever so slightly, just enough to show that she had teeth. A quick squeeze on the perfume atomizer and she was ready. After introductions and explanations for the surprise visit, Josie started to relax. "Welcome to Miltonberry." Josie wished she could give such a broad smile as this young woman. What was her name? Oh yes, "Em Lucas." She was a striking young woman with intense eyes, in her early twenties, perhaps. Even with no makeup and in overalls, she was attractive.

"My daughter tells me you are from Massachusetts. What brings you all this way?"

"I'm visiting Louise and my grandparents. I'm very interested in cranberry bogs. I know that the bogs here are managed differently from those in Massachusetts. I study agriculture at the University of Massachusetts."

"How interesting!" Josie could fake sincerity with the best of them. "Marie, would you please show Em the way down to the warehouse? I think your father is there, showing a young man around."

Turning to Em, Josie explained. "He's interviewing a young man for the job of foreman. Mr. Milton will be glad to see you. He may be quite busy talking to this young man, but he would be delighted to have you look around. If you would like, please join us for lunch here at the house. We'll be serving it at noon."

"Thank you very much, but I really don't want to intrude, I…"

"I insist. We would like to get to know you."

"Well, thank you. That would be lovely."

Josephine turned around and re-entered the house to look for Louise. In her mind she madly ran through possible menus for the noon meal. Press told her before he left for the bog that the young man, Joel somebody, might be staying for lunch. Fortunately, we have tomato aspic already prepared, she thought.

Marie began to escort Em down the sandy road to the warehouse. Josie watched them from the open kitchen windows. The two passed the large playpen in which their two-year-old was playing, supposedly being supervised by their middle daughter, Susan.

"This is my baby sister, Lucy. And here comes trouble!"—Marie's way of introducing her sister, Susan. The two were usually competing with each other for something, Josie lamented.

Marie asked Em if she spelled her name with just the letter "M." They would soon be out of earshot but Josie thinks she heard Em's answer correctly.

"No it is 'e-m'—short for Emma."

CHAPTER 15

Walking along with Marie as her guide gave Em the opportunity to let down her guard and allow her mind to drift. She was glad to come again to Springbrook to visit her grandparents, even though she thought they were strange people…well, no, not her grandmother, but definitely her grandfather. He was such a grim, unfriendly man, so unlike Mom she thought. He must be the reason she will never come back here. Em hadn't told her mother the main reason she wanted to visit her grandparents—she wanted to figure out who her real father was. She figured he must be someone from the Springbrook area.

Yesterday, at the Springbrook store, Em had heard for the first time that there was a cranberry bog outside of Springbrook. Why had her mother never told her about it? You would think with all the stories about Emma Cranberry, Mom would have mentioned it, unless she had a reason for not bringing it up.

Em went back to the store and struck up another conversation with Louise, whom she had learned periodically worked at the Milton home, owners of the cranberry bog. As an agricultural major at the University of Massachusetts, Em thought she had an excuse to visit the bog, an excuse that would arouse no suspicion. Louise was willing to take her the next day, as she was going there to work.

Everything was going well, she thought, but she had better stay concentrated on what Marie was telling her—something about this smallish house on our left.

"This is where the foreman lives," Marie was saying. "He's getting a bit old and doesn't like to spend all night checking thermometers. That's why Dad is looking for a new foreman."

The building, like the Milton's house, was wooden-frame, painted white with green trim. They passed a large vegetable garden. There were many rows of corn and a section devoted to other vegetables and flowers.

"That's our garden, and the smaller section in back is for the foreman, Mr. and Mrs. Hopscotch." She giggled. "Their name is really Hodgekiss."

Em was enjoying Marie's bluntness. She must be around ten years old she thought. The road deepened with sand as they went. A big warehouse came into sight with a sand pit in back. Em could see two cabins in the woods. The warehouse was built on a hill. It appeared to have three stories. The top level had doors that opened to face the woods.

They were getting close now. It was a huge frame building, also painted white with green trim. Marie led her to the bottom end of the warehouse, the end that faced the bog.

"Dad has his office down at this end."

"Do you and your family live here all year round?" Em asked.

"No. We live in Kenilworth in the winter so we can go to school."

"So you haven't been to school in Springbrook?"

"No, we have to go back before harvest."

The sunlight was so bright that Em had trouble adjusting her eyesight when she entered the warehouse, walking on the cement floor. She heard voices further back inside, and after a minute, deciphered a tall, young, good-looking man wearing glasses talking with a shorter, older man with gray wavy hair and a mustache.

"Dad, this is Em. She wants to see the bog."

"Excuse me, Joel. Marie you shouldn't just walk in and interrupt. I want to talk to you about this after lunch in private."

"Sorry, Dad." She slipped quietly into a side room.

"After lunch, don't forget," Press called after her. Then he turned to Em. "I'm sorry, did Marie say your name was Em?"

"Yes, I am Em Lucas. I didn't want to interrupt your interview. Are you Mr. Milton?"

"Yes, but please call me Preston. You're very welcome here, Em. It's just that I am interviewing Joel here for the foreman's job. I will be showing him around the bog in a few minutes. You could tag along then if you'd like."

"Thank you. I'll keep out of your way," said Em, retreating towards the door. She looked around without moving much, so as not to be distracting. She couldn't help but overhear their conversation but she pretended to not be listening. Preston sounded kind but firm. Em spent most of her time concentrating on the pleasant looking man whose name she had overheard was Joel Helmer. She wished she had not worn her overalls. He had dark-ish skin, a muscular build, with large facial features. He wore glasses. He didn't look like a typical farmer, she thought.

Preston invited her to walk with them while he pointed out to Joel some details of the warehouse and how it functioned during harvest. They saw the sorting room, climbed up to the third floor, saw how the side panels of the upper two stories could swing open to help the berries dry in their crates. Em was a silent observer. She could have asked many questions but knew that would be inappropriate. She overheard the men talk and discovered that Joel had lived most of his life in Rice Lake, a city that she had seen on the map, maybe 25 miles from Springbrook. His parents were schoolteachers. Aha, just as I thought. He's not from a farming background.

When Preston turned to Joel and asked him point blank why he thought he would like to be the foreman of a cranberry bog, Em stepped away, realizing the seriousness of this question, but remained just close enough to hear Joel's answer, while pretending again not to be listening. "I have always loved the outdoor life."

Before Joel could continue, Preston broke in, "There's some wonderful hunting around here, and of course you probably know how people come from all over to fish here, Hayward being the muskie capitol of the world," he said laughing a bit. "Do you hunt and fish a lot?"

"Eh, no, I'm afraid I don't do either."

"Really, you mean you haven't had the chance?"

"No. I don't want to. I'm a vegetarian."

"Good grief," said Preston. "You've never eaten a sirloin steak?"

"Well, I have, but I no longer want to. I want to be involved in helping things grow, in preserving what we have. Like I said in my resumé, all my work experience has centered around nature. I trained at the University of Wisconsin in forestry and have worked as an amateur naturalist ever since."

"So I guess I don't have to worry about you're running off and joining the French Foreign Legion," he said smiling.

"No worry of that, I'm a Quaker…and a pacifist. I hope I'll never get called up."

Em couldn't help herself. She turned and looked at Joel and saw the two men stare at each other for a few seconds before the interview continued.

After fifteen minutes or so, Susan came into the warehouse to tell Marie that Lucy had gone down for a nap and that their mother needed both of them up at the house. They ran around. Susan jumped up on a cart that was used to carry the drying crates and Marie gave it a spin, much to Susan's delight. Preston stopped this horseplay and sent them both back up to the house.

"Oh, I forgot to ask," Marie called back to her dad, looking at Joel. "Will *he* be coming to lunch? Mom wants to know."

"Yes, I certainly hope so. I'm sorry I should have asked you right from the start, Joel. I hope you will have lunch with us. We eat at noon."

"Thank you. I would love to."

Em felt Joel looking at her. Not knowing how to respond, she smiled and looked back at him. Preston continued with the interview. "You come with good recommendations. People say you are very dependable. That is fine, but how will you take being alone here for the winter months?"

"I love to read and like to write as well, so it isn't a worry to me. Yes, I'll be somewhat lonely, but I won't be at a loss for how to spend my time."

After a few more questions in the warehouse, Preston moved them on. "Well, lets go down to the river."

Em followed the two men but lagged well behind them, not wishing to intrude. She began to realize that Mr. Milton might be hard of hearing. Joel must think so too, she thought, because he is speaking louder now. This gave her the opportunity to hear more of what they were saying. Preston told Joel about the Indians who worked on the bog, how most of them only worked during harvest time, but that one, John Pete Kingfisher, worked on the bog most of the year. He went back to the reservation only during the winter months. "I think you would enjoy working with him. He is hard-working and enthusiastic—very reliable, too."

They walked on the road past hazelnut bushes and quaking aspen, circling the bog clockwise. Rounding a bend, the reservoir came into full view. It was a lovely sight. Em immediately spotted two goldeneyes swimming through the reeds and cattails. A squirrel was chattering away close by them. In the distance they could see a man leaning over the bulkhead. As they got closer Preston said, "Ah, there's John Pete now." Em saw Preston frown, seemingly perplexed over what the worker was doing. He appeared to Em to be dribbling sand into the water by the main floodgate. After introductions, Preston asked him for an explanation.

"Oh boss, you know how water is leaking through between these planks."

"Yes, I certainly do, but I don't know how to stop it without draining the reservoir and putting in new planks that are tighter fitting."

"I thought I would try an old Ojibwe trick. The water in the reservoir should push the sand against the planks. Hopefully, the sand will get stuck in the gaps and the gate will no longer leak." They stood around watching John Pete dribble more sand from his hand.

"My goodness, it seems to be working."

"It is probably only a temporary solution," John Pete added modestly.

Twenty seconds passed while John Pete studied Em. She thought she detected some sadness in his voice as he said, "It's been a long time since I've seen a smile like yours." Then he added almost to himself, "May the birch leaves dance and the flowers of heaven blossom."

Em didn't know how to respond to this. She looked at Joel with a quizzical look on her face.

Bending close to her he said: "You do have a wonderful smile."

Em tried to cover up the pleasure that Joel's remark gave her by saying, "John Pete's comment was more like a prayer."

"Yes, beautifully expressed."

They returned to the house and entered through a back porch, containing the icebox and entrance to a root cellar. It was quite messy and disorganized but gave access to a large kitchen, which had been newly constructed just two years ago. It was unusual in that two walls were made of fieldstone. There were many windows, whose glass panes were hand-painted with scenes of birds and flowers. Later on, Em learned from Mrs. Milton that the panes had been brought from Mexico, as had the large tin rooster and candlesticks on the table. There were six place settings, but the table was large enough to hold more than twice that many. It was made of five enormously long planks of pine. A bench flanked its long side next to the stone wall.

"That's where younger people sit," Marie told Em. "You might have to climb behind someone to get in and out of your place."

In the fieldstone wall, there was a fireplace that started at waist level with a compartment below for wood. On another wall was a wood-burning stove. Marie told Em and Joel that after dinner they would scrape their plates into the fire.

"We always light a fire at night to burn the food scraps."

"So we don't attract more mice," added six-year-old Susan, in a voice louder than necessary.

"And so the mosquitoes won't swarm down the chimney," said Marie. "As Mom says," (putting on a posh voice), "'It's all a part of country living.'"

"What do you do with your other trash?" Em asked with a smile.

"We have a garbage dump way over there, in the woods. Susan's afraid to go there."

"So are you," Susan said. "Once we heard a bear there."

"Really!" Joel exclaimed smiling at Em.

"Yes, now we only go there together, right Susan? You have to go with me," Marie said, eyeing Susan pointedly. She turned to Em and Joel to explain further, "We don't like going down in the cellar either. Its floor is dirt and there are spider webs that you have to break through."

"And we know there are mice down there!" Susan dramatically shuddered. "That's where we store our canned vegetables and fruit."

"Girls, that's enough," Josie interrupted. "Go help Louise serve up the plates."

Em heard Joel say to Marie on the side, "Marie, I don't eat meat. Would you please be sure no meat is put on my plate?"

Marie looked delighted to have this responsibility. "Yes," she answered.

"Thank you," Joel said.

"Oh Joel," Mrs. Milton said. "Do tell me about your family. We have Helmers in our family. Do you have relatives in Indiana?"

"I suppose it is possible, but I have no idea."

"You know our little Lucy—she's just two so she won't be eating with us—but she was named after her great-grandmother on Preston's mother's side, Lucinda Helmer, known to the family as Puss."

"Oh, I see. I'm afraid I don't know much about my ancestry. I'll have to see what I can find out when I get back to Rice Lake."

"Rice Lake? Oh, I thought Preston said you were from Minneapolis."

"No, my grandfather on my father's side was from Trego."

"Trego! Oh, that is very close by." Em noticed Mrs. Milton's enthusiasm slightly diminished. "I know we pass it on the way to Spooner."

"Yes. That's right."

Just then the phone rang.

"That's us," squealed Susan, "Four shorts."

Josie turned to Em to say, "We still have a party line here in Springbrook."

Preston quickly pulled Joel aside to say: "Joel, every day the weather bureau sends us a telegram giving us a three day forecast. I record it in a notebook. If they say the temperature will get as low as 40°, we have to be sure there is plenty of water in the reservoir in case we have to flood. We never want to flood unless we have to. Mr. Lee, the station master, receives the telegram and then phones us to read what it says." Preston led Joel through a pantry into a small, older room where there was a telephone mounted to the wall. He held the receiver so Joel could hear as well. Em couldn't help herself. She followed them through the pantry into the small room where the telephone was located.

After hanging up, Preston wrote down the weather report in a notebook which he kept by the phone. Then, turning to Joel he said: "Tonight's low is expected to be 42°, so we're safe. If there was a worry of frost we'd begin pumping water into the reservoir by 3:00 P.M. Starting about eight o'clock, we'd read the thermometers every hour. The thermometers have been placed in five beds, in different sections of the bog. Your job will be to take readings late in the night, from 11:00 P.M.–5 A.M. You'll read all five thermometers and come by my bedroom window and report them in to me. This is the least fun part of your job. To give you an idea, during June and August we might have 15 nights of frost watch. We may have to actually flood only about 7 of those 15 nights. Of course, in September and October the flooding is more frequent still."

"Sometimes, we just raise the water in the ditches, but we don't actually have to flood. There are certain beds that need to be flooded more often than others. When you come to my window to give me the five temperatures, I will tell you the number of planks you should pull out of each gate, if any. I'll do the frost watch with you the first three or four times. This is the part of the job that Elmer Hotchkiss thoroughly dislikes. After lunch, I think you should have a good long talk with him, because there may be other things that he'll want to warn you about. Anyway, you should also see his house because that is where you will be living. There's still more to tell you but I can see Josephine wants us to eat."

Before they sat down to eat, Josie suggested that they may want to "freshen up." From the pantry adjacent to their large kitchen, Joel was directed to a bathroom up the stairs, whereas Preston suggested that Em use the bathroom on the same floor, to the right off the living room. Em was glad to have a chance to look around inside the house. As she left the pantry, she re-entered the room where the telephone hung on the wall. Here was another fireplace—one made out of rounded cobbles. This room's ceiling was low. How odd, she thought, as she saw another stairway. The two stairways were so close to each other. Why have two? Then she realized that this one was quite steep and narrow. Joel would really have to duck if he came down it. Oh, I see, this must be the original part of the house. She stood there and just soaked in its aura.

"May we pour you a glass of sherry?" Josie asked Joel and Em, when they returned to the kitchen.

It embarrassed Em when she realized that Louise was not going to be sitting at the table with them. She raised her eyebrows at Louise to express her discomfort. Louise bowed her head slightly while opening her hands, implying this is the way it is here, and to just go along with it.

Preston sat at the head of the table with Josie on a chair at his side. Joel and the girls were directed to the bench, leaving Em to take the chair next to Josie. Em and Joel hardly dared to look at each other or they might burst out laughing. For one thing, thanks to Marie, Joel's plate consisted of a heaping pile of tomato aspic. Joel could say nothing.

Finally, Josie noticed: "Joel, you must be quite fond of tomato aspic. Did you not want any beans?"

"No," said Marie, not allowing Joel to speak for himself. "The beans have bacon in them."

"Oh, did you serve Joel's plate, Marie?"

"Yes. He can't have the chicken and the other salad has tuna fish in it. That means he can only eat the red stuff. But that's good because no one else usually likes it."

"Excuse me young lady, that remark gives us something else to talk about after lunch," Preston said.

"Well, I'm sorry, Joel. I didn't know you were a vegetarian," Josie said. "Have some more powder-milk biscuits. We'll try to make things up to you with dessert."

"Please, don't worry. This is delicious and you took good care of me, Marie."

Mrs. Milton had the most elegant hands Em had ever seen, long fingers with beautifully manicured nails polished to match her lipstick. On the fourth finger of her left hand, she wore a large diamond and sapphire ring, yet no wedding band. Her brown hair was drawn up in wavy mounds on both sides of her face. Em thought she must appear very dull sitting next to Mrs. Milton.

No one took Josie up on her offer of a glass of sherry. This did not discourage her from having another glass during the dinner.

Em was embarrassed to see Louise sitting on a stool using the butcher's block as her table. Louise often stopped eating and hopped up to serve someone when needed.

Having already discovered that Joel was local, Josie began asking Em where in Massachusetts she was from. In the process, Em let her know that her father was a farmer.

"Oh what type of farming do you do?"

"We have a small farm with many different types of crops and animals. We're able to grow and raise most of what we need."

"That must mean a lot of work."

"Yes," Em answered, "there is hard work, even drudgery at times, but it's also very satisfying." Em was a little out of breath, nervous because they were all intently listening. "Satisfying because we use what we produce. To me, farming is a satisfying lifestyle because you are personally related to what you use. It's hard to explain, but I don't think you get that satisfaction when you just buy everything you use."

"Nonetheless it must be difficult for your parents to get away," Josie commented.

"Yes, but we don't have cause to get away often."

"Well, what brought you to Springbrook?"

"I'm visiting Louise and my grandparents," Em turned and smiled at Louise. She quickly added that the university encourages its agriculture majors to travel around and observe different farming techniques. "I've always been interested in cranberries. In Massachusetts most of our bogs are dry-harvested."

From that point the conversation began to center around cranberries. At dessert time, Marie reminded her mother that she had promised her they would be able to play the birthday game. With much reluctance Josie said: "OK, Marie, you can ask for two volunteers—only two people."

"That's easy." Marie took charge, "Em and Joel, will you volunteer because we've played this game with everybody else here? The way it goes is we all guess your birthday and whoever is closest gets the prize."

Susan piped up for the first time, "Can the prize be another piece of blueberry pie?"

Marie was already prepared with pencil and paper. Em guessed the closest to Joel's birth date. She felt herself blushing.

When it was time to speculate on Em's birthday, Josie delayed her guess until last, then said, "April 15?"

"That's right, exactly right," Em said to her amazement. She noticed Josie looked rather pleased with herself.

After thanking Mr. and Mrs. Milton for the wonderful lunch, Em asked if it would be all right if she wandered around the reservoir to look at birds until Louise was finished with her work.

"It certainly is," Preston replied. "I hope that someday one of our daughters will become as interested in cranberries as you are." He turned to Joel to say goodbye and reminded him to go to Elmer's house to talk with him. "Elmer is expecting you. Then give me a call in a few days when you have had a chance to think things over, and we can talk further."

"Mom, may I go with them?" Susan asked. "I haven't had a chance yet to be with them like Marie has."

"You can walk them as far as Mr. Hodgekiss' house, but then you have to turn around and come back. OK?"

The Miltons escorted Em and Joel out through the back porch and said goodbye to them on the terrace. Then they went back in the house. Mrs. Milton seemed excited and in a hurry, Em noticed. Left alone the three of them walked out onto the road. Em could feel that Joel was trying to pull her aside, but little Susan had latched onto her hand. So as they proceeded to walk towards the foreman's house, Joel asked Em in front of Susan how long she would be visiting in Springbrook.

"Two more days," Em said.

"Are you actually staying in Springbrook?"

"Yes."

"Can I come by tomorrow sometime? Perhaps we can go on a walk?" By the time they reached the Hodgekiss's house, Joel had the directions to the Ellsworth's house and knew how to telephone Em.

"We're not on the same party line as the Miltons," Em said.

"Good." Joel gave her a broad smile and went up to the foreman's house and knocked on the door.

Still holding onto Em's hand, Susan began pulling her across the road. "I can show you another way you can go down to the warehouse by the front of our house," Susan said. "Some of my favorite hiding places are there."

"Hiding places?" Em inquired.

"For 'kick-the-can'—do you like to play that?"

They walked back toward the main house around the large playpen and through a stand of blue spruce, before they came out on the side of the house that faced the bog. Em admired the view, backing up so she could keep it in sight while she listened to Susan explain the rules of the game. When she turned around to look at the house from this angle, she noticed two faces at a window inside the house. They quickly disappeared behind a curtain. They must have been looking out of a window in that big living room that she had passed through on her way to the bathroom, Em thought. Then, she realized that she was practically standing on a grave marker flush with the ground. She bent over to better read the inscription engraved in granite:

Timothy Zearing Milton

1889 - 1919

Cranberry Pioneer

Springbrook, Wisconsin

Driving back from Miltonberry to Springbrook, Em could hardly contain herself. She must have asked Louise three times what she thought of Joel. When she was back in her grandparents' house, Em immediately washed out a blouse so she could look her best tomorrow when she and Joel went out for a walk. In between thinking of Joel, Em considered the curious things that occurred that day. There was that sweet but strange way the Indian man reacted to her. What was that about? And why hadn't her mother ever told her about a cranberry bog outside of Springbrook? My real father must have a connection with cranberries. Em knew Steve had adopted her when Steve and her mom got married, but why, after all these years, does Mom refuse to tell me who my blood father is?

While her grandparents were out of the living room, Em took down the family album from a shelf. She had looked at it nine years ago during her first visit to Springbrook. This time she noticed that some photos had been removed. Maybe they had been removed prior to her first visit. She wasn't sure. At that time, she wasn't looking for clues. Why were they removed? There were no photos more recent than the ones of Aunt Sarah's wedding. She had never met Aunt Sarah, but she knew she lived in Minneapolis. She wished so much to meet her. "Oh my goodness," Em almost declared out loud. One photo was rather formally posed of the bride and groom and on it was written: Sarah Ellsworth and Tim Milton, married August 16th, 1916.

"Milton!" thought Em. That name hadn't meant anything to her nine years ago, but now it did. And it was Tim Milton's name on the grave marker!

Em examined the photo closely. Sarah looked very pretty. She was almost the same height as the groom. Even though they were sisters, Sarah didn't seem to resemble her mother. Looking closely she couldn't tell much about Tim. What was odd was that neither one of them looked very happy. At their own wedding! There were no photos of her mother. Perhaps Mom took the pictures, she thought. Two other things were curious. There were several empty pages at the end of the album and there were no photos of anyone after the wedding. It was as if nothing important happened after that which was worth keeping. There must be another album showing Sarah and Richard's wedding. Perhaps, they thought it would be inappropriate to have both of Sarah's weddings shown in the same album.

After minutes of deep deliberation, it struck Em that everything could be explained if Tim Milton was actually her father. Mom had to give birth to me away from Springbrook. Aunt May and Uncle Ed's home in Massachusetts is far away and safe. Then Em recalled the stories of Emma Cranberry. Of course! The illustrations that went with the stories were so crude. It wasn't a professional artist but her father who drew them. She would always treasure those stories.

My father has been dead for a long time, she thought. I'll never get to know him, but at least I know who he is. Maybe someday Mom will tell me about him and I'll learn more. Em decided that when she went back to Massachusetts, she wouldn't tell her mother that she had figured out her father's identity. It's obvious that Mom has experienced a lot of pain over this. I know she'll tell me all about him when the time is right. My father being Tim Milton explains why Mom and her sister never communicate, and why they seldom receive letters from her grandparents.

Still, it puzzled her why her granddad was so unpleasant. Sure, he is old and ailing, but he was this unpleasant nine years ago, too. Not so with Grandma, she is softer and friendlier. Did her grandparents know that Tim Milton was her father? Why did they never talk about Sarah?

CHAPTER 16

Riding on the train to Springbrook to see Em, Joel thought about his job interview of the previous day. He didn't know that Mr. Milton was a Navy man. He chided himself for recklessly divulging that he was a pacifist. And perhaps, he thought, I should have given in on my principles and eaten meat at lunch. I'm sure that being a vegetarian didn't endear me to Mrs. Milton. He sighed, thinking about the challenges of being a Quaker. I have to constantly explain to people why I don't want to do this or that. It makes me feel out of the mainstream. Normally, I don't mind not fitting in, but I really want this job, and my chances of getting it are slim enough already—knowing nothing about cranberries. This is exactly the type of work I want. I could spend my days outdoors dealing with all aspects of nature.

Joel had good reason to worry about getting the job. He had been trained in forestry at the University of Wisconsin, yet he couldn't, for the life of him, find a job in forestry. Times were hard. He had felt lucky that he found work as a naturalist, but it was only temporary and the pay was almost nothing.

There were many sad stories. Several grocers went belly up because they gave too many desperate families food. It was quite common to hear of three families living in space appropriate for one. It's funny how everything happens at once, Joel thought. There he was, trying his darnedest to present himself well to Mr. Milton, when in walks the loveliest girl that he has seen in years. If she looks that good in overalls, how would she look in a dress? He tried his best not to be distracted by Em, but her eyes were so intense they almost commanded his attention. Then, when she smiled—that broad warm smile that seemed to go from ear to ear—it made him feel both joy and relief. She was only in Springbrook for two more days. He hoped they could become friends quickly before she returned to Massachusetts. There were probably several men back at the University there who had their eyes on her.

Joel's train arrived in Springbrook at around 10:30 A.M. Driving the car two days in a row had been out of the question. He had to be sure to catch the 4:00 P.M. train home, the last one of the day. Em had told him that her grandparent's house was within sight of the depot. There it is, he said to himself. As he walked towards it, he couldn't help but notice that the house was very run down. Not surprising, he thought. Poverty was rampant in Rice Lake as well.

Em suggested that they walk out of town to the Namekagon River. From the old bridge that crossed it, they'd be able to watch the rapids and have a place to sit in the shade, as there were tall stands of alders and willows on both banks. They started to talk about the Miltons and Miltonberry.

"I was impressed that you were able to eat all of the tomato aspic piled on your plate."

"When you need a job you'll do anything."

They spent hours telling each other about their backgrounds. Em explained that her Mom was estranged from her grandparents. Feeling embarrassed about the state of her grandparents' house she explained, "Years ago, my grandfather was forced to retire from the church. Apparently, the candidate chosen to be the new reverend would not take granddad's job if he was required to live in his home. The Board of Governors decided that instead of giving granddad a pension, my grandparents would be allowed to live in the house until they died. Then, I guess the church used the pension money to build the new minister a house out of town. So this is why they can't afford to repair their home."

"Well, that's too bad. I'm sorry to hear they're having trouble. My dad lost his job as a teacher. The school board referred to it as early retirement with no pension. He was only fifty-three when that happened to him. The board had to get rid of their more expensive teachers. Fortunately, my mom was kept on in her teaching job, but at a much reduced salary."

The Depression had affected everyone they knew. Each had many sad stories of friends and family trying to cope with the collapsed economy. Joel had been lucky compared to his best friend Billy Henshaw.

"Billy's father had been a plumber and pipe fitter. They lived in a beautiful home in Rice Lake, but when Mr. Henshaw's clients couldn't pay him for his services, he lost both his business and his house. The Henshaws had to move into a rundown cabin outside of Rice Lake. Billy had to wait in line at the grocery store for welfare food packages. He walked the railroad tracks looking for coal. Fortunately, Mrs. Henshaw had acquired some chickens. They could trade the eggs for other food. In fact, this was so important to their survival that whenever Billy's mother heard a chicken squawk, she ran to the hen house to grab the freshly laid egg."

Joel usually didn't talk much, but Em seemed interested and encouraged him to continue by asking more questions. "Let's see what else did Billy do? Oh yes, he collected Arco Coffee cans. For each one he brought to the movie theater, he could see a movie free…. My favorite Billy story is about crows. Our county wanted to help save food crops so it paid 25¢ for each dead crow. Billy told me that whenever his family killed a chicken to eat, he would take the head, color it black as best he could, and leave it in the sun so it developed a ripe odor. Then he carried the head in a gunny sack into Town Hall. Once the gunnysack was opened the inspector lost his will to closely scrutinize its contents. Billy always got his 25¢."

"How's he doing now?" asked Em.

"Smart as he is, his family couldn't afford to send him to college. The advantages I had, he deserved. You see, we both took college entrance courses in high school, but come graduation, Billy had to stay home because he didn't have the money to pay for his cap and gown. He later received his diploma but he wasn't allowed to participate in the ceremony. So what's he doing now? Odd jobs that he can pick up, but he also taught himself the banjo. Now, in his spare time, he plays in a small trio, touring the local dance halls."

"My family is better off than most," Em said. "We grow so many of the things we need." She paused and looked indecisive. Finally she blurted out, "I love my parents." She paused again and finally said, "Actually my dad is not my real father." She looked down. Joel could tell that Em had something important to tell him. He didn't respond because he thought she was trying to decide whether to tell him or not. "My real father called me Emma Cranberry." She began to cry and then she laughed. Joel put his arm around her and held her tenderly, kissing her forehead.

She recovered, and told him with laughter about the little stories her real father must have sent her mother when she was very young. Emma Cranberry had to eat cranberries in order to be healthy and keep her rosy cheeks. The stories were about the constant struggle protecting the cranberries and Elm Grove against Rusty Muskrat and Bertie Beaver, who had destructive tendencies. Their worst fear, however, was Wendy North Wind, who tried her best to freeze the cranberries…. Then the stories stopped. I think my father died. Mom never has told me about him."

The next day, Joel came back to see Em again. The two of them walked to Spring Lake, a mile-and-a-half outside of town, for a swim and picnic. Joel told her that he had called Mr. Milton that morning before he left for Springbrook.

"He definitely offered me the job. He said Mr. Hodgekiss will be moved out in nine days and I can move into the foreman's house then. I didn't tell him that I really don't have anything to move in. I'll come with a suitcase. Mom said she can give me a blanket and towel. Dad said that I could take my bed and mattress—they'll drive them here—putting them on top of the car. Then I would be free to ride my horse to Miltonberry."

They went swimming. She's lovely to look at even with wet

hair, Joel thought. Now it was drying into soft waves and curls. They sat on an old bedspread from the Ellsworth's house and ate sandwiches.

"I wish I could see you working on the bog. You are going to love it."

"I wish you could too. Do you have to go back tomorrow?"

He bent over and kissed her.

CHAPTER 17

Joel's lack of cranberry farming experience didn't bother Preston. Most people don't know anything about cranberries. Just about everybody he hired had to be taught from scratch. But the foreman would have considerable responsibility, so what Preston was looking for was integrity and honesty. Preston thought Joel had those qualities. He was a bit young, around twenty-five, if he remembered correctly, but he appeared strong, healthy and energetic.

"Well, I have to admit he had charm," Josie said.

"There was charm in somebody who grew up in Trego?" Press teased. He recognized that Josie was snobbish at times, but her snobbishness was due more to loneliness. She was constantly hoping to find someone with whom she had something in common. When it came right down to it, she liked lots of types of people. Nonetheless, he continued to tease her, "Charm wasn't exactly high on the list of attributes I was looking for in Joel."

"I liked the way he treated Marie. He seemed kind."

Press and Josie had already discussed Em. Josie told Press that she had overheard Em say her full name was Emma. Once they learned her birthday matched that on the back of the photo, they realized who she might be and watched her through the living room window.

"Do you think she kept her identity secret so she could come here to see what we were like?" Press asked her.

"I've been wondering that myself. Did she ever ask you about the history of the bog?"

"No, but why would she ask if she already knew it?"

"Did you notice," Josie asked, "that when she read the engraving she looked puzzled?"

"I would have noticed that had you not edged me out of the

way so you could get a better look at her."

"Do you think she looks like Tim?" Josie asked him.

"Well I spent the morning concentrating on Joel. Maybe her smile is like Tim's."

"She seemed so...so...uncomplicated. I think she doesn't know."

"But it's too much of a coincidence that she would come here all the way from Massachusetts entirely by accident."

CHAPTER 18

The next afternoon, Josie found herself relatively alone. The girls were helping Louise dry dishes. Then they went on the front porch to play with little Lucy. Josie was not feeling very happy. She couldn't put her finger on just what was bothering her. Perhaps, if she played the piano she would cheer up. She had settled on playing an old favorite, a Chopin scherzo, but realized her mistake too late. For as soon as little Susan heard the music, she entered the dining room with a series of arabesques and continued to pretend she was a ballerina as long as Josie played.

Susan had picked up Josephine's flare for theatrical displays and saw herself as a ballerina. Her little body was supple and strong, but she was too forceful for a ballerina. There was no indication that her soul felt the subtleties of the music. Nonetheless, Josie hoped that when Susan's enthusiasm for ballet flagged, it wouldn't be because she realized that she lacked talent.

Josephine was struggling with motherhood. She loved her three girls, but had no example to draw on as to how to bring them up. She knew it was important for them to have the best schooling money could buy, but she never viewed motherhood as an opportunity to teach or guide her children. Women in her class didn't do practical things for their daughters to mimic. The miniature tea service that she and Press gave Susan last Christmas was the best she could offer. Josie could hear Susan imitating her during her pretend tea parties. Marie was somewhat of a tomboy, no, not actually a tomboy, Josephine thought, because she wasn't interested in the outdoors. She was more like a bully, good at asserting herself and maneuvering opinions so she got what she wanted. Preston's pursuits outdoors and with machinery were wasted on her. For Susan and Lucy only time would tell. So far, for Preston at least, it was unfortunate that none of their children were boys.

Looking back on her own early upbringing, Josie realized that much of it was relegated to various servants. When her parents were present, she was expected to be beautifully dressed and curtsy. She was instructed in table manners, how to write thank-you-notes and was given years of piano lessons. Josie was a reader, but reading and piano playing were solitary pursuits. They didn't satisfy her social needs.

She discovered as a young girl that she could get people's attention if she made witty conversation. Trips with her family gave her plenty of material to talk about. They also inspired her love of history, languages and the fine arts, but even on these family trips, she and her brother were always left in the care of someone other than their parents.

What was it that Em had said at lunch? That it was "satisfying to use what you produce." Josephine had never produced anything other than delicious dishes to eat and most often, she just directed others on how to make them. Here, in the North Woods, it was expected that a mother tend to her children, and Josie realized that she really didn't want to. In their Kenilworth home, Lucy's crib was kept next to the maid's room, far from the other members of the family. She must stop these thoughts. What Josie did love to do was to plan the trips that she and Preston took during the winter months.

The Miltons went on these trips each winter. Broadening and entertaining as they were, Josie felt without direction when she returned. Her months at Miltonberry with house parties—guests from Chicago—were fun and had their challenges, but there was no single pursuit that carried her interest throughout the year, continuously, like Preston had with his cranberries.

Their annual patterns of migration were offset from each other's. Preston was at Miltonberry seven months of the year, whereas Josie was in Kenilworth nine months of the year. For four months they were separated from each other. This way Josie could ensure that their girls received an excellent education.

Sending them to the Springbrook School was out of the question. Louise told her that there were only two teachers for its eight grades. Each classroom had four rows of desks—one for each grade. The principal was one of the two teachers. He spent 30 minutes instructing the children in one row before going on to the next row/grade, and so on. Through no fault of their own, the two teachers had to make the students spend most of the day working in silence so as not to disturb the others. To avoid this, Josie went to the other extreme and sent her girls, at great expense, to a private school on the North Shore.

While Josie's parents were alive, she and Preston could afford private schools, trips and entertaining their friends and relatives. They gave numerous parties while they were together in Kenilworth, and with house parties at Miltonberry, Josie could maintain a lifestyle (albeit a bit truncated) of a socialite, in keeping with her upbringing.

She was aware that she could make more of an effort to assimilate into the Springbrook community, but she had not been brought up to do physical work. The proper thing to do was to arrange for others to do things you wanted done. That took time, organization, and forethought. She was not lazy. Why did such disturbing doubts occur to her only while she was at Miltonberry?

How could she get out of this sad mood she was in? Reflecting on Tim's death brought up her nagging concern about why there was no death certificate. Maybe Clarence Ellsworth had lied? Tomorrow she resolved to drive into Shell Lake—the Washburn County's seat of government. She had already found out that she needed to go to the Register of Deeds in the court house, but that was the limit of what she could ask over the party line. She didn't want anyone to know that she had doubts about some aspects of Tim's death.

Preston gave her clear directions to follow. Josie wasn't afraid of getting lost, but she worried about staying in the tire tracks when there was thick sand. She didn't have much experience driving and still couldn't negotiate the clutch smoothly. She was pleased to have arrived at the County Courthouse without a hitch. Unfortunately, there was no record of Tim Milton's death. She learned that twenty years ago there was no coroner in Washburn County.

"When someone died, the normal thing for people to do was to call the sheriff or a doctor," she was told.

"Would the sheriff's office have a record of being called out to verify a death?" she asked.

"You'll have to inquire there. They should still be open." Josie rushed over to the county jail, where the sheriff's office was located, only to find that there was no record of the sheriff being called out to verify Tim's death.

"Would the cold weather be a reason why the sheriff hadn't been summoned?" Josie asked the officer on duty.

"No, that shouldn't do anything but delay matters by a day or two."

Josie started back home, disappointed that her excursion proved useless but pleased that she would be able to tell Press that she had no trouble driving. She nearly made it home when all of the sudden she felt the car swerve. Try as she might, she could not steer the car away from the ditch. The car stopped at a 35-degree angle, with the right front tire deep in sand. Shaken and mortified, Josie got out of the car and started walking down the road. Their nearest neighbor was plowing in his field and had witnessed the whole episode. You don't get away with a thing around here. She thought she remembered his name. Wasn't it Guy Wade?

She couldn't approach him because the ditch was in the way. So she just stood helpless and watched him come toward her. Mr. Wade had no trouble jumping over the ditch despite the fact that he was in his mid-sixties.

"Ain't that sand somethin'? Take you eye off the rut for a second and it gits you into trouble."

She introduced herself, and he said, "Oh I knows ya. Sure,

Preston's wife. Good to meet ya."

Josie wanted to be sure he knew that she was a perfectly capable driver. "I made it into Shell Lake and almost got home without a hitch."

"Why did ya go all that way?"

Josie took a moment to think and decided, why not? "You knew Preston's brother, Tim Milton, didn't you?"

"Oh sure, such a shame a young man like that. I went to the Congregational Church in town. So I knew them all."

"What can you tell me about how he died?"

"The story is that he fell down stairs."

"Do you believe that is what happened?"

"No reason not to. Why do ya ask?"

"Well there is no death certificate for Tim. That's why I went to Shell Lake. And the sheriff wasn't called out either."

"Hmm, well maybe that's not so unusual for them days. Oh, that was a bitter winter. I remember a woman on horseback rode into Tim's place the day after the rest of them left. I was a little worried for her because it was so cold—15 below, or something like that."

"What do you mean 'the rest of them?'"

"Let's see: Clarence, Rose and Sarah, they all went to Minneapolis. They often did that after Christmas to visit their relatives there. Tim didn't go."

"You have a pretty good memory for something that happened twenty years ago."

"When the Ellsworths went somewhere, Clarence would let the whole congregation know, because then others of us would have to take over. He asked me to do the sermon that week while he was gone."

"Do you remember when they left and came back?"

"Friday to Friday."

"You do have a good memory."

"It was the first and last sermon I ever gave. Nervous as can be, I was. Then, when I found out that Tim died sometime in that week, I felt guilty. I was here, so close. I wish I had known he was in trouble. Ya know how ya go over and over things in your mind? Tim used ta borrow things and would ask me for practical advice. He was a serious person, not what you would call a chatterbug."

"Who was the woman on horseback?"

"Don't know. I didn't get a look at her face. She was all wrapped up, of course, kind of bulky-like."

"Was there anything unusual about the horse?"

"Na, just a brown thing.... Ya know we didn't find out that Tim had died until a couple of weeks after the family returned from Minneapolis. Clarence had the family zipped up about it. I did think that was strange. They didn't want a memorial service, said they wanted to wait until spring to have a proper burial, when Tim's family from Chicago could be there."

"Did you go to the memorial service in the spring?'

"Far's I know there weren't none.... Well's, I better help you out of that ditch."

Chapter 19

April 1940

Preston no sooner arrived from Chicago for the growing season than Joel asked if he could take a day or two off. "I want to go to a funeral."

"Anyone from around here?" Preston asked.

"Clarence Ellsworth. He was the pastor of the Congregational Church in town years ago."

"But Joel, I thought you were a Quaker?"

"Well yes, I am, but do you remember Em Lucas, the young woman that came the day you interviewed me for the job?"

"Yes, I do. I think you were a little sweet on her, weren't you?"

"I still am." Joel laughed. "She's coming to the funeral and I'll get to meet her mother if I go. Mr. Ellsworth was Em's grandfather."

Josie is going to be thrilled to hear this, Preston thought. "What time's the funeral? I only ask because I think I may go myself. I knew Clarence a long time ago."

"Ten o'clock tomorrow morning."

"Sure, Joel, take a couple of days off, more if you'd like, but just inform me what needs doing on the bog and I'll get on it." Josie will be so disappointed that she isn't here for this, Preston thought. She sees Tim's death as a mystery—one she wants to solve. I wish I could call her, but I don't want those people who listen in to know we are concerned.

Over the years, he and Josie had asked Clarence and Rose over for dinner perhaps three times. Each time, it seemed to them that Rose wanted to come, but Clarence was very firm in rejecting the invitation. He still disapproves of us, Preston thought. Oh well.

He didn't want to go to the funeral to pay homage to that severe man. What he wanted was to have a chance to look at Em, now that he knew for sure that she was Tim's daughter.

Em's mother would be there. What was her name? It came to him at last, "Meg." Probably Meg doesn't want Em to know that Tim's her father, so I won't say a thing. I can just hear Josie. If she knew I was going to have this opportunity she'd say STAY AWAKE, keep looking for clues and write me all about it immediately.

After the service, he wrote Josie a long letter.

I don't think I would have recognized Meg. Not that she has aged any more than the rest of us, but because she was never very memorable looking. I arrived late and slipped in one of the back pews. I noticed Joel and Em were absolutely smitten with each other. Then, I'm afraid, I did go to sleep for a bit, but surely you don't want to know what the preacher said.

Em is a lovely young woman. I see a resemblance between her and Tim when she smiles. She has Clarence's eyes, intense but not as frightening, thank God! Fortunately Em does not have the shape of her mother, who is definitely on the chubby side, but both mother and daughter are energetic and enthusiastic. Rose, Clarence's widow, looked relieved and happy. To be fair, that probably had more to do with being reunited with her family than being unhitched to Clarence. I'm sorry. One should never talk badly of the deceased, but he was not a pleasant type. No tear was shed for him and that is sad.

When Joel introduced (reintroduced) me to the three women, it was Meg that seemed uncomfortable. She made little eye contact with me. I may have more chances to see Meg and Em, as I think they will come to Miltonberry to visit Joel.

Oh, one thing was strange. Sarah, Tim's wife, was not there. I heard Meg express disappointment that bordered on anger that her sister was not there to help with the funeral arrangements and care for their mother, Rose. She said something like: "We had to come all the way from Massachusetts and Sarah couldn't make it from Minneapolis?" Em was disappointed too. Evidently she has never met her Aunt Sarah. No explanation was given for Sarah's absence.

Josie please don't ask me to describe the few cakes and sandwiches that were served after the burial. I just ate them hungrily. They were served on a mixed assortment of plates with paper napkins. Will that do? Oh yes, the reception was in the church proper and not in the Ellsworth's home. That is an eyesore, if there ever was one.

I'm tired now, so good night my little 'Humpafine.' If any further 'clues' come to my attention, I will telegraph them to you in code without delay.

Love,

Press

Before they got engaged, Joel explained to Em that he was a birthright Friend, "Birthright because I grew up in a Quaker family. When I was young, we lived in Trego, near Spooner, and about 16 miles from Sarona, where my meetinghouse is."

"You don't call it a church?" Em asked.

"No, we get attached to our meetinghouse, but it is really nothing more than a building to us. Anyway, each Sunday we'd ride in our horse-drawn wagon to Meeting in Sarona. When Mom and Dad decided to move out of Trego, they chose Rice Lake because we would be just as close to Sarona, only we'd be coming there from the south, not north."

"It sounds like the meetinghouse is pretty important to you."

"Well, what is important is to have the opportunity to meet as a group, and in silence. The meetinghouse is just a convenient way to do that."

"Are you Christians?"

"I can only speak for myself. I guess I consider myself a Christian in spirit and tradition. We don't have a creed or anything like that. Rituals, preaching, singing and music that are usual in church services would be distractions to us. We spend the time together to focus on what we call the 'Inner Light'—the spirit of God that we believe is in every person. We are all equal in that respect."

"Is that why you don't have a minister?"

"Yes."

"Well, I can understand that," Em replied. "I don't believe any of us need an intermediary in order to talk with God. To me, a minister is a manager of a congregation. He helps to keep the congregation focused on God."

When he became the foreman at Miltonberry, Joel tried to

continue to go to Meeting in Sarona, as it was still the closest
meetinghouse to Springbrook, but the distance he had to cover
each Sunday was double what it had been when he lived in Rice
Lake. During that first year, he couldn't afford to buy a car, so
he rode his horse to Meeting. He enjoyed the ride each Sunday.
When the Depression ended with World War II, he could finally
afford to buy a car but then he had to worry about exceeding his
ration of gasoline. He compromised: during the coldest part of
winter, when it was risky to ride a horse so far from home, he
drove his car.

The Sunday after Clarence's funeral, Joel took Em and her
mother to Meeting in Sarona. The meetinghouse was on a
rise, surrounded by white pines. It was originally built to serve
a Presbyterian congregation. In time, however, the number of
Presbyterians dwindled in that area. Those who remained decided to sell their small white frame church to a group of Quakers,
which included Joel's family. "When we took possession of the
building, we removed the stained glass from all the windows except the high circular window above what had been the altar. We
couldn't easily reach it, so we just left it as it was. We knew a day
might come when we might have to sell the building as a church
so we carefully bundled up the glass and buried it in back."

"Pretty frugal of you I'd say," Em said.

Joel laughed. "Yes, I guess you're right. We wish the building
didn't have a steeple, but it was simpler to keep the structure as
it was."

As they approached, they could read the hand carved sign
that said: "Sarona Friends Meetinghouse." The entrance was a
plain, small door next to which was another sign which read:
"To live in the virtue of that life and power that takes away the
occasion of all wars."

Joel told them that there were about twelve families and eight
individuals like Joel who came to Meeting fairly regularly. The
benches were arranged in a circle, connoting their testimony of
equality. Most were people Joel knew quite well, but he made

sure Em and her mother met the Scattergoods, the Boyntons and his favorite "dear little Abby," in her nineties. Later he told them, "Abby has the sharpest mind in Washburn County. In Meeting sometimes when we think she is asleep, she will suddenly rise to her feet and minister us with a poignant message.

"I rarely miss Meeting on Sundays. Once a month, we have a potluck lunch. On the other Sundays, my parents and I bring a picnic, so we have a little time together before I have to ride back to Miltonberry."

Joel found Em's mother pleasant and friendly, but he couldn't understand why she held back from telling Em who her father was. Especially now that they would live on the very place that Tim had homesteaded. Did she think it would embarrass Mr. Milton and strain my relationship with him? Joel asked Em when they were alone, "Why don't you ask your mother again about your father?"

"You know, I have been tempted to ask her many times, but then I think she must have a significant reason why she doesn't want me to know. Anyway, I already know who my father is, so I feel I should respect my mom's need to not discuss it with me."

～

In 1941, like all young men between the ages of 21 and 36, Joel had to register for the draft. He was determined not to contribute in any way to a war effort, but he dreaded the consequences of that decision, if the country went to war. His father had had a terrible time as a conscientious objector during World War I. He was exempted from combat because of his religion, but he had to perform an alternative service in an army camp in Michigan. Once there, he was verbally abused and had to repeatedly convince officials that he was a sincere pacifist. His father's only other option was prison. Even after the war, some of the Helmer's neighbors continued to be rude to them. Living and teaching in Trego was no longer enjoyable. This was the real reason his family decided to move to Rice Lake.

By 1942, even men of Preston's age were required to register for the draft. A registrant claiming to be a conscientious objector (CO) had to fill out a questionnaire explaining his beliefs. Joel could easily prove he was a Quaker and so he would be exempted from combat, but he would have to join the Civilian Public Service (CPS). Thank goodness the military no longer mixed COs with other servicemen. They learned that lesson in WWI. Now, COs were kept by themselves in CPS camps that were located in remote areas of the country. The army didn't want COs to sway public opinion against the war and they also wanted to protect COs from people who might want to mistreat them. The government spent no money on CPS camps. COs had to work without pay and their families and congregations had to provide their food, plus whatever else it took to maintain the camps.

The men in the CPS camps worked on soil conservation, forestry and agricultural projects. How ironic, Joel thought. For years I wanted a job in forestry but couldn't get one. Now that I can get one, I don't want it. He loved being Miltonberry's foreman. He and Preston had often discussed with some alarm how the draft might affect them personally. Fortunately, soon after the war started, cranberries were declared a war crop. During the war, the Army shipped out a million pounds of dehydrated cranberries to the troops. Any full-time worker involved in producing a war crop like cranberries was exempt from military service.

Joel and Em had been engaged for a year. Now that there was no fear of Joel being called up, they were free to marry.

CHAPTER 21

1941

Harold had become so fond of Sam and his family that he often rented a cabin near their home so he could be with them over an extended period of time. It got so he didn't even want to return home. The night he died, he had just driven back from Hayward to his eight-bedroom home in Minneapolis. His gardener waved to greet him when he drove into his estate. The cook prepared him a meal of white fish, parsley potatoes and succotash—all his favorites. After dinner he tried to phone Richard. They must be out. It had been five months since he had talked to him. Richard's butler always gave a reason why Richard was unavailable, out of town, or in a meeting.

Harold died that night in 1941. He never did tell Richard that he had a half-brother. His will didn't show any money going to Sam. Clarence Ellsworth had died the year before. This meant that there was no one except the members of Sam's family who knew that Harold was Sam's father. Harold no longer thought of this as unfinished business. Sam understood the reason for maintaining this secret. Harold Morris died that night in his sleep feeling at peace with himself.

Sam didn't find out about his death until a week later when he read an article in the newspaper. It wouldn't be appropriate for him to attend the funeral in Minneapolis, so he and his family had their own ceremony on the shores of Chief Lake to honor Harold. Sam knew about the secret trust and vowed to use whatever money he might inherit to further education on the reservation.

CHAPTER 22

Preston's mother, Emily, was so frail in her last years that she gave up living alone in her South Side apartment, and upon Preston's insistence, came to live with his family. Although Emily was quiet and unobtrusive, Josie felt her disapproving eye when it came time to serve cocktails. Most days at Miltonberry, she sat on the front porch alternating between snoozing and reading from her *Science and Health*. Sitting there, she could see Tim's gravesite and had a nice view of the bog. I think she sees this as her territory, Josie thought. When we enter the porch, she makes us feel like we have to ask permission.

Em and Joel had already been married at the Congregational Church in Middlefield, Massachusetts, where Em grew up, but when they returned to Miltonberry after their brief honeymoon, they decided to have another celebration to include Springbrook, Sarona and Rice Lake friends. Josie immediately offered Miltonberry.

The following Saturday morning, Josie was seated in her usual spot at the kitchen table where she could view the back door entrance, which most people used, and the other entrance into the front porch. Was that Emily talking, she asked herself? Without looking up from her book, she thought Emily's probably going senile—after all she is 87 years old. Josie knew only the two of them were in the house. Maybe she had better look to make sure Emily was all right.

As Joel and Em entered the porch from the outside, Josie came from the inside to see Emily staring at Em. She looked surprised and unsure as to whom they were, Josie thought, so she introduced them to each other. Now, Josie noticed Em staring at Emily. That clinches it, Josie thought, Em knows that Tim was her father. This is ridiculous. Emily would love to know that Em is her granddaughter. She would have to speak to Preston. This secrecy has got to end. Josie couldn't help but enjoy the thought of Emily discovering that her darling Tim had been a naughty boy.

Joel got straight to the point: "You are very kind to let us have our wedding celebration here at Miltonberry, Mrs. Milton. We've talked it over and would like to be married under the care of Sarona Meeting, but at Miltonberry. Would that be alright with you?" Joel explained further what that meant.

"OK, I understand that," said Josie, "but why in silence?"

"Because, Josie dear, it's a contemplative religion," Emily interjected.

That woman talks down to me, thought Josie, but I am not going to get upset about it. "So you all sit in silence every Sunday?" (She felt like asking, "where did this religion come from?")

"Josephine, I know you are keen on drama and music, but to some of us, pageantry is rather detrimental to serious spiritual inquiry," Emily said.

Preston's mother is so formal and stiff, Josie thought. I bet Tim was the same. Josie was ready to drop this topic. She was outnumbered. Quakers must be one of those weird religions that nobody ever hears much about. More like something you'd find in...in San Francisco, not six miles south of Spooner! She heard Joel say that there was no minister and that everybody signs the marriage certificate. That is sweet, but no music?

Josie moved onto thoughts about the reception. She suggested to them that she could serve some of her pet hors d'oeuvres and quarters of sandwiches without crusts; also cranberry bars, wine, sherry and beer, or if they would prefer, Bloody Marys or even Mint Juleps.

On hearing all this, Joel quickly replied. "I think most of the guests would love iced tea."

How boring, Josie thought.

"Weddings should be sober occasions," Emily said pointedly. Preston's mother has an uncanny knack of reading people's mind,

Josie thought.

"We would like to sit outside in a circle, Mrs. Milton, between the front porch and the bog."

"Where my fine Tim is buried, yes, he would approve of that! He can be a part of the wedding, so to speak," Emily said.

"What about mosquitoes. They can be frightful in August," Josie added.

Emily again spoke up: "Most people are used to them by now."

There is another remark that is directed at me, even though she doesn't look at me, thought Josie. In fact, she never stops looking adoringly at Em, Josie realized. Does she know? No, she probably sees a resemblance to Tim—her darling!

"Is there any way we could get folding chairs so we could sit outside in a circle?" Joel asked.

"Maybe we could rent them from the Town Hall. I could ask Louise, her husband's head of the town council," Em suggested.

"How many people do you think will come?"

They added up all the people that they wanted to come. "Let's see, my aunt Sarah I know won't come…so that's around 45, including all of us."

Joel quickly said: "Mrs. Milton, that is probably many more than you were anticipating. If…"

"Oh no, that's easy."

"Also, the Quakers always bring food to things like this."

"No, I want this to be a treat for everybody," Josephine said hastily. Good grief, I can see it now: tuna casseroles, deviled eggs, celery sticks and Kool-Aid. Oh no, no, no. "How long would people sit in a circle?"

"About 45 minutes to an hour."

"Really I hope the mosquitoes behave! We'll have to put out those incendiary repellants."

"Then it takes a few minutes for everybody to sign the marriage certificate," Joel added. "I guess we would need a card table to place it on."

Chapter 23

Once Em and Joel were engaged, Press asked them if they would mind taking care of goats if he purchased some. Joel didn't mind, but he admitted he didn't know how to take care of them. Em, however, knew just what they needed. Her family had raised goats on their farm. Preston had a chicken coop built with an extension to barn seven goats. The goats arrived two days after Joel and Em came back from Massachusetts. Press wanted to be sure that Joel and Em would have eggs, meat, and milk at hand throughout the cold winter. If vegetarian attitudes prevailed, he and Josie would eat any old hens over the summer months.

Em was going to be an asset to life at Miltonberry, Preston was sure, not only because she loved farming, but she also enjoyed showing Susan and Lucy how to take care of plants and animals. She taught them how to milk the goats and to clean out their stalls. Sadly, Marie showed no interest in these things. She was a reader and somewhat lazy, Preston had to admit. She seemed to lack a sense of responsibility and left it to Susan to look after Lucy.

Preston didn't want to take advantage of Em's goodwill. He heard that Susan often knocked on Em's door first thing in the morning, and recently, he heard little Lucy was following suit. In the evening, his girls often told him what they had learned that day. Evidently, if Em was sewing, she would give them a piece to work on for themselves. In the afternoons, Em spent a couple of hours in the garden. She and Joel grew a great variety of vegetables. Typically, Susan and Lucy helped Em for fifteen minutes. During that time, they were learning how to weed and hoe as well as how to recognize the different vegetables.

Josie expressed gratitude to Em, but on another level, Press knew it saddened her.

"I just can't teach them how to milk the goats," she lamented to Press.

Press tried not to laugh, but the vision of Josie sitting on a small three-legged stool surrounded by muck, her beautifully manicured fingers pulling on teats, was definitely ludicrous. Josie did like the garden. She would take notes of what needed doing and then asked her girls to weed this row or hoe that bed. She prided herself in designing the arrangement of the planted flowers around the house. She made copious lists of what had to be done and taped them to hanging light fixtures in the kitchen. She made sure that there were fresh flowers on the long kitchen table everyday.

Preston was pleased with the relationship he was developing with little Lucy. Each night after dinner, the two would walk through the garden inspecting which plants had come up, which vegetables needed picking. Occasionally, they would walk down to the edge of the bog to see if they could spot deer grazing on the other side. Lucy usually searched the sky for stars so she could make a wish:

> Star light, star bright,
> The first star I see tonight;
> I wish I may, I wish I might,
> Have the wish, I wish tonight.

On these warm summer evenings, Preston kept his shirt sleeves rolled up. "Daddy, you're getting bitten by mosquitoes. Don't you mind?" Lucy asked.

"I'm just used to them by now I guess."

"One, two, three," Lucy tried to count how many were biting him at once. "Don't you want to brush them away? I can't stand them." She watched him smoke. "Is that why you smoke Luckies? Do they keep the mosquitoes from bothering you?"

Lucy usually slept with Susan on the sun porch. "I love listening to the whip-poor-wills. Em says that at night from her house she can hear the loons on the reservoir."

Marie slept next door in the blue room, which had two doors.

During the day, the room was used as a hall between the new and the old part of the house. "Last night, Marie said that Uncle Tim walked through her room and left the doors open. I hope I never hear him. Mom says Uncle Tim is a friendly ghost."

That reminded Preston of how Josie had cornered him earlier in the day and tried to convince him to tell his mother about Tim, so she could enjoy knowing that Em was his daughter.

"How can I do that?" he had asked her, "when Em's mother won't talk to her about it. Surely that has to come first."

"You should see how your mother looks at Em. Maybe she can't know the truth, but I sense she feels that Em is special."

Susan was being a bit of a problem concerning the wedding. Preston noticed that she was irreverent when it came to religion, in general. He overheard her telling his mother that she was an atheist. At the same time, she managed to let everyone know, including Joel and Em, that she was disappointed that she wasn't going to be a bridesmaid. And now Josie tells him that Lucy, who doesn't even know what a bridesmaid is, wants to be one. Susan wanted to participate in the theatrics of the wedding. Joel and Em tried to explain that there couldn't be a bridesmaid because there was no aisle and no bridal procession. The wedding had to be simple and everybody was expected to be quiet. Marie, just to be different and ornery, pretended the whole topic was boring.

It pleased Press to see Joel and Em tackle such problems, minor as they were. To soothe the girls' feelings, they decided to give all three girls a job. Susan and Lucy were assigned to usher people to the circular gathering on the other side of the house. On the way, they could explain to guests that it was a Quaker wedding, so it would be different, and that there would be long periods of silence. They asked Marie to see that everybody remained quiet during Meeting. They explained to her that every now and then someone would stand up and give a message that was important for everyone to hear. They should not be interrupted.

"What if they talk too long?" Marie asked.

"The clerk of the Meeting will take care of that."

"Who's the clerk?"

It was then that Joel and Em struck on the idea of taking the three girls with them to a Meeting in Sarona at least once before the wedding. Josie and Preston gave their consent.

Preston's mother overheard this arrangement and commented to Preston alone, "Well, at least some religion is better than none."

A week or so later, Joel asked if it would be OK if a couple of his friends brought some instruments, a fiddle and a banjo, to play after the wedding.

"Of course, that would be wonderful," Josie said promptly.

Later that night Preston said to Josie, "Wouldn't it be nice if they could dance. You know, when we made that wooden floor in the living room, I always thought it would be fun if some day people could dance on it. What do you say, Josie?"

"Fine, but we'd have to remove some of the furniture and roll up the rug."

"We have some strong men around to help with that."

"OK, I'll serve the refreshments and food on the front porch and that way the living room can be used for dancing. The girls will be thrilled."

"Oh, wait a minute. Do Quakers dance?"

"Sure, Joel and Em have gone to dances in town."

"Oh, that's right, but we had better ask them if they want the dancing."

Not only did they want dancing but Joel asked, "Mrs. Milton, would you consider playing the piano?"

"Oh what a wonderful idea," Preston said. "We can move the upright into the living room."

Josie gasped and blushed a bit.

"I'd love to, Joel, but I need some sheet music. I've never played country dance music, you know, like the schottische or a polka. What I do play doesn't go with a banjo and fiddle. I don't want to cause last minute complications, but if I could get the sheet music a couple of days ahead of time to practice, that would help."

"My friend Dwayne, the fiddler, was part of a three-piece band, but recently they lost their piano player to the Army. I think we can get hold of his sheet music.

CHAPTER 24

Meg and her husband, Steve Lucas, came out a week ahead of the wedding and stayed with Joel and Em in the foreman's house. Josie was grateful for Meg's offer to help her with last minute preparations in the kitchen, especially since her usual helper, Louise, was a guest at the wedding and therefore was unavailable. While chopping celery and preparing sandwiches, Josie was pleasantly surprised when the conversation turned to discussing a couple of books they both had read. Josie realized that Meg was a far more complex individual than she had previously thought.

Steve and Joel picked up the chairs from the Town Hall and arranged them in a circle around Tim's headstone on the lawn, facing the bog.

Marie usually wore her straight brown hair in braids, but for the wedding Josie noticed she tried to do herself up. She overheard Marie say that she was "the manager of the Meeting." All day long, she kept her hair set so the curl would hold. By the time the guests arrived she had successfully propped up an enormous pompadour with bobby pins. The rest of her hair fell in soft waves below her shoulders. She was wearing her favorite green and white cotton dress. In spite of Marie's efforts to look older, her plump shape and freckles revealed that she was only 13. "She must have bought an eyebrow pencil on the sly during our last trip to Spooner," Josie said to Press. Marie had used the pencil liberally, well beyond the boundary of her faint eyebrows.

Everything was going like clockwork until people started arriving. "It's time for you to leave the kitchen, Meg. I can manage from here. Go out and socialize with your friends and family. Thanks for all the help you gave me." While Josie completed the final touches on the food, she glanced out the kitchen window and noticed Press and others collecting more folding chairs. The circle of chairs must have become full, Josie thought. She finished the sandwiches and started to carry large platters of them out to the front porch. Thank goodness for wax paper, she thought. The sandwiches will stay fresh and sealed off from flies. Looking through the porch screens Josie could see that there were already two concentric circles and still more people were coming. Back in the kitchen, she saw cars parked up and down the road to the warehouse. Press, Joel and Em were greeting people as they arrived.

Susan burst into the kitchen on her way to the bathroom. "Oh boy, they brought their kids." Josie tried to catch her when she came back through to ask her what she meant, but she rushed out again. Where did all these people come from? Josie felt humiliated when she realized that there would probably not be enough food. She had always prided herself on feeding people well. Then she began hearing voices on the front porch and that made her furious. The porch (and more importantly the food on the porch) was off-bounds until after the marriage ceremony. With steam coming out of her ears, Josie walked quickly through the living room and out into the porch. There, she found various women bringing in dishes and placing them on the table. Her frown changed to a smile as she realized that there would be enough food, after all. Of course, there was no guarantee about the quality, and the positioning of dishes on the table made no sense. Perhaps I should just let go of all this and stop worrying. She stripped off her apron and continued walking, passing through the front porch door to join those outdoors.

Josie didn't know many of the people there. Several smiled at her and told her how beautiful her house was, but conversations with her went no further. Josie didn't feel slighted. She wanted to give Em and Joel a chance to be with their friends and relatives. Besides, there was an advantage to being virtually ignored. She had time to make observations and analyze what she saw. Her thoughts were interrupted by Marie's commanding voice: "Children cannot sit in chairs. Blankets and bedspreads should be placed in the center." Marie stood with her arms folded across her plump tummy. Just look at those eyebrows! She looks like a Samurai warrior. "All children should sit on the blankets in the center," Marie repeated. Josie just stood and watched. She had lost control. At this point there was nothing she could do.

Em and Joel came to the circle and took their seats in front of Tim's grave. Press came up to Josie and silently took her arm and directed her to a seat in the outer circle just behind Em and Joel, and next to Press's mother. Josie noticed that Meg appeared overwhelmed with emotion. She took the hand of her white-haired husband, Steve, and closed her eyes. The guests settled down, taking their cue from the Quakers who sat still in their chairs. Many had closed their eyes. Someone must have brought out some dressing table stools. Surveying the two circles, Josie noticed all the chairs had been taken, but the stools were still unoccupied.

There was silence. A gray-haired woman with glasses rose to her feet. "I am Margaret Scattergood, clerk of Sarona Friends Meeting. We welcome you all and thank you for coming to help us witness the marriage of Joel Helmer and Emma Lucas. We know that most of you are not familiar with Quaker traditions, so we thought it would make you feel more comfortable if we explained how a marriage in the manner of Friends proceeds...."

Just as Clerk Margaret's explanation finished, around the corner of the house came an elegant middle-aged couple led by Susan and Lucy. Susan directed them to the dressing table stools and said in a very loud whisper: "Quakers meet in silence."

Josie was mortified. Press reached out and held her hand. His grip was as strong as when they first met, only now his hand was somewhat rough, weathered from working outdoors on the bog. Josie wanted to find the new guests better seats and tried to squirm loose, but she couldn't free herself from Press's clasp. He's trying to hold me back, she thought. Who is that couple? That woman is beautiful—not just pretty, but beautiful. Oh, I bet she is Tim's wife, Sarah, with her very wealthy husband,

Richard Morris. Josie knew access to money could enhance one's looks, but Sarah must pay special attention to her appearance. Everything about her was done to perfection.

Josie was to learn that a Quaker Meeting imposes a regimen of silence from which one can't get away. If you were alone, you could get up and do something else, but Meeting protocol keeps you sitting quietly, so you can't escape your thoughts. Josie remembered that Em thought her aunt wouldn't come to their wedding. How strange that Sarah wouldn't go to her father's funeral and yet would come to her niece's wedding.

Josie's thoughts calmed down the longer Press held her hand. She wanted to look at Press and tell him how much she loved him. His hair was almost white now but he was still a handsome man. His poor hearing made him seem slow-witted to others, but Josie knew better. It also made him appear detached, whereas he was actually always sensitive to people's feelings.

Lucy's giggle broke the silence. Lucy's eyes were focused on a dragonfly that had landed on Sarah's knee. Each time Sarah brushed it off it came right back.

Josie tried to keep her eyes closed like Meg was doing. How could they be sisters, she thought? Meg was so plain. She clearly put little effort in the way she looked. No, she just couldn't keep her eyes closed. There was too much of interest right in this silent circle. She smiled to think she was getting away with analyzing people, her favorite pastime, because no one was looking at her. Richard is nice looking, she thought, but also seems a little shifty. Aha, there is Emily snoozing her way through this "contemplative" service!

The next time Josie looked at Sarah she saw perspiration running down her face. The day wasn't warm. Maybe she is having a hot flash, Josie thought. She looked over the bog in the distance. It all seemed so peaceful and innocent. Another quick scan of the people brought her attention to John Pete. The fierce expression on his face did not emanate love and kindness, so unlike the John Pete she knew. Josie realized he was fixing his stare on something or someone. She tried to determine what he was looking at. It was in the direction of Sarah. Was he putting a curse on her? Of course not!

Every now and then, one of the guests stood and said a few words about Em or Joel. Josie listened and then forgot what they had said. The last to speak was John Pete. His spell of anger must have been temporary, for now he appeared composed.

"It seems to me that the purpose of this day is not just to bless the union of Joel and Em. This day offers more than an opportunity to let them know that we love them and wish them a long, happy life together.

"Marriage is also a special opportunity because it brings families and friends together. A marriage reminds us of the value of union. It helps us to erase old grudges. It washes away any desire we may have for vengeance. It reminds us of who we came from.

"We can see in Joel or Em a father's smile of sunshine, the warmth of a mother's love, the gentle guiding of a father's whispers, the unending energy of a mother, and we can sense a father's on-going wish for peace in the world. It is easy to forget what we have been given by those who came before us. A wedding helps us to remember and be appreciative."

Josie once again marveled over John Pete's eloquence. She wondered whether the oral tradition among Ojibwe had contributed to his talent for speaking. After five more minutes of silence, the clerk shook someone's hand. With that signal, everybody shook hands with those around them. Guests were asked to sign the marriage certificate, which was a 20" x 30" sheet of paper. A fountain pen, ink bottle and blotter were on hand. The Meeting was over, so Josie stood up and stayed standing behind Em. She saw Sarah coming towards them. Josie decided to listen carefully, while pretending her thoughts were engaged with something to her right.

"Hello Em, I'm your aunt Sarah from Minneapolis and this is my husband, Richard Morris. I'm sorry we were a little late.

We want to give you our blessings." Before Em could even reply, Sarah quickly continued, "I wish we could stay and talk with you and the others, but I am not feeling well." Sarah turned to her mother, Rose, and quickly gave her a kiss on the cheek, apologizing for not feeling well enough to stay. Then she and Richard left with haste.

Josie saw that Meg had been occupied talking with the clerk. Now that she was free, Meg began scanning the circle with a frantic look on her face. She must be looking for Sarah, Josie thought.

Rose moved closer to Meg and said: "Sarah and Richard had to leave. She wasn't feeling well.… I know you're disappointed, Dear, but at least she came. She did not look well!" Meg looked like she was about to cry, but she saw Josie looking at her and she seemed to pull herself together.

When most had signed the marriage certificate, Josie began to encourage people to come onto the porch and have some refreshments. Many guests stayed until 11:00 that night. The two dairy farmers had to leave earlier, as they had to get up at 4:00 A.M. to milk cows. It was the music and dancing that kept things going. The lovely aspect of country dancing, Josie discovered, was that anybody could dance anytime they wanted to—with anyone they liked. People in the North Woods had danced these lively dances for decades. Swing, jitterbug, and Charleston were dances of urban areas. Josie and Joel's two musician friends hammered out schottisches, polkas and waltzes all night. Older folk who no longer danced could enjoy watching the fiddler bend down, tap his foot, and sometimes skip. The banjo player was quite the opposite. He sat very straight on a stool with no expression on his face all evening.

Josie had assumed that there would be a hideous amount of cleaning up to do afterwards, and was surprised to find that the dishes had been washed, dried and put away, except for a few serving plates and bowls left on the kitchen table. Earlier in the evening, Preston and John Pete had quietly put all the folding chairs in the truck, ready to be returned to the Town Hall in the morning. For Josie, this was an entirely new way of giving a party. Work, food preparation and accolades were shared. She had to admit that the broccoli casserole that someone brought would be considered delicious on Lake Shore Drive, Chicago.

Josie had a whale of a time. Playing the piano removed her from the hostess role, but she heard later from others, mostly from Susan, that Marie told everybody what to do until Johnnie Ferguson asked her to dance.

As they were going to bed, Press explained: "Johnnie is about three years older than Marie, I would say. He must have been taught all the dances by his older brothers and sisters, of whom there are many, I have heard. Yes, Johnnie would be a nice look-ing lad—glossy black hair, clear light complexion—except his teeth stick out even when his mouth is closed."

Josie immediately sympathized with the boy. Now she re-membered noticing him before playing the piano.

"Well, the kid looked like he loved to dance and was quite patient teaching Marie."

"Marie is not very agile, is she? How did Susan react to all this," Josie asked.

Press laughed. "Susan kept pointing out that Marie had no sense of rhythm. Yes, sadly, she was a bit jealous of her sister getting all this attention. I guess she sees herself as the dancer of the family."

"Don't tell me she tried to do sautés to that kind of music."

"I'm afraid so, until a man, I forget who, almost knocked her down while waltzing with his partner."

The next day, Josie heard Susan ask Marie if she had kissed Johnnie's teeth yet.

CHAPTER 25

END OF SUMMER 1941

Emily was enjoying the summer as much as she could, being tired all the time. Everything was such an effort. Her grandchildren were far too rambunctious for her to want to be in their presence for long. Only little Lucy was a pleasure. How she loves to sit down beside me and listen to me read. Thank God I still have my eyesight, she thought. That child is starved for attention.

The wedding was special, she thought. What was it John Pete said? "It is easy to forget what we have been given by those who came before us." I will never forget you, Chauncey. I am ready to be with you forever. Emily snoozed a bit in her chair on the front porch. When she awoke, her thoughts carried on from where she'd left them. It was a special wedding even though it only lasted a few minutes. Emily shook her head thinking of how Josie dreaded 45 minutes of silence. I could feel Tim's presence. He would approve of how things at Miltonberry are going.

It's a good time to die, but I want to hang on until we are back in Kenilworth. Then I will be sure to be buried next to you, Chauncey. Emily did not look forward to the drive back. Marie has to sit in the front seat so she and Susan won't fight. Marie always gets her way and Susan makes sure that everyone knows that Marie always gets her way. Then there's the problem of Josie's driving. Whenever I fall asleep, she manages to jerk the car, scaring all of us half to death.

Leaving Preston will be hard. Josie doesn't appreciate him. She thinks he's too passive and dull. She should realize that he doesn't challenge people or make witty remarks because he is never sure he has heard the conversation correctly. If he asks people to re-

peat themselves, they are mildly annoyed. Josie likes a fast rep-
artee. I am proud of Press. He has learned to accept the isolation
that his poor hearing has imposed. Josie either is embarrassed
by him or ignores him. She just carries on, not expecting him to
respond, treating him like an old man. Emily started laughing,
because at times, she realized, Press used his poor hearing to get
out of situations he didn't like. When he doesn't want to respond
to Josie's endless stream of gossip, I think he pretends he can't
hear it. Press is at peace with himself. He doesn't need to drink.
He accepts who he is and, as a result, others feel comfortable with
him. He is non-threatening and well-liked. My goodness, this
family needs more people with placid dispositions!

Emily was amused at the thought that perhaps Josie had developed the ability to hear a pine needle fall to compensate for
Press. That might be the one way they are a good match. Nothing
auditory passed her by unnoticed. She was quick to interpret a
hint of sarcasm in Susan's voice. She could hear Marie's kick land
on Susan's leg under the far end of the dinner table. Without even
looking at Preston, she could decipher from his breathing that he
was asleep.

The two of them ruled their realms in their own way. Preston
was a good boss. Emily was sure he gave clear instructions and
made nothing but reasonable demands on his employees. He often worked with them and enjoyed their company. Josie guarded
her indoor realm seated at the harvest table in the kitchen. She
was perched like a leopardess ready to pounce if necessary. It
was rarely necessary, so her method was as successful, in its way,
as Preston's. Emily noted their way of handling payday. Most
employees came to the house to collect their checks. Josephine
usually wrote checks from her account for people who worked in
the house and Preston paid the others out of his checkbook.

Emily knew Press and Josie didn't have money worries, even
during the Depression: salaries were low and equipment for the
bog was not expensive. Furthermore, as long as the Haylocks
were alive, money just appeared when needed. Even though they

were more fortunate than most families, they still canned fruits and vegetables at the end of the summer. The household was taken over by this activity for a week or two. Marie and Susan did their part. They even helped to carry the canned goods down to the dirt cellar, if someone went ahead of them to open the trapdoor and break the spider webs. It was during the canning season that Emily woke up one morning and immediately sensed that something was wrong. When the children were out of the kitchen, Josie explained in hushed tones what had happened. "After fourteen summers, falling asleep at Miltonberry has become easy for me."

She can't get to the point, Emily thought, but has to make a big drama out of this.

"Whip-poor-will calls, crickets chirping and frogs croaking have become the *Brahms Lullaby* of the North Woods."

Emily took a seat at the kitchen table. She knew she was in for a long tale. Josie was going to play it for all it was worth.

"Last night however, I awakened about two in the morning because I heard a different noise. On listening closely, I became convinced that I heard the screen door on the back porch make its usual creaking noise. So I crossed the room to Preston's bed and gently woke him up. We both went in bare feet, as quietly as possible, close to the kitchen. Preston peeked his head around the kitchen cupboard so he could look through the window in the kitchen door that leads to the back porch. He saw light from flashlights, and holding very still, he realized that people were going in and out of the cellar. He quietly told me that...," here Josie's voice was almost a whisper, "...there were Indians on the porch and in the cellar helping themselves to the canned goods stored there. We stood motionless, except for shivering, until the intruders left."

At last Josie paused to hear Emily's reaction. "Were you scared?" she asked.

"Yes, of course, before they left. Then once they left, we couldn't sleep the rest of the night. We know that people are hungry. Indians are probably desperately hungry. We can understand that some would resort to stealing food. We figured the canned goods could easily be carried back to the reservations. We've been putting up fruit and vegetables for several years, and in one year, we don't eat more than half of what we store in the cellar. By early morning, we had decided that we wouldn't investigate further. The food was probably very much needed to feed some poor and hungry families. What we can't figure out is how they knew that we had food stored in the cellar."

"Probably every farm puts their canned goods in a root cellar. What is different here is that you have some extremely poor people living on your farm, " Emily suggested.

"The only Indian who has come into the house is John Pete. You know we always pay the others down in the warehouse at the end of the month. They never came up here to the house. Preston is absolutely confident that John Pete had no part in the theft. He pointed out that Indians come and go from Miltonberry. Not all are workers here. Some are friends of workers. What we did resolve to do is to put secure locks on all the doors. In fact, Preston is in Hayward now buying locks and padlocks."

"Good," said Emily. "John Pete is a dear. He couldn't do anything like that."

"Oh, one more thing, Emily—please don't say anything to the girls about all this. I don't want them to become frightened. Louise is discretely cleaning out the cellar. And from now on, we aren't going to let them carry canned goods down there, so they won't know what's happened."

"Both Marie and Susan hate going down into that cellar anyway. I remember them squealing about cobwebs, mice and spiders."

Josie laughed. "Yes, it should be easy to keep them out."

Two days later, in the middle of the afternoon, Josie was having her nap while Emily quietly left her chair on the porch to go into the kitchen for a glass of water. She heard Susan and Marie scurrying up the cellar steps. Susan entered the kitchen holding an envelope and Marie followed carrying a flash light. Oh dear, Emily said to herself. She didn't want to deal with them, but felt she had to fulfill her promise to Josie. With a playful tone, devoid of accusation, she said, "So you've been down in the cellar. What did you find there?"

"This letter," Susan answered her grandmother excitedly. Marie put the flashlight in the broom closet while Susan handed the envelope to her grandmother.

The letter was addressed to Ryan C. Berr. "How exciting, it looks quite old. Let's see what it says." Inside was a knitted pink baby bootie.

"It's the size that Lucy wore when she was first born," Susan said.

Tucked in the baby bootie Emily found a little curl of hair and a note, which said simply, "She has your smile." The note wasn't signed. Marie grabbed the envelope. "There is no return address."

Emily took the envelope from Marie. Oh, a 2¢ stamp she thought. That could be from before or after WWI but not during the war, because she remembered that they had raised the postal rate to 3¢ during the war. Emily thought that she must quickly divert the girls' attention. Holding on to the envelope she asked, "What else did you see down there?"

"The cellar is cleaned out."

"Really, but I thought it was full of cobwebs, and spiders."

"So did we, but Louise must have cleaned it out. Where did all the jars of food go?" Susan asked.

"I think I know," Marie answered. "Mom doesn't want us to know, but the Indians stole our food."

"Why in heaven do you think that?" Emily asked.

"I know because I heard her talk to dad about it…. Promise you won't tell, Grandma. I often sit and read in the wing chair in the living room, the one with its back to the downstairs bedrooms. No one notices that I'm there if I'm perfectly still."

"You know—where Marie hides so she doesn't have to dry

the dishes? That's where I look to find her," Susan said.

"I heard Mom tell Dad that she didn't want us to go down in the cellar, so we wouldn't find out that the Indians stole our food."

Perfect, thought Emily, she could strike a deal. "Well, I won't tell her that you went down in the cellar, but you had better let me keep this letter, and don't say that you found it, because she probably knows it was down there, OK?"

"OK, Grandma. Thanks."

As they walked away, Susan said to Marie, "So, you knew it wouldn't be scary to go down in the cellar. That's why you suggested we investigate it. For a moment I thought you were getting brave."

"Girls," said Emily, "You had better not talk about it because your mom will overhear you. You know what sharp ears she has."

After they left, Emily went out to the porch where she knew she was safe to examine the envelope more carefully. There was no return address, as Marie had said, but maybe the postmark could tell her something. It was barely legible. All she could make out was "Mid….. Mass.… July ..17." The year had to be 1917. "Mass" has to be the beginning of Massachusetts. Em's father and mother were from Middlefield, Massachusetts. It has to be from Meg, but why would it be addressed to Ryan C. Berr? Who is he? The address was a Post Office box in Spooner. Before she fell asleep again, Emily had the foresight to put the letter in her pocket so no one would see it in her lap. As she was almost dozing off she thought of another thing that was strange. The address was written in capital letters and printed, whereas the note was in cursive. She would look in the telephone book to see if she could find any Berrs. An unusual name! Of course, the man had probably moved. She suspected that this letter might explain what she felt in her bones. She didn't know how, but she felt Em was connected to Tim.

Emily had long known that while one sleeps, one's mind

can work on puzzles. "Trust your mind" was a basic Christian Science principle. But the next day, after a good night sleep, she had progressed only a little. She found no Berrs in the telephone book. She decided if the letter was intended for Tim, there must have been many times that he and Meg had communicated because they took the trouble of using a Post Office box in Spooner. Writing in capital letters must have been done to conceal the author's handwriting. Was there any clue in the name Ryan C. Berr, she asked herself?

Emily went into her little bedroom on the ground floor. She could remember it when it served as the kitchen in Tim's small house. Now what was it she came for? Oh yes, pencil and paper. She carried these in her pocket along with the letter out to the porch where usually no one disturbed her. She wrote down the name and inspected it for several minutes. It could be an anagram, she said to herself. Suddenly it came to her: Ryan C. Berr had all the letters needed for cranberry. That clinched it. Em must be Tim's daughter and her granddaughter. She tried not to think about what Tim had done. That is probably why the Ellsworths were so cool to Preston and me when we came up north to bury Tim. No one need know this. Think of the positive, she told herself. I have a lovely granddaughter. Tim lives on.

During the day, Emily planned to ask Susan to help her walk over to Em's house. Thinking further, Emily asked Susan to run over to Em's house first, and ask Em if she could come over to visit at around 3:00 in the afternoon. Josie should be asleep then. Meg and Steve had long since returned to Massachusetts, so Em should be alone. Before sending Susan off on her mission, she sat her down to explain something to her. "Susan, I'd appreciate it if you wouldn't tell your parents that I'm walking over to Em's house. Your mom and dad would probably think I shouldn't strain myself—that I may die if I make such an effort at my age. I want to live my life fully, until I die. I am going to die anyway. I'm ready to die. Just because I'm weak and feeble doesn't keep me from wanting to do things. Would you please not tell them that I am paying Em a visit and that I want to talk to Em alone?"

"Sure, Grandma, but does that mean I can't stay at Em's house while you're there?"

"Well, we'll see. Maybe Em has something important that you can do for her."

~

Emily died the following winter in Kenilworth and was buried next to Chauncey in the Milton section of a cemetery on the South Side of Chicago.

CHAPTER 26

1942

Soon after World War II began, the War Department officially notified Preston that because cranberries were a war crop, he would be receiving some benefits in addition to the one Preston already knew to expect, that is, exemption from the draft. "Cranberries are high in vitamin C, can easily be dried and stored, and can be shipped inexpensively overseas to the troops." Miltonberry received an army truck and discounted gasoline.

So, unlike most people for whom gas was rationed, Preston was able to have as much gas as his cranberry business needed. He had an underground gas tank installed with a hand pump just like those at gas stations. He located it between the warehouse and the main house so he could keep an eye on it from both places. Although he could order the tank filled whenever necessary, Preston wasn't to let the gasoline be used by anybody else.

The war both enlarged and guaranteed the market for cranberries. At the same time, the price of cranberries steadily rose. Having such good fortune as well as a superb foreman encouraged Preston to think it was time to expand his business. He had his eye on a large piece of land that was for sale on the Totogatic River, twenty miles from Miltonberry. It was an extensive area of peat bog surrounded by a mixed woodland of conifers and deciduous trees. Preston wanted Joel and John Pete's opinion first. Using county maps, the three of them drove in the pickup on all the roads that existed on the property. They spent the day walking over places where there were no roads, shuffling through high grasses and swarms of insects.

"The land seems good to me, because where there isn't the peat bog, the soil is sandy," Joel noted.

When they reached the river, they walked along its banks. A doe and her fawn were grazing on the opposite side, oblivious to their presence, while a beaver worked its way upstream. The men stopped where the river cascaded over large boulders and dropped in elevation 27 feet.

"Here's where I would build a dam—just before these boulders. I figure a small, narrow lake would be formed. It would really be just a flowage. The river would pass through it. Water from the lake could be taken when necessary to fill the reservoir, which we could build over there. A sluice would connect the two. We could build a high dike that was quite wide to separate the reservoir from the lake.

"Would it be in effect an earthen dam, then?" Joel asked.

"Yes, the sluice would have a gate to control the flow at its end by the river. The reservoir would be lower than the lake so it could be filled by gravity. No pump would be necessary."

"How wide would the lake be?" John Pete asked. "Remember the disaster when they dammed up the Chippewa River...."

"I won't know for sure until we do it, but I would guess it will be about 300 yards wide or more."

"We like small bodies of water with lots of shoreline for ricing and picking wild cranberries. They're better for fishing as well. The treaty excluded the Totogatic from our reservation, but it's always been one of our favorite rivers."

"Well, this land meets the three crucial requirements for a cranberry marsh—water, sand and peat bog, but what I like most is the river and its surrounding woodlands." Joel turned to John Pete and added, "I can see why your people would love it. It's pristine, beautiful and abundant with wild life." Then, Joel looked at Preston and said with some hesitation, "This'd be a big undertaking. Are you sure you want to take on something so large? I mean, won't it be several years before the bog would make money?"

A bit presumptuous of Joel, Preston thought. Should an employee talk to his boss that way? But then, *I did ask his opinion,* and Joel and John Pete are not just employees. "Well, I guess that's a legitimate question. Let's see, I'll be 58 before the bog is producing. This bog will have three times the capacity for growing cranberries that Miltonberry has, so it is a large undertaking, but not all of it has to be developed immediately. I want to do it piecemeal." In his mind, Preston thought, perhaps Mr. Haylock will no longer think of me as just a small cranberry grower.

On the way back to Miltonberry, John Pete reminded Press and Joel that the damming of the Chippewa River had produced the third largest lake in Wisconsin. After acknowledging the injustice done to the reservation and its people, Preston assured John Pete that this flowage would be tiny compared to the Chippewa Flowage and that no one lived in this area.

A few days later, Preston heard from a clerk in the county office that there was another party interested in buying the land for timbering. Preston's heart sank, especially when he heard that the other potential buyer was an agent of Richard Morris. The land will be ruined, he thought. Press quickly raised enough money for the down payment by asking his father-in-law for a loan of several thousands of dollars. Mr. Haylock was glad to give him the money, with the proviso that any amount of it not paid back by the time of his death would come out of Josie's inheritance. Press bought the land under the nose of Mr. Morris's agent. He hoped that the agent wouldn't tell Mr. Morris who bought the property because it was rumored that Mr. Morris retaliated if he didn't get what he wanted.

A couple of months later, Press was told by a Totogatic neighbor that Richard Morris did not want the land for timbering at all. Far from it! "Them's great hunting woods. For at least 35 years, the Morris men have hunted them. They have a plush hunting cabin that they and friends camp in for a week during hunting season. In fact, the land you bought, Mr. Milton, is damn close to that cabin."

CHAPTER 27

1943

Preston finished building the dam and reservoir for the Totogatic bog in 1942. Once the water system was in place, he had ditches dug, built the dike system, and planted the beds. Each acre was planted with one to two tons of cranberry cuttings. He needed the water system established right away so the vines could be protected from frost. Once that was done, it would be another four years before it was safe to harvest because it would take that long for the vines to root securely in the peat. If they harvested the berries before four years, the vines might be pulled out during the raking process.

Preston's second bog quickly acquired the nickname "Toto," for Totogatic. It was in a remote area twenty miles from Miltonberry. Press had a simple house built with outdoor plumbing for Toto's foreman. Only one cabin was built for men hired from the Lac Courte Oreilles Reservation, because until Toto was producing a harvest, there would not be a need to house many workers.

During the construction stage, Press had to be at Toto almost daily to supervise the work. He was not worried about leaving Joel in charge of Miltonberry. Joel knew what to do and rarely needed Preston's advice.

Often the girls and guests at Miltonberry would go with Press to Toto for the day to watch the bulldozer at work. They fished from the dam, usually catching a sunfish or perch within ten minutes of dropping a line in the water. Susan and Lucy could put worms on their own hooks, but Marie always wanted someone else to bait her line.

Josie hardly ever went to Toto, but before the "crowd" took off in the morning, she and Louise prepared a large picnic lunch. At lunchtime, Preston would build a small fire on the rocks near the dam's cascade of water and everyone pitched in sautéing onions and hamburgers.

Preston hoped for but did not expect Josie to come on these outings. He knew that the rugged outdoors was not something she appreciated. Josie didn't even like to expose her skin to the sun. Press couldn't remember ever having seen her in slacks or shorts. She avoided discussions of toilet issues. He knew that she must loath the thought of using the bushes. He could easily understand if she wanted to stay home just to have the experience of being alone in a quiet house. Did she also want the liberty to drink without the disapproval of prying eyes? He hoped that was not her reason.

~

One day late in August, Joel heard the weather report and wasn't surprised by its frost warning. The sky was clear and it was nippy even at noon. He went down to the pumphouse on the Namekagon to start the diesel engine so the reservoir would be filled by evening time. He had asked John Pete to fix the broken drying crates on the third floor of the warehouse so they would be ready for harvest. At lunch, Em told Joel that she planned to spend the first part of what promised to be a cool afternoon in the garden. Em was eight months pregnant, so Joel expressed his concern that she might overdo it. "Please go back indoors if your back hurts or if you're tired." Joel had noticed she was beginning to slow down. He loved coming home to find her settled in a chair with her knitting in her lap, having drifted off to sleep.

Josie was alone in the main house. It was a bit too early for her afternoon nap. She had just poured her fourth sherry of the day. Usually, she would have walked back to the kitchen table where she sat in the afternoon, but today, being all alone, she thought of stepping outside via the front porch. No one was home to see her. Once outside she decided to walk down to the bog— just to have a look at its great expanse of green. She sometimes imagined herself as the mistress of a large estate, overlooking her formal garden—the well-manicured type, with hedges dividing different sections and forming a symmetrical pattern. There was a slight resemblance. The dikes and ditches did form sections, but the pattern wasn't very symmetrical....

It was then that Josie noticed smoke coming out of the lower end of the warehouse. She threw her glass to the ground and ran back into the house to the phone, and rang it hysterically. Between rings she shouted, "Fire, fire, fire at the warehouse," (forgetting to say "at the *Milton's* warehouse"). She repeated this sequence about five times until she remembered the gong. Grabbing it from its perch outside the back porch she ran with it back down towards the bog and proceeded to beat the hell out of it.

One worker had been swinging his scythe cutting the grass on a dike near the reservoir when he thought he smelled smoke. Looking up he saw a plume emerging from the warehouse. His first thought was to note the wind direction. The wind was bringing the smoke towards the bog. He was grateful it wasn't in the opposite direction, towards the woods, where his wife and kids were. Then in a flash, and to his great relief, he remembered that all the women and children had gone far away to pick blueberries. Dropping his scythe, he heard the clanging of the gong. He spotted Joel at the floodgate to the reservoir and yelled "Fire!" to him, pointing towards the warehouse.

Joel had been filling the reservoir since noon. He was standing at the floodgate about to add more planks to allow the reservoir to fill even higher when he heard the gong and someone yelling "Fire!" Then he saw the plume of smoke coming from the bottom of the warehouse. He had rehearsed in his mind what he would do if there was ever a fire in the warehouse, so within a second or two he put his plan into action. Instead of putting more planks in, he pulled a few out so water poured into the main ditch, which followed the road to the warehouse.

Em woke to the telephone ringing incessantly. Lifting the receiver she heard Mrs. Milton screaming "Fire!" When Josie finally hung up, Em called the Spooner volunteer fire department. Her heart sank when she realized that they wouldn't arrive sooner than 25 minutes. Then Em called the telephone operator in Springbrook.

"Don't worry, Em dear, the whole town knows about the fire. They're on their way," Hazel replied. How did they find out so soon, Em wondered? She grabbed three buckets and went as fast as she could to the bog side of the warehouse where she saw smoke.

A nearby neighbor, Bertha Hamilton, listened in on the phone and realized there was a fire at Miltonberry. She phoned other neighbors to alert them of the emergency. Being well into her seventies, she was too old to be of any help when it came to putting out the fire, but she could bring the oatmeal cookies she just took out of the oven. She started down the sandy road towards the Milton's.

Within five minutes of Josie's anonymous telephone alert the first neighbor arrived, joining all the others alerted by her gonging in fighting the fire.

"Why hasn't John Pete come out?" Joel shouted. Joel and two other men ran to the top end of the warehouse where John Pete should have been working. Some smoke was coming out of the upper door now. The three men went in, shouting John Pete's name.

"Here he is," one called out choking. John Pete was barely conscious and slumped over at the top of the stairs. From his position, it looked as though he had been coming up the stairs. Coughing and with stinging eyes, the three men lifted and carried him outside and laid him down far away from the building. Em shouted out, "I'll call the ambulance." She ran as best she could to their house to telephone.

Many townspeople and neighbors had arrived with buckets by this time. A bucket brigade immediately started. One man was in the ditch lifting buckets filled with water up to a man on the dike who passed it to the next man, and so on. Women ran the emptied buckets back down to the man in the ditch. Joel was inside the warehouse directing where the water should be thrown.

After several minutes of this they had managed to save the milling room where the sorting equipment was. Joel directed the next buckets to the thick wooden pillar that helped to support the wooden floor above. When that was out, Joel had to step outside because the smoke was smothering him. Another man ran inside to take his place. If the fire reached the second floor, the whole place would be in flames in a matter of minutes. The drying crates that filled that floor were made of flimsy lathes which would act like kindling. "Get the stairs," was all Joel could tell his replacement before coughing consumed him. He just had to breathe some fresh air.

In spite of coughing, Joel was relieved to see the Spooner fire truck barreling down the road towards the warehouse. Within a minute the firemen were pumping water from the ditch through a long hose that reached the stairs. Two firemen erected a ladder to get into the second story from the outside. Unlike the firemen in Rice Lake, these rural firemen were all volunteers and they didn't have the benefit of gas masks. Joel had heard that they called themselves "smoke eaters." Two went inside the second floor and hosed down the area around the stairs. They had to come out a minute later and another two firemen took their place. After switching back and forth, the crucial parts of the warehouse were hosed down and the fire was put out. Most of the warehouse was saved.

Joel noticed that Em had brought out a folding chair for Bertha Hamilton to sit on so she could watch everything. Em looked like she needed one herself. Bertha's oatmeal cookies were quickly devoured. Josie and some women appeared with peanut butter and jelly sandwiches and bottles of pop. They disappeared quickly. Then two huge pots of coffee with just a few cups appeared. At this point people didn't mind sharing. The Indian women and children returned from their blueberry picking. The ambulance had already picked up John Pete, but the fire truck was still there when Press drove in with the girls and guests from their trip to Toto. Most of the helpers from town were still there.

Joel and the fire chief entered the warehouse, looking for clues about where the fire started. Preston quickly followed.

"Can you remember what was here?" the fire chief asked.

"Yes, some of it at least, an old box with conveyor belts on top.... Oh, my goodness...that's right. The conveyor belts were made out of canvas. I put that box on the cart.... Oh, the cart's gone. These are the wheels."

"It looks like the cart was about here. How big was the cart?" the fire chief asked.

Joel indicated its size. "It was placed here between the mill room and that pillar and to the side of the stairs."

"Before we arrived, where had you all been trying to put out the fire? This wall here, I see, was burned."

"Yes, that's the mill room's wall—we went for that first because there is a lot of expensive equipment in there."

"Then where?

"The pillar."

"Were the stairs already on fire?"

"Yes, maybe we should have worked on that next instead of the pillar, but I was afraid the floor above would come down. I knew it was critical to not let the fire get upstairs."

"That's fine, what you did. It looks like we got here just in time. One or two minutes later and we might not have been able to save the warehouse. The canvas of the conveyor belts produced a smoldering fire. That put out a lot of smoke, allowing the fire to attract your attention and give you time to respond, but it wasn't until the wood on the cart started to burn that the fire rapidly progressed. Yep, smoldering fires are slow burning. They produce a lot of smoke, giving you time to notice them and work to put them out without too much damage. You were very lucky. I'm guessing about this. If the wood had started burning right away, I'm afraid the building would have burned to the ground."

A fireman spoke up to say how fortunate it was that the fire was on the bottom floor "cuz we's were lucky to have that water in the ditch so near to draw on."

Joel explained to Preston about the frost warning for that night, and how he had started filling the reservoir early. Once he noticed the fire, he was able to quickly fill the main ditch by the warehouse.

"Thank God for that, but what could have started it?" Preston persisted. "We don't keep any paint or rags down here or anywhere in the warehouse for that matter."

"Do you think it could be electrical, I mean, could a short or something have caused it? It isn't likely that John Pete would have even turned on the lights, though. He was repairing crates up on the third floor and could see well enough in the daylight," Joel added.

The fire chief went to an electric light switch and turned it on. "Looks like you still have your electrics. Was there anything else in that box with the conveyor belts or anything else that you can remember on the cart?"

"There was an old blue comforter in the bottom of that box, if I remember correctly," Press put in.

"I can't remember more," said Joel. "I wish John Pete were here, because he might remember something."

"Who's John Pete?"

"He's a long-time employee whom we found slumped over...." Joel went on to explain how they found John Pete and what he was doing in the warehouse.

Preston spoke to the entire group of volunteers to thank them for their quick response in helping to put out the fire.

Joel slipped away to return to the floodgates. He had to put back the planks so water in the reservoir would build up in case they had to flood that night. Then, he quickly returned to the warehouse just in time to hear the fire chief address the crowd of people.

"Mr. Milton and everybody else here, I have an important announcement to make that you all must hear.... It appears to me that this may be a case of arson.... I know you are all tired and many of you would like to go home, but we have called the sheriff and he should be here at any minute. He will have to take your names and statements. Nobody should touch anything in here. I am asking all of you to go outside and wait in front of the warehouse until the sheriff arrives. Thank you for your cooperation."

By seven o'clock that night, the sheriff dismissed everybody except Preston and Joel. He wanted to talk just to them in the warehouse. "I seem to have only two pieces of information that could be clues. One worker said that he had noticed a fellow worker, the one who is now in the hospital for smoke inhalation," he paused to look at his notes, "John Pete Kingfisher, this worker saw him going into the lower end of the warehouse thirty to forty-five minutes before he noticed smoke coming out. I asked him how he could know it was John Pete at that distance, from where he was working in a ditch, and he said," referring to his notes again, "It was a dark-skinned man and he was wearing a hat just like John Pete always wears. I didn't think anything of it."

"So I asked him if he had noticed which way the man approached the warehouse door. And he said from the right side. Then he said that was odd, because he must have come down to that level from the outside. If it was John Pete, he would have just come down the stairs in the warehouse."

Preston said, "I know John Pete would never have done this."

Joel said, "I absolutely agree."

"So it appears that who ever it was didn't want to be seen by anybody in the warehouse." The sheriff paused again before asking Joel and Preston to follow him outside. "Please stand with your backs to the bog and look at the warehouse.

"If you had to come down from the top end of the warehouse

to this bottom end from the outside, how would you come?"

"You would use the road on the left. There isn't even a path on the right," Preston said.

"Unless you didn't want to be seen by someone outside," Joel added.

"That's how I see it. Anyway you look at it, the man wearing the hat didn't want to be seen.... According to the worker who saw this man, he was not carrying anything."

He paused and added, "That is puzzle number one. For puzzle two, we go to one of the Indian women I interviewed. She had gone blueberry picking with the other women and children. Evidently, where they went was a spot quite far away. It was recommended to them by a..." he referred to his notes, "by George White Feather. Does he work for you, Mr. Milton?"

"I've never heard of him before," Press answered. "Have you Joel?"

"No. No one works for us by that name." Then Joel explained that friends and relatives of the workers occasionally stay here. "We don't like it but it's hard to control."

"Well, I asked this woman if it had been a good place for berry picking. She scowled and said that it was pretty bad. 'A waste of time,' were her words.... It turned out this fellow, George, had spent a couple of nights with them. Supposedly, he had been looking for work on the bog, but Mr. Milton wasn't hiring more people, so he left a couple of days ago. He supposedly came from the reservation but none of them knew him.

"Then here's something interesting, when I asked her about John Pete and what he was wearing she said, 'He usually wears his hat but it went missing a couple of days ago. He looked everywhere for it. He asked us if we had seen it.' I checked with others and it appears that no one saw John Pete wearing his hat for a few days."

Joel went back home to check on Em and told her about the sheriff's two puzzles. "Quick," she said, "We've got to catch him." Joel rushed outside after her. The sheriff was just driving by their house, about to leave by the new driveway. He spotted Em, stopped his car, and rolled down the window.

"I'm sorry," Em said, panting hard. "I'm sorry to stop you," she paused to catch her breath.

"Take your time."

Joel was at her side holding on to her arm. "It just occurred to me that perhaps I should tell you that there is an old Indian trail that runs from town through the woods and ends here at the Indian cabins. You can take the trail from behind the Post Office in town. I'll show you where it is…."

"Well, that's very interesting. Yes, I think I had better take a look at that trail right now to see if there are any clues…. I don't think you should come with me, however."

"No, Em, you can't go. I'll go with you, Sheriff." He turned to ask Em: "It's the trail that goes by the elm grove, right?"

She nodded her head. "Yes. Please be careful. Take a flash light, it'll be dark soon."

The sheriff asked his deputy to drive the car in to town and wait for them there, behind the Post Office. "And while you're waiting, see if you can get any information on a George White Feather. Be sure to call the reservation."

Joel and the sheriff set out on foot.

After being gone for more than an hour, the sheriff brought Joel back to Miltonberry. They found John Pete's hat on the trail, but no other evidence. The grass was matted down off the trail by the elm grove. Possibly, someone had spent the night there, but there would be no way of proving it. The deputy that met them in Springbrook said that no one seemed to know a George White Feather at the reservation.

"If he is the arsonist, would he have used his real name? I don't think so. Why would someone light the fire and then go away? Usually arsonists want to see the fire, unless the reason to start a fire was to do harm, but in that case, the fire could have been lit in another place, where it would have been more effective."

The sheriff asked if Em and Joel would come with him to the main house so he could talk further to Preston.

"Mr. Milton, do you know anyone who would like to do you harm, hurt your business, that sort of thing."

"No... I can't think of anyone."

"What about Mr. Morris?" Joel injected.

"Oh...yes...I forgot about him.... You see I bought another piece of property over a year ago. It turned out that Richard Morris really wanted it for himself. Rumor has it he was furious that he couldn't buy it before I did. I have heard, but I don't know if there is any truth to it, that he fired his agent over it—the man who was supposed to buy it for him. Someone told me that he was going to do what he could to drive me off that land, but that property is twenty miles from here...so, no...it doesn't make sense to me. I don't think the fire here could have anything to do with Mr. Morris."

"We have many people with sad stories that implicate that man," the sheriff said. "The trouble is we can never pin anything on him. We think he buys people off."

"Maybe he thought if he ruined your business here," Joel said, "you'd have to sell the property on the Totogatic. It would be a way of getting it, indirectly."

"Possibly," Preston said, "but I don't think he could care so much that it would lead him to try to burn my place down." Joel and the sheriff exchanged glances.

Later that night, when Em and Joel were back in their own house, Joel said to Em that Preston was a bit naïve. He was too optimistic, too positive about people.

"Yes, but that's why he's so endearing. He thinks everybody is wonderful. Most of us try to live up to his high opinion of us." Considering this further, Em added, "Of course that makes him very vulnerable to people like Mr. Morris, doesn't it?"

"Did you notice Mrs. Milton's reaction when she heard everything?"

"Yes, her eyes narrowed. She won't forget this, I believe. I don't think it was just the alcohol in her. I have the feeling she would relish going after Richard Morris."

∼

Days later, John Pete returned from the hospital and explained what happened. While he was repairing crates on the third floor he smelled smoke coming from below and went downstairs to investigate. When he reached the bottom floor, he couldn't get through the fire to get to the door on that level. He had no way to put the fire out, so he went back up to the third floor. Before he reached the top, he succumbed to smoke inhalation and collapsed on the steps. Since John Pete never saw the arsonist, Press, Joel and the sheriff assumed that immediately after starting the fire, he must have left the warehouse by the same way he got in—through the bottom door.

George White Feather was never found. No further evidence turned up, so the sheriff put the case of arson at Miltonberry in the unsolved mysteries file.

CHAPTER 28

1947

One July evening in 1947, Preston and Josie were drinking cocktails on the terrace in front of the back porch. They would soon have to cook dinner, but now they had a little time to talk to one another. Josie looked nice, Preston thought, in a flowery pinafore dress.

Something had occurred to Press and he was glad now to have the chance to talk to Josie about it, "Have you noticed," he said, "how the war didn't affect the daily lives of people in Springbrook very much?"

"What do you mean?" she asked.

"Well, nothing dramatic happened up here, no black-outs, that sort of thing."

"No, the Germans would hardly have wanted to bomb Spooner, let alone Springbrook." She chuckled.

"Well, what I mean is that people up here have always had vegetable gardens. No one here ever called them 'victory gardens,' like they did in Chicago."

"I see what you mean," Josie said, and after thinking a bit she added, "Farm women up here have always canned food too. How else could they get through the winter months?"

"That's right," Press agreed. "You could be snowed-in for weeks. Even if there wasn't that much snow, the temperature could get down into the thirties below zero. A trip to the store could be dangerous."

"I think the people up here have always lived this way, war or no war. When haven't they knitted or sewed most of their family's clothes?"

"Yes, and take driving, people up here weren't accustomed to driving much so gas rationing wasn't such a huge inconvenience to them."

"To me," Josie said, "the big difference between living in Chicago and Springbrook is how little news you get up here."

"You mean because we don't get a daily newspaper?"

"Yes, that, but also the news on the radio is so poor. First of all, the reception is crackly, and what news we get is very skimpy."

"I suppose they'll do more broadcasting up here once everyone has electricity."

"What percentage has electricity now, do you think?"

"I would say about 50%."

"I bet that explains why the war was never a big topic of conversation like it always was in Chicago." Josie was deep in thought before she added, "The only program at Miltonberry I look forward to listening to is Paul Harvey's *The Rest of the Story*."

Press smiled thinking of their girls singing while they washed the dishes in the kitchen. How they loved '*Hit Parade.*'

Josie bent over to pick up a smoldering insect-repellant stick so she could hold it closer to her. "The girls have to entertain themselves when they're at Miltonberry. Susan has taught herself to play the ukulele and Marie loves to read. And cards, they play cards constantly! And jitterbugging, they practice dancing on the living room rug so much that it will soon be worn out."

"You know what they like the most is when you read to them," Press told Josie. "Yes, they seem really taken by *The Bridge of San Luis Rey*. I'll have to read another chapter tonight, which means we better get started cooking dinner."

By 1949, Preston began to notice that the system of farming in Wisconsin was undergoing a major change. Several people in the Springbrook area remarked about how men who served in the war did not return to work on farms. Cities offered educational opportunities that these men could now pay for through the G.I. Bill of Rights. No doubt higher salaries and better healthcare also lured them to take up urban residences. The decrease in rural population was just part of what was causing farming to change, though, Press thought.

Year after year, he had driven around all of northern Wisconsin, and several times a year he drove through the south on his way to Chicago. After the war, Press noticed that there were fewer and fewer farms in the north, and many of those in the south were very large and devoted to only one crop. Since the war, chemical fertilizers and big farm machines made it possible to farm large plots of land, but only if the soil was good and the farmer could afford to buy the equipment. In the lower-half of the state, the land was starting to be owned mostly by big agri-businesses, but not so in the north, where the soil was poor, the growing season short, and the winters severe. Small family farms were disappearing in the north. In many cases they were simply abandoned. No one bought them and nothing took their place.

His neighbor Guy Wade's descendents moved to St. Paul and abandoned his farm. Bertha Hamilton died at the age of 78 and had no relatives to inherit her house. Press noticed that their barn and sheds had become rundown. The two farms closest to Miltonberry were left vacant. Grass, hazelnut bushes and jack pines were taking them over, making it difficult to see the remnants of the buildings. Press missed having close neighbors, but he was also grateful that these trends had not affected cranberry growers. Cranberry bogs continued to be one-family operations.

Preston's cranberry business struggled for different reasons. Just when he expanded his production, the secure market that he counted on during the war was no longer there. Consumers thought of cranberries only as a condiment for Thanksgiving and Christmas dinners. The berry's nutritional value was relatively unknown to the public.

Mr. Haylock's death in 1947 removed a source of funds that had been available to Preston in times of financial emergency. Without that safety net, the challenge of having a second bog increased Preston's stress. He was diagnosed as having angina. In addition to the pack of Lucky Strikes in his shirt pocket, he also carried a little white box of nitroglycerin pills packed in cotton.

~

In the summer of 1949, Northwest Wisconsin experienced a deluge of rain that lasted eleven days. The waters of all the rivers were very high. Many parts of Washburn and Sawyer Counties became flooded. Engineers feared that the Lake Nelson dam would not hold, as the lake water had risen near its capacity. This dam regulated the water on the Totogatic River, upstream from Milton Flowage.

Without any warning, three feet of water was let out of Nelson Dam. Within an hour, Milton Flowage began to swell up. Preston had all the planks in his cement dam lifted. So much water gushed over it that the boulders on the other side were barely visible. The river held its course until a channel of water began pushing its way through the earthen dam that separated the reservoir from the flowage. Within a few hours, the channel became huge and the reservoir level rose to the same level as the flowage. The river soon bypassed the cement dam and chose a new course through the reservoir. A tremendous gorge was created where the reservoir had been. Josie referred to it as "Milton Canyon" in her letters to Chicago friends. The damage was truly devastating. Preston had to close off the end of the gorge, construct a new reservoir, drain beds and shore up some of the dikes on the bog.

Weeks after the earthen dam burst, Preston finally had the time to start making inquiries. Why had no one downstream been warned of the sudden discharge of water? This was particularly important if, as rumored, the water had been released from the bottom of Nelson dam, making the discharge faster and more forceful than if it had been released from the top. Preston understood that Nelson Dam had to release water, but any hydraulic engineer worth his salt should have realized that people downstream would have to be warned! Preston filed a complaint with the Water Authority of Sawyer County, where Lake Nelson was located. He explained that the repairs had cost him tens of thousands of dollars.

Fifteen years prior, the governors of Sawyer County had decided to dam up the Totogatic River to make a large lake—Lake Nelson. By creating a sizable resort area, these planners hoped to attract tourists and thereby generate revenue for the county. Lake Nelson was an expensive investment for the local government. Preston's complaint was ignored. Infuriated he prepared to carry his complaint to higher authorities until his inquiries revealed that Richard Morris was on the board which oversaw Lake Nelson and its dam.

Upon hearing this, Preston asked Joel if he might do some discreet investigating, so it wouldn't appear that Preston was involved. Joel found out that Richard almost never attended board meetings, but was on hand at three such meetings during the week of the floods. Shortly thereafter, Joel also learned that a "good friend" of Richard's was the Sawyer County District Attorney.

Joel suggested that maybe Richard Morris had waited all these years to inflict another blow to Preston's cranberry business. "No, too much time has gone by," Press said. "Besides, we really don't know if Richard had anything to do with the warehouse fire."

Any lawsuit would become long and nasty, and Preston did not have the funds or the energy to take one on. As it was, he was working long hours each day. It took months of work to repair the earthen dam and get the river back on its original course. The money he had set aside to finish developing this bog was now spent on the repair work. Toto was only half-developed and would have to stay that way for a long while, perhaps forever.

Chapter 29

Late summer, 1949

A few days later, Josie got up earlier than usual and immediately showered and dressed. She said goodbye to Press, who had to leave by 8:00 A.M. to go to Toto. She watched him from the window as he went to the Chevy pickup. He had rolled up his white shirt sleeves to below the elbow. Looking at his neckline, she was reminded that he still wore those cheap undershirts which he bought in bulk at the Spooner Mercantile—the kind that showed if the top two buttons of his shirt were undone. She didn't mind the pith helmet. It made him look like he was going on a safari. It kept him cool, shaded his eyes, and enabled her to spot him when he was out on the bog. But the pith helmet had the disadvantage of covering up his beautiful, wavy, white hair, (even though it was so unfashionably styled in a "bowl" cut he got from that cheap barber in Spooner).

As soon as Press had driven off, Josie went outside to the yard opposite the foreman's house and puttered around with secateurs until Joel came out to go down to the bog.

"Oh, hello Joel." She tried to sound nonchalant.

"Good morning, Mrs. Milton."

He looks surprised to see me, Josie thought. "Isn't it a lovely morning?"

"Yes it is."

"Say, Joel, tell me about Mr. Morris. I heard a little of it from Preston. What did you find out?"

Em must have heard them talking because she came out with their two children, Timmy and Amy, to join the discussion.

Joel retold the findings of his investigation of the flood at Toto to Josie.

"Yes, I heard that from Press. Was there anything more?"

"Well," Joel began, "there were some other stories. Who knows if they are true?" Joel felt uncomfortable in this gossiping role. "One story I heard was about a Minnesota man who had refused to sell Mr. Morris the timber rights to his large tract of land. A few years later, that same man wanted to construct a retirement home on his property. It was rumored that Richard Morris arm-twisted officials to ensure that the man never received a building permit for the project. Of course, that may just be gossip."

"Is there any more gossip?"

"Well, another story was that Mr. Morris wanted to build a bridge over a tributary to the St. Croix River so he could easily transfer lumber from one of his mills to the railroad in St. Croix. Evidently, environmentalists and recreation people got together and opposed the bridge. They said the bridge would be an eyesore to people enjoying the rapids. There was a beautiful bend in the river where he proposed the bridge, and those very rapids prevented Mr. Morris from moving his lumber downstream by boat. Apparently, Mr. Morris owned much of the land surrounding his lumber mill. Since he couldn't build the bridge where he wanted, he changed the course of the river so it would bypass the rapids. People can no longer enjoy the rapids or the bend. He simply eliminated the treasured site altogether."

"Not a nice man, I would say. Although you're right, Joel, one shouldn't judge him on just stories." Josie knew from affluent friends in her Chicago circle that great wealth can give one unusual power. It is important not to misuse that power, but Richard appeared to arrogantly believe that he was entitled to get whatever he wanted.

As much as she wanted to, there was nothing Josie could do about Richard Morris. She went back inside and reflected on her financial situation. Two years ago when her father died, she received from him a lump sum and a trust which sent her a healthy check each month. Josie had decided to use the lump sum to take the entire family to Europe for three months. She thought this was an important extension of the girls' education. Preston could join them for only part of the trip. By the time the earthen dam broke, that lump sum had already been spent.

Aware of the need to economize, they developed a quieter social life. When Preston came down to Kenilworth they stopped going into the city to attend the theater or symphony. He couldn't hear well anyway, and often fell asleep during performances. Even with little money to spend, Preston could still put on his city polish. He looked dignified with his white wavy hair and mustache. His posture was still erect, but Josie knew he had another side to his life. When he was in Springbrook, he fell into another way of talking that increasingly annoyed her. She was reminded of this just the other day, when a workman asked him which way to do something, Josie heard Preston answer, "It don't make no diff." She consoled herself that at least he had picked up only the North Woods pattern of speech and not the nasal twang.

To be honest, she had declined in some ways herself. It was hard for her to look glamorous now that she was overweight. When at Miltonberry, she went into Spooner once a week to get her hair done and her nails polished. She bleached the hairs on her arms so they would be blond but stayed out of the sun so she wouldn't get wrinkles on her face. She knew her smooth, white skin was an asset. She had stopped playing the piano altogether and blamed it on the arthritis in her fingers. Some of the fingers on her beautiful hands were becoming crooked. Press never liked hearing me play anyway, she thought.

Several months later, her mother passed away. She inherited no trust, just a lump sum. Josie knew the curtain was falling on her life as a Chicago socialite, but she would spend the lump sum on one last encore and give her girls the experience of living abroad. She turned down Preston's request to pay some of the flood repair bills. Bog expenses would never cease, Josie thought. Living abroad would be a truly memorable experience for her girls. It would be her last hurrah.

Josie rented an apartment in Lausanne, Switzerland, where

she and the girls attended a language school five days a week. The money lasted nine months. Upon returning to the States, Josie realized that she and Press could only keep the house in Kenilworth for one more year. Susan would be able to graduate from high school, then they would have to sell it. When the Kenilworth house was sold, Lucy would have to live with her father in Springbrook and go to school there.

CHAPTER 30

It was a cold night for early June. Preston and Josie were both sound asleep. Their beds were separated by the large bay window which faced the bog. Josie had gone to bed with a glass of sherry and the latest detective magazine, but had soon given up reading and turned out her light. Preston had left the window ajar so he could hear Joel when he gave him the temperature report. He left the light on next to his bed, supposedly to make Joel feel less intrusive when he had to interrupt Preston's sleep. Actually, Press often dozed off without turning the light off.

"Press…Press…"

"Oh…yes, Joel"

"It's midnight. The thermometer on the bed farthest to the west reads 34°," Joel reported.

"If it's only midnight it will go down below freezing for sure before dawn." It was not necessary to tell that to Joel. For years Joel had known that the coldest part of the night was just before dawn, but Press was still trying to wake up. "We'll have to flood then. But we may be able to get by without flooding the eastern beds. What's the temperature on the bed closest to the house?"

"36°."

"Good. We can wait a bit on those eastern beds then."

Press recalled the previous foreman, Hotchkiss, and how he hated hearing that he should flood only in specific areas of the bog. Hotchkiss knew he would be up all night reading thermometers, lifting up this plank and then that plank to let water into certain ditches. Press was pleased that Joel has a more proprietary attitude. He wanted a successful crop as much as Press did.

He picked the cookbook back up that had fallen over on his tummy. Now where was he? Oh yes, reading the recipe for "popovers." Tomorrow he hoped to cook them properly so they would rise far above the wrought-iron muffin tin. Soon, however, he drifted off and the cookbook again collapsed on his stomach.

A while later Press awoke to hear some alarm in Joel's voice.

"Press?…Press?"

"Yes, Joel. What time is it now?"

"3:00 A.M. At 2:00 A.M. I started to flood the middle beds. When I went out just now I found a considerable amount of water in the ditches around two of the beds near the house. I think there must be a hole in one of the dikes."

"Probably a muskrat's been at work. Did the middle beds get flooded in time?

"Yes, the thermometers there are at 33°, and those beds are flooded now, but regretfully the two beds near the house are only at 34° and they are also close to being flooded."

"Well, there is nothing that can be done about it now. We'll see to mending the dike in the morning." Press remembered that John Pete knew exactly what to do.

Josie was snoring quite loudly now, but it wouldn't keep Press from sleeping. She never snored in the first years of their marriage. Then, she used to go to bed with an apple. He smiled to remember how loud her bites were. It was almost a nightly routine. Now, sherry had replaced the apple. He became distressed thinking about the progression of her alcoholism. He didn't have anyone he could talk to about Josie's problem, nor anywhere to turn to get advice. When they were engaged, he remembered his mother's disapproval of the Haylocks for their excessive drinking and partying. He never thought at that time that Josie would become an alcoholic. Would he have married her had he known? His eyes began to mist—yes, he would, because he loved her.

Press wondered if he was somewhat to blame. She was left alone so much of the time. Even while they were together at Miltonberry, he wasn't able to be with her during the day, and by night he was exhausted. She was probably bored with him. He often dozed off at the end of dinner, before he even left the table.

She had given up the piano a few years ago. She claimed that she lost interest because he didn't like to hear her play. Hearing tests had shown that he had lost the hearing of certain frequencies. The mix of those that he did hear was not always pleasant, but he had never told her he didn't like to listen to her play. Press thought Josie had trouble accepting the fact that she wasn't as good as she used to be. With excessive drinking, she had to take a nap in the afternoon. By dinner time, Josie was usually fractious.

There were several alcoholics in Josie's family. Press noted that each of the Haylock families produced at least one alcoholic per generation. Josie probably had the cards stacked against her. Had he known from the beginning, could he have steered her away from drinking? He didn't think so, because drinking was so thoroughly sown into the fabric of the Haylock style of living. Josie grew up in the twenties, when people were hell-bent on having fun after the war. He knew there were programs that treated alcoholics, but they required living in the same place year-round. He also knew that Josie wouldn't be willing to participate in such a program. She wouldn't even admit that she needed help. He drifted off again.

After Joel's final temperature report, Press continued worrying about Josie. She spent much of the day seated at the kitchen table and got little exercise. Nevertheless, Press was sure it was her drinking that made her overweight. The weight seemed to collect around her middle. The rest of her was not really fat at all. She was becoming much more relaxed about her appearance. If there were no houseguests, she might not even get dressed, and just wear a long, elegant bathrobe all day.

From Josie, Press moved on to worrying about Susan. She spent much of her time in her room, claiming she needed to sleep. No one needs that much sleep! Josie's alcoholism was taking its toll on each of the children.

Marie was now out of the nest. She had Josephine's flare for spending money, her good taste and her concern for possessions. Press worried that she was showing the early signs of becoming a drinker too. She definitely took after the Haylock side of the family. Her disposition was sunny and light-hearted but also self-centered. She couldn't be more different from Susan, who was ruthlessly honest about everything she said or did. It was touching to see her care about Lucy's upbringing. She got furious at Marie for trying to teach Lucy drinking songs. Susan thought about the consequences of her actions. She cared about people who were poor and wanted to correct injustices in the world. That was lovely but she also seemed sad. She couldn't act on anything, always procrastinated, and had a hard time getting herself going in the morning.

Before he could consider Lucy, Press had fallen asleep again.

~

The following winter, money was so tight that Josie had to find a job while she was in Chicago. Having traveled all her life, she applied to be a travel agent with International Travel. They hired her because she had first hand knowledge about many of the places her clients wished to visit and she also knew people with money who could afford to travel.

Susan had started studying philosophy at the University of Wisconsin, but there was not enough money to send Lucy to a good school in the city, so she stayed at Miltonberry with Press until Christmas time and went to the Springbrook school.

Press took advantage of this opportunity to teach Lucy about Miltonberry's wildlife at that time of year. He pointed out flocks of Canada geese resting on the flooded bog before they pushed on further to the south. Lucy had never seen the winter migrants. Pine siskins were all around the house once cold weather set in. She said her favorite birds were the evening grossbeaks, probably because they were easy for her to identify. When the snow came, she began noticing snowshoe rabbits for the first time.

"They're here in summer too, but during the summer they're brown, so you don't notice them as much."

"Really! Its coat can change from brown to white?"

"Yes."

"I get it. Now they're the color of snow so they can't be spotted easily."

"Yes, and notice their large hind feet. Their toes can spread out for better traction."

The only problem with staying at Miltonberry beyond September was that the house had never been properly winterized. Press felt it was too expensive to run the furnace more than once a week. That meant they had only one shower a week. They were only warm in the kitchen, and then only when they sat next to the stove.

IV

REGAINING STEADY FLOW

CHAPTER 31

1954

After her husband Steve passed away, Meg moved from Massachusetts to Wisconsin to live with Em and Joel. Press and Josie invited the Helmer family over for a barbecue dinner as a way of welcoming Meg to Miltonberry. Meg fit right into the life on the bog. She was often seen wandering around Miltonberry with binoculars in hand, bird watching.

It was a beautiful mid-June day in 1954 when Preston noticed the blue spruce trees had two-inch tips of new growth. That promised a good growing season, he thought. Too bad he and Joel were stuck working in the warehouse on such a lovely day.

Joel was installing a light fixture on the ceiling of the bottom floor of the warehouse. "Yesterday, Meg spotted what she called a Kirtland's warbler," Joel told Preston. "She has talked of nothing else since. Evidently the bird is quite rare, and it loves to nest in jack pines. She is determined to find the nest."

Climbing up on a ladder, Joel noticed a metal box resting on a supporting beam and told Preston about it. "Hand it down to me," Preston requested. "Oh, my goodness. I was not expecting it to be so old. The metal is no longer shiny."

"It was tucked back completely out of sight. You couldn't have seen it from the floor," Joel explained.

Press recalled the time his mother thought she had seen a metal box in just the same sort of place. She had been able to see it from the floor so somehow it must have been moved out of sight. Who moved it?

Press savored the memory of his mom. He remembered how encouraging she had been during those dark days when he was trying to decipher how to operate a cranberry bog. He wished he could tell her that he had found the box. He smiled to himself thinking of her practicing 'mind-over-matter' whenever she had misplaced something. It usually worked, but not in the case of this metal box.

He slowly carried the box over to his make-shift desk outside the milling room and sat in his captain's chair. He loved this chair with its thin cushion, not so much for its comfort as for the chance it gave him to get off his feet. He tried to pull off the lid. He was having so much trouble that Joel came over ready to give him a hand. Finally, the lid sprung free and some of the box's contents spilled out on the floor. Joel bent over to pick up what appeared to be letters. Press watched Joel glance at them and noticed that he hesitated before handing them over to Press. "Hmm, some old letters. How puzzling," Press remarked.

"Really?" said Joel.

"Yes, letters written to Ryan C. Berr—who in heck is Ryan C. Berr?" Preston looked up at Joel and noticed that he had turned white.

"Do you want me to get rid of them for you?" Joel said quickly.

"Well, hold on. Let's see what they're all about.... They all have a Spooner address...but a P.O. box.... Why would they be here?" Press opened a letter, and read briefly, and quickly put it back in its envelope. He paused and then told Joel, "Well, it's time for lunch." Press left the warehouse immediately, taking the metal box with him. He realized he was going for lunch a bit early, but he had to show these to Josie.

Walking quickly back to the house, Press gasped for breath and felt that familiar chest pain, so he put the metal box under his arm and held it there firmly. With both hands free, he took out the little white box he carried in his shirt pocket and carefully extracted a nitroglycerin pill to put under his tongue. This was a matter that needed to be handled with great delicacy, he thought.

Josie was in the kitchen preparing lunch when Press walked in. She was removing a hot casserole from the oven. "You're here early," she said without looking at him.

"Yes, for good reason."

Josie looked up. She could tell from the tone of his voice that something was wrong. "What's in the box?"

"I think they're love letters that Meg wrote to Tim. I haven't had a chance to look at them, yet." He went to the table and sat down at the head. "They're addressed to a Ryan C. Berr but inside they say 'Dear Tim.'"

Josie came over and took a seat next to him and without asking his permission she took a letter and began to read it.

"Josie, I don't think we should read them."

"I don't want to read them, but I think we should establish that they really are love letters. After all, they may give some clue about Tim's death. We would be derelict if we didn't bother to know what they say." Josie and Press exchanged letters as they read them.

"Well, these are definitely love letters," Press declared.

"So far, yes," Josie agreed, "but we have to read them all."

Press thought he noticed a little smirk on her face. Then he read one that was quite explicit and put it firmly back in its envelope, slamming it down on the table, saying, "That's it. We really shouldn't read more."

Josie grabbed it. "Think of your brother," and started reading it as fast as she could.

When they were finished reading them, Press suggested, "Perhaps I should have let Joel open a letter and have him decide what to do, but I'm such a terrible actor."

"Yes, you are a bad actor," Josie agreed.

"I couldn't have just pretended that I didn't know what the letters were all about."

"How did Joel react?" Josie asked.

"Well, he actually looked a little scared and offered quickly to take the box from me."

"Not surprising," said Josie. "I've always maintained that they know Tim was Em's father. Their boy's name is 'Timmy.' Too many coincidences! They know."

"OK, you may be right, but why haven't they said anything?"

"Why haven't you? No one wants to rock the boat."

"No, the reason I didn't want to say anything was that I wanted to be sure that Meg had told them first. That's her right."

"I wonder why she's not forthcoming. After all, her husband is dead. She doesn't have to keep it a secret from him anymore. Her parents are dead. Sarah is far away and never in contact, as far as I can tell."

"She may feel it would strain our relationship by adding another dimension...you know...we'd no longer just be employee and boss, Joel and I."

"No, but plenty of people have their son-in-law working for them and Joel is your nephew-in-law."

Maybe Meg didn't want Josie's drinking to have an influence on her family. This thought really hurt Preston. Josie was a wonderful woman in her way.

"Press, let me handle this," said Josie. "Tomorrow morning I'll ask Meg over for a cup of coffee. This can't go on any longer."

Press felt grateful. There were some things Josie was much better at than he. Just before falling asleep that night it occurred to Press that perhaps the box had been moved. He recalled that years ago when his mom saw the box, John Pete had still been on the reservation. Then a few days later, when he and his mother failed to find it, John Pete had returned to Miltonberry, so John Pete could have moved it back out of sight. Was John Pete trying to protect Tim's reputation?

The bedroom was pitch black now but Preston was wide awake, reviewing so many things about John Pete. It occurred to him that it might have been John Pete who had brought out of hiding the Eatmor cranberry crate containing the *Tales from Elm Grove*. Press knew that crate wouldn't have been under the warehouse stairs all those years without his noticing it. And then there was the red-winged blackbird myth. Preston finally fell asleep with a smile on his face.

CHAPTER 32

After a few minutes of general conversation, Josie asked Meg to take a seat at the kitchen table. She poured her a specially brewed cup of coffee and sat down to drink her own cup. She wanted to add a drop of brandy, but decided against it. "There is something I have to give to you," she said to Meg as she handed her the metal box.

"Should I open it?"

"Yes, please do," Josie replied.

"This is old."

Josie noticed that Meg had become pale. "Yes," Josie replied. Meg fumbled with the box but managed to open it, and gave an audible sigh, sitting back in her chair, not looking at Josie. "We thought you should have them. They were found on a beam in the warehouse. Preston's brother must have kept them hidden there...." Meg still hadn't looked up at Josie. "I never met Tim," Josie continued. "I'd love to hear about him." Still, Meg kept her eyes averted. "I know this is such a personal matter. If you don't want to say anything, I understand completely." Meg's lack of response was agony for Josie. She knew she should just wait, give her time to respond, but Josie was not good at handling silence. "Did Joel say anything to you, yesterday?" she asked. "He and Press found them yesterday."

By this time Meg had turned crimson. "N-No," she stammered, "he didn't say anything. I was going to tell them, but the timing never seemed right."

"But it's been more than three decades. Doesn't Em want to know who her father was?" Josie couldn't help herself. Meg's statement seemed ridiculous.

"Yes, of course she does.... It was just that there were so many people's feelings to protect that I thought it best not to say anything all these years."

"You seemed so close to Steve. Didn't he know?"

"Yes, of course he knew, right from the beginning."

"When did you and Steve get married?"

"Mrs. Milton..."

"Please call me Josie."

"I hope you understand but I would like to talk to Em and Joel about this right away. It doesn't seem right to discuss it with you before I have explained it to them."

"Are you sure they don't already know? After all, they named their boy Timmy."

"Yes, but they said it was for Joel's great-grandfather, Timothy McLean. I thought it was a coincidence." This time, when Meg paused, Josie kept quiet.

"I would really love to explain it all to everybody in the family," Meg finally said. "It's quite a complicated story."

"I understand."

Meg got up from the table. "Thank you for the coffee, Mrs., ...I mean, Josie," she said, leaving the house.

CHAPTER 33

Throughout the fifties, Preston steadily made improvements to the bogs, when he could afford them. He stuck with the decision to not fully develop Toto. By 1958, the two bogs were producing three times what he had harvested during the war. The increase in production was one factor that caused his financial situation to improve. Another factor was that the Miltons had learned to economize. Now they stayed up at Miltonberry until Christmas time. Then, for the two weeks over Christmas, they rented a small apartment in a hotel in Chicago, after which they drove to Cuernavaca, Mexico, where they rented a small house for the rest of the winter. In Spring, they drove back to Miltonberry. All of this was possible because they could leave the bog in the capable hands of Joel and Em.

Nonetheless, Preston felt the stress of being a cranberry grower was straining his weak heart. He had reached the age of 66 and was ready to retire. His bills were finally under control, and at the end of October, he had harvested a bumper crop, so he put his bogs up for sale, thinking that there would never be a better time to sell. Events proved otherwise.

On November 9, 1959, thereafter known as 'Black Monday,' Secretary of Health, Education, and Welfare Arthur Flemming forbade the sale of cranberries or cranberry products produced in Washington and Oregon States because some of the growers there had used aminotriazole, a weed killer that had been shown to cause thyroid cancer in laboratory rodents. The ban affected the sale of cranberries throughout the nation, however, because cranberries were pooled. A housewife had no means of telling where the cranberries she bought were grown. Flemming's announcement came too late to have most cranberries tested before the holiday seasons. Across the country, people stopped buying cranberries. The cranberry industry lost millions of dollars.

"It is particularly unfair because only a few growers in Washington and Oregon States actually used the weed killer," Preston argued.

The Department of Agriculture had approved the weed killer the year before. However, it was clearly stated on the label that the herbicide should be used only after harvest. Perhaps the growers who used it were expecting it would soon be approved for use during the growing season, or perhaps they just didn't read the label carefully. Nonetheless, all growers were furious. An executive of Ocean Spray Company expressed their feelings well when he said: "The government is killing a thoroughbred in order to destroy a flea."

Susan and Preston argued back and forth about whom to blame for Black Monday. Both understood that this was a new phenomenon. Chemical innovations spurred on by the war effort had produced many artificial (laboratory-created) insecticides and herbicides, some of which had unknown repercussions. The Food and Drug Administration had not yet determined the tolerance level of aminotriazole, so, according to Susan, "Flemming was right to follow the law, as written by the Dulaney Clause, which 'prohibited the sale of any food shown to contain any amount of a cancer causing chemical.'"

"But," Preston argued, "A person has to eat 15,000 lbs. of cranberries every day to develop cancer."

"Yes, but the law, as written, says 'any amount.' They found some. Even though it was a small amount, the cranberries had to be taken off the market."

"Just because aminotriazole kills rats, doesn't mean it'll kill humans."

"Maybe so, but that has nothing to do with whether Flemming was right or not. They found aminotriazole in some cranberries. To follow the law, he had to withdraw them from the market."

At moments like this, Preston wished Susan had taken up home economics.

"You see, Dad," she went on, "it doesn't matter that a human's physiology differs from that of a rat. Flemming had to obey the law, as written."

She doesn't realize that I am about to become bankrupt over this technicality, he thought.

"If you want to blame somebody, blame the farmers that didn't use the herbicide according to the label."

This carcinogen scare was devastating to all growers. The government compensated them to some extent, but it wasn't enough to keep many from going out of business. For Preston, it dashed his hopes of retirement by making a quick sale of his property. In fact, in order to produce cranberries the following year he would have to borrow a lot of money. Well over half of a farmer's profits are usually needed to invest in the next year's crop.

The last thing Preston needed was more stress. He talked things over with Joel and John Pete. It was then that Joel said how much he and Em would like to buy the Miltonberry bog. Preston was really touched by this. For one thing, Joel had developed a love of the cranberry business, and it meant that Preston's bog would continue to operate under someone in the family—Em being Tim's daughter and all. But when Preston heard how little Em and Joel had to offer as payment, he knew he couldn't afford to sell the bog to them. They knew that as well. A week later, Meg said that she would throw in the money she inherited from her husband Steve, but it still didn't come to even half of what Preston was asking.

In the spring following Black Monday, Josie and Preston drove into Miltonberry, their aging Dodge sedan packed with the items they used to set up housekeeping in Cuernavaca. They were returning without any idea of what they were to do. Press feared that at his age, no bank would loan him the money needed to start up the bogs. They had to use Josie's money to pay for salaries at both bogs as well as their own living expenses. There wasn't enough money for all of this. The workers realized the situation and were dreading being laid-off. One day, a week after they returned, John Pete came to Preston with a suggestion. "I have a friend who is President of the Bank of Hayward."

"Really?" Preston tried not to sound surprised or skeptical.

"Yes, he's a very good friend. He used to live at Post when it was above water. I don't see him often. Ever since the power company formed Chippewa Flowage, there is no direct route from our home to his, but we have been friends for over forty years."

"And he's President of the Bank of Hayward?"

"Yes. His name's Sam Cloud. He is well educated and a very good person. I think he would give you a loan."

"Really, that would be wonderful."

Preston was skeptical, but owed it to John Pete to follow through on his suggestion. He might as well go into the bank and ask for a loan from this Sam Cloud. Imagine, an Ojibwe as president of a bank!

When he met Mr. Cloud in the bank, Preston was surprised to see a man older than himself. Sam had very white hair. He was stout and a little round-shouldered. His face showed that perhaps he was of mixed breeding, not only because his skin color was not very dark, but there was something about his facial features that didn't seem all Indian.

Mr. Cloud knew all about the 'cranberry scare' and realized that Preston really did need help. He remembered that his good friend John Pete had spoken highly of the owner of the cranberry bog a few years back. He asked Preston to come back in a few days, after his bank had looked into things, and they might be able to offer him a loan.

Upon Preston's second visit to the bank, Mr. Cloud offered him a $40,000 loan at a 2.5% interest rate. Preston was ecstatic and signed the papers immediately. Preston walked out of the bank beaming with joy. He had just about reached his car when he heard Sam's voice calling after him. Oh no, thought Preston, something has gone wrong! Mr. Cloud walked up to him and asked, "Do you have a minute?"

"Sure do, yes."

"You know, I was just thinking about it. I believe I was on your cranberry bog about forty years ago. It's just outside of Springbrook, isn't it?"

"Yes. That's right.... Quite a coincidence."

"Yes, a man paid my brother and me to dig two graves there, and we were asked not to talk to anybody about it. Did you own the bog forty years ago?"

"No, but my brother Tim did. My God, he died about forty years ago.... Do you think you dug his grave?"

"Well, I don't know. We were asked not to talk about it, as I said, and we were given little information as to what we were doing, but we were paid a lot of money, and he was a minister, so we figured it couldn't be bad. I was a young married man at the time with lots of bills. I couldn't resist making that much money, and my brother needed the money even more than I did. You're the first person aside from my wife that I've told about it. I know I shouldn't say anything, because I promised not to, you know, but the person who hired me has long since died and my brother, the one who helped me dig the graves, died, a few years ago."

"Two graves?"

"Well, it was all a bit strange. Yes, two...two graves. Why did we have to keep it a secret if everything was on the up and up? That was my question...The man who asked us to dig the graves was a minister, as I said, from Springbrook."

"What was his name? Do you remember?"

"Mr. Ellswood, or something like that. Did you know him?"

"Yes, Clarence Ellsworth. He was the father of my brother's wife. Why did he ask you both to dig the graves? Surely there must have been someone closer to Springbrook who might have done the digging."

"That's what I thought. Mr. Ellsworth was a bit intimidating. You knew him, I guess. He was probably a very nice man, but those eyes would frighten anybody."

"Oh yes, I remember those eyes."

"You say your brother died about then?"

"Yes. He died at the bog late in December, 1919."

"Well, we dug those graves in the spring of 1920. I know that because we did it the day after we saw Chief George dance at the end of the maple syrup gathering."

"I don't suppose you remember where you dug the graves, do you?"

"Yes, at least I know for sure where one was dug. It was in front of the house, the side facing the bog."

"And the other?"

"Well, that was what was strange. At first, I thought the two bodies would be buried next to each other, but Mr. Ellsworth explained that the other body was someone they found in the woods. Since no one knew who he was, they thought they would bury him in the woods. They had to wait until the ground had thawed to dig both graves. The bodies themselves had been kept in the icehouse until the burial. They were really heavy to lift."

"Weren't they in coffins?"

"The one buried in front of the house was. It was in a simple pine box, but the other body was just sewn up in a shroud— a white cloth. That was the messy one. I had to dig down into muck. At least the peat held things together. Do you have any idea who the other body was?"

"Not in the least, but I am quite sure the grave in front of the house was for my brother, Tim."

"Mr. Ellsworth got impatient with me because I insisted doing some burial rites. I figured if no one knew the other man's identity, he was probably an Indian. In fact, I tried to mentally note the location. We take the burial of an Ojibwe very seriously. You'd think a minister, of all people, would understand that, but he kept telling us to hurry up. It took us all day and we only went as deep as 4 to 5 feet. I thought it was strange too, that he didn't give a little prayer at either grave especially for the unknown man, whom we covered with muck. Well, the whole thing was odd and somewhat suspicious."

"You know your friend John Pete Kingfisher, who works for us, he was convinced that Tim wasn't buried in front of the house. Did you ever talk to John Pete about this?"

"No. I have only told the story to my wife."

"How did Rev. Ellsworth find you?"

"Well, that's another thing. When a white man had some dirty work to do, it was not uncommon to hire someone from the reservation to do it. They would come to Post because that was the largest village on the reservation. My mother was still living in our family home at Post. This was about three years before it was flooded under. My brother Jack and I had ridden our horses over to visit with our mom. We were outside, unsaddling our horses to spend the day with her, when Mr. Ellsworth rode up and asked us if we wanted to earn some good money.... There are many things about that day that don't add up."

"Mr. Cloud, would you mind coming to my cranberry bog and showing us where you think you buried the other man? We wouldn't have to involve you any further in this if you don't want, but I feel obligated, since he's buried on my property, to try to find out who he is. Of course, we won't be able to tell much from a skeleton."

"Oh, I think you would. Critters buried in peat don't decay, you know, so why should a man? You know that acidic soil preserves them. In fact, when Mr. Ellsworth led me across the bog to an area in the woods for the second grave, I suggested another spot that was quite marshy because it would be easier to dig there. I didn't say anything to him about the preserving qualities of peat.

"You see, I was scared. As an Indian, you were never safe. You could be used to do someone else's dirty work and then be eliminated yourself. It was no surprise that Al Capone chose our reservation for his hideout. He could easily terrify us and nobody off-reservation would protect us. Occasionally, we'd see him and his thugs driving in their fancy cars. If you were walking on the road, they might stop to offer you a lift. We were too scared not to accept. You had to stand on the running board and hold on. They never let you in the car. Then they drove faster than usual just to scare you, I think. You see, also in the back of my mind was the thought that the dead man was somebody that some big shot had ordered to be killed without a trace."

Preston drove home to Miltonberry full of energy, relieved that he was to get the loan he needed and excited about the stories Mr. Cloud told him. At last, he was finding out about Tim's burial. He had heard about Al Capone's hideout, but had no idea that it was so close by. There were so many things to tell Josie when he got home.

The next morning, Mr. Cloud came dressed in outdoor work clothes. As Press walked him around the house, he asked him if he would mind if two members of the crew helped to exhume the body.

"Mind?" laughing, he added, "My days of digging in muck are over!"

Joel approached from the other side of the house when they neared Tim's grave site. As Press was introducing Mr. Cloud to Joel, John Pete ran up from the bog. The two men hugged and chatted away in Ojibwe. John Pete couldn't stop smiling.

"You know, I am actually relieved to finally be doing something about this. It's been on my conscience for forty years." Sam paused and looked around. "My, how this house has grown! I remember the grave as further from the house, but then the house used to be much smaller. I guess the house has been added onto and the additions were made in the direction of the bog."

"That's right," said Press.

"Well considering that, this seems to be where I buried the coffin."

At that moment Josie rushed from around the corner of the house wearing a billowing muumuu. Her hair was hastily pinned up and her lipstick slightly off kilter. On her feet she wore some old boots of Preston's that made it awkward for her to walk. Holding out her hand, she greeted Sam.

"Hello, Mr. Cloud, I'm Josephine Milton."

This was one time Press did not want Josie to come outside. He was trying to minimize the exposure of what they were doing. He had specifically asked Joel and John Pete not to let anyone else know what they were about to do. He didn't want the emotions that Em and Meg might resurrect to embarrass Mr. Cloud.

"Oh my golly, this is so different from how I remembered it. The bog is so much bigger now—I mean the part under cultivation is so much bigger. Let's see, as I remember it, we stood here and then started walking around the bog on the right to this dike. Only the dike goes twice the distance that it did when I was here. Is that possible?"

"Yes, that's very possible. Should we walk along this dike then?" Press suggested. "There was only one cranberry bed on this side of the dike when Tim was alive. So the dike would have turned left at the end of this bed."

"So this dike is in the same position as it was back then?" Mr. Cloud asked.

"Yes, we added three more beds as you can see, and we just extended the dike in a straight line. This dike has always been the northern border of the bog," Preston explained.

"That's right, Boss," John Pete spontaneously concurred. Then he ran along the dike to the end of the first bed, stopped and turned around to face them. "The dike would not have gone further than this point," he said.

What has gotten into John Pete? I've never seen him so excited, thought Preston.

Josephine was trying to cope with walking on the dike's uneven surface. Preston's boots were too big for her, so she had to shuffle along. Press wished she would go back to the kitchen.

When Mr. Cloud reached the spot where John Pete was standing, he turned to face north, asking Preston: "Why, didn't you plant a bed in this direction?"

"We considered it, but it would have been a lot of ditch digging and dike building for such a small bed, because the peat bog doesn't go very far in that direction."

"I see. Well, it's lucky you didn't, because…hmm…see that tall white pine? It still stands above the others. You haven't cut down any of the trees on this side of the bog, have you?"

"No."

"Well, I tried to make a mental note as to where we buried the body. I always had it in the back of my mind that the body should be transferred to a sacred Indian burial mound. We had to be careful that Mr. Ellsworth didn't suspect us of trying to remember where we buried the body." He paused to survey the surroundings, then asked, "Does anyone have boots on?"

"I do," piped up Josephine.

"Well, I think this might be too difficult for you, Mrs. Milton. I should have thought this morning that I would need boots." John Pete ran to the warehouse and came back with four pairs of hip boots.

Once again, it registered with Press how excited John Pete was. Joel and John Pete put on boots.

"Please walk 30 paces, big paces, from here, where I'm standing," Mr. Cloud directed, "towards that white pine in the distance. The ground is awfully mucky, isn't it?"

Josie's muumuu was blowing in the wind. Press could tell that she wanted to follow Joel and John Pete. Fortunately, he thought, she must have realized that she couldn't walk well enough through the peat, so she stood by him on the dike. Being so consumed with the task of finding where the unknown man was buried, it hadn't occurred to her how ridiculous she looked. He liked that about her—the way she could become so obsessed with something. Of course, it could also be maddening at times.

Mr. Cloud remained on the dike as well. He directed Joel and John Pete from there. He asked them if they could see the trunk of the oak tree in front of the house from where they were standing.

Both men called out, "Yes."

Mr. Cloud said: "Stand so your line-of-sight with the oak is tangent to the corner where the dike meets the road—the road running in front of the house. "I have to do better than this," said Mr. Cloud reaching for a pair of boots. Preston followed his example, and they walked out to join Joel and John Pete. "If I'm going to ask you to dig in this peat, I better be sure I select the spot carefully," Mr. Cloud explained to the two workers.

After checking the line-of-sight, Mr. Cloud marked out an area where he thought they should dig. "I suggest you dig two holes here a yard apart from each other."

The men dug for a couple of hours. Josie gave up waiting back on the dike and went to the house. She returned after an hour or so with sandwiches and a thermos of coffee. By this time, Joel and John Pete had each dug a hole five feet deep.

"I think that would be deep enough, so let's start two new holes: here and here," Sam said.

Joel climbed out of his hole dripping in perspiration. Preston noted that he looked pale. Josie offered him and the others a sandwich and coffee. Joel said, "No, thanks," without looking at her and walked over to Preston. "I'm glad to stop digging. I dread hitting the body with the shovel. This whole thing spooks me." He rested a bit and was about to start digging the next hole when John Pete called out something in Ojibwe. Mr. Cloud whipped around and went to where John Pete was digging. A rapid fire of Ojibwe ensued. John Pete bent over and brought up a part of a finger and some brown cloth. He apologized for harming the body.

Josie set the refreshments down, lifted her skirt and quickly made her way to John Pete's hole. "This is truly amazing," she said, reaching out to hold the finger herself. "I never believed that you would find the body. This finger looks perfectly intact. All the flesh is here."

From where the finger had been found, they all agreed as to the likely position of the rest of the body still covered in muck.

Joel suggested that they should phone the sheriff, so he could see them digging up the body.

"You know, I think you are right, Joel. How would you feel about that, Mr. Cloud?" Preston asked.

"I think you had all better call me Sam. Yes, by all means, let's do this right this time. Call the sheriff."

"Mr. Cloud, or Sam, do you remember if the bodies smelled when you buried them?" Josie asked.

Sam laughed and then answered, "No they didn't, not even the one in just a shroud. It was stiff and hard, still mostly frozen, I think."

Josie offered them the sandwiches and coffee, before they continued with the digging.

"I'm going back to call the sheriff," she volunteered. "Let's see, I must call the sheriff in Washburn County, not Sawyer."

Preston was glad Josie got this straight, because it could be confusing. Springbrook was in Washburn County. Its closest city was Hayward, but Hayward was in Sawyer County. The sheriff there wouldn't respond to calls from Springbrook.

"Why didn't Clarence call the sheriff when he found this body in the woods?" Preston asked.

"Maybe he did, but when the sheriff realized it was an Indian, he didn't bother to come," John Pete conjectured.

"Possibly, but Tim didn't have a death certificate either. Clarence didn't call the sheriff out when Tim died."

"That's interesting. Was there an obituary in the *Spooner Advocate*?" Sam asked. None of them responded. Finally Preston explained, "None of us were here when Tim died. He died in late December, 1919, but my mother and I didn't come up here from Chicago until the following April." Press explained the reason for the delay. "I never thought about checking obituary notices in papers up here. I told you, I think, that my brother was the original owner of the bog. He was only 31 years old when he died."

"Hmm, intriguing complications," said Sam. "Well let's keep digging and maybe we can uncover this man by the time the sheriff gets here. Maybe the sheriff will have something in his records that will clear the whole thing up."

Joel threw another idea out for general discussion, "You know now that you mention the *Spooner Advocate*, how's about if I call our friend Bob Olson? Bob's a good friend of Em's and mine. He's an investigative reporter for the *Spooner Advocate*. Awhile back, he was telling us that he never gets a breaking story. They always assign him columns like the 'News from Earl.' This might help his career.... Of course, perhaps you'd prefer not to have the publicity, Press?"

"It's fine by me. We have nothing to hide," said Preston. "How do you feel about getting the press here, Sam?"

"Fine, I want this all out in the open. It probably wouldn't go beyond the *Spooner Advocate*, anyway."

CHAPTER 34

The sheriff came promptly after Josie called. The men were still digging out the body when he arrived, and he walked straight out to them on the bog. Josie spotted Em and her mother a good distance behind him. "Em dear, are your children at home?" Josie shouted, walking quickly out to meet them.

"No, they're in school."

"The reason I ask is because they are digging up a body."

"Oh, my heavens! Mom and I saw the sheriff's car go down to the bog, so we wanted to know what was happening."

Josie noticed that Em and Meg were dressed in overalls and long sleeve shirts. Great protection against mosquitoes, she thought, then she realized that she might be missing something where the men were digging, so she scurried back to them. They had uncovered the shroud and only cut it with the shovel in a couple of places. "We're trying to carefully dig all around the shroud so we can lift the body up out of this muck," said Joel. "OK, I think we are ready to try to lift it out, but I'm afraid John Pete and I are not going to be strong enough to do it by ourselves."

Em and Meg volunteered to go to the warehouse and get some more boots. They soon returned each carrying a pair. The sheriff took a pair from Meg and began to put them on. "I can help."

Em hesitated and then started to put on a pair herself. "I've always wanted to try these on," she said catching Joel's eye. He laughed.

The four of them managed to raise the body and transfer it to dry land. The sheriff took out a knife and cut the shroud in places it had already been torn and carefully removed the pieces. Everybody crowded around to get the first look. Standing next to Press, Josie sought Meg's eye to give her a "Can-you-imagine-this?" kind of look. Meg's eyes, however, were fixed on the body, when suddenly her face expressed horror.

A second later she heard Press say, "Oh my God, it's Tim…oh my God." Josie took hold of his hand, wrapping an arm around him, then looked herself. Meg and Em both stared down at Tim's body. Press started crying. Josie expected Meg to break out into tears and need comforting like Preston, but Josie saw in her expression more fear than sadness.

The sheriff scrutinized Tim's body and then exclaimed, "Look at that nasty gash on his head."

"I remember that shirt," Press said. Meg didn't say anything, but Em got on her knees to get close to the body. Then she must have felt this was inappropriate and immediately stood up. Preston went on his knees and gently touched Tim's face. He held Tim's hand that was nearest him—the one with the missing finger. He noticed the chain coming from Tim's watch pocket and withdrew his pocket watch.

"Wait a minute. Mr. Milton, put the watch back," the sheriff said with apprehension. "I have to ask all of you not to touch the body again." Before he could go on to explain, a young man came running up with a camera. He politely asked if he could photograph the body. The sheriff took his name and made him promise to give him copies of the photos, as he hadn't brought his camera. The sheriff proceeded to ask many questions until he was caught up on the basics in the story of Tim's death and burial.

"From the looks of that head wound, maybe he died from something more than just a fall down stairs," the sheriff said. "Yeah, this is going to require an autopsy."

Press and Meg almost simultaneously said, "Oh no."

"Yep, this may be a murder, especially considering that you all were told he was buried in front of the house.… No one touch anything from now on. Mr. Milton and Mr. Cloud, please stay here and watch that nothing happens to the body. Nobody should get near it. I'm going to call my deputy and have the body picked up and taken to the coroner. Joel and John Pete, if you don't mind would you please start digging up the grave in front of the house. God knows who's in that one! Then, when I come back, I'll need to talk with each of you. Please don't leave. Stay right here. I'll be back in a few minutes."

When the sheriff came back, Meg asked if she could go to the house and tend to something. Soon after she left, Josie announced that she was going back to the house. The sheriff didn't seem to mind. Rather than just going in through the front porch, Josie decided to check a bed of mixed flowers she had planted in the front yard opposite the foreman's house. While there, she heard Meg talking inside and started to listen. That's funny, she thought, she's not talking to children. I think she is on the phone. Why would she be calling someone now? Perhaps the phone had rung and Meg was answering a call, but the phone rang in both houses. Josie hadn't heard it ring. Josie admitted to herself that she was too curious for her own good, but she couldn't help herself. She retraced her steps and went back into her house through the front porch. She very quietly picked up the receiver, putting her hand over the mouthpiece first so the parties wouldn't hear her breathing. She heard Meg say: "… to do an autopsy."

A female voice answered: "Call Earl tomorrow at 4:00 P.M." Josie heard both receivers click. The phone was dead. Josie poured herself just a little glass of sherry. She didn't want to muddle her mind. She had some important thinking to do. The only person she could think Meg might be calling would be Sarah. On the other hand, Meg was good friends with Louise in town. I suppose it could be Louise, but who was Earl?

Josie went out the front porch. John Pete was digging up Tim's grave, but Joel was out on the bog with Em, who was looking at her father. Rather than interrupt them, she simply announced to John Pete that she had to go into town to get some milk. Josie rarely went into town by herself, but she wanted to see if she could find out what the telephone number was that Meg had just called. The Post Office was where Springbrook's telephone operator worked the switchboard.

The only vehicle keys she could find hanging on the hooks in the pantry were those to the old Chevy pickup. She still found the sandy roads treacherous, so she drove carefully into town and parked in front of the Post Office, killing the engine. Holding a letter that she had written to her cousin MaryAnn, she explained to the post master that she had missed the mail carrier.

"I hope this can still go out today," she said to him.

"Not to worry, Mrs. Milton, the mail goes out on the 4:00 P.M. train and it's only noon now."

Noon, Josie thought. I need to get home soon, I should have started preparing lunch long ago. I hope Sam will stay, and maybe the sheriff too. "Is the operator here?" she asked trying to sound nonchalant, but struggling to remember her name.

A woman wearing a cotton dress and cardigan came out from behind the switchboard. She held one hand up to her head trying to cover the fact that her hair was up in pin curls. "Yes, hello Mrs. Milton."

"Hello, Hazel." Thank goodness Josie remembered her name in time. "I am going to make a call to Minneapolis tonight. We have already made one call there today, I believe. Do you happen to have a record of that?"

"Yes, I do."

"Well, I'm afraid, in the short time since we made that call, I've lost the telephone number. You wouldn't have it would you?"

"Yes, I should have it." She went back to the switchboard to look and came back with a slip of paper. "Here it is."

"Thank you so much."

As Josie left the Post Office, another car drove into the small parking area. A man got out and called back to the woman who remained seated in the passenger's seat, "After this," he said, "I have to go to Earl to pick up the plough."

Earl, said Josie to herself. Of course, she's to call *from* Earl, not *to* Earl! Feeling a bit smug, she said through her teeth—

"Avoiding party lines, no doubt." To hell with lunch, it's about time men learn how to fend for themselves. Josie got back into the old Chevy and with some gnashing of gears, she managed to get back on Highway 63 and drive the four miles to Earl.

She didn't know what she was looking for exactly. Like Springbrook, Earl was an unincorporated town. Most of its buildings flanked the highway. Besides houses, Earl only had a few public buildings, one of which was the general store. In the parking lot, was a red telephone booth. I'll bet Meg is going to call this number in Minneapolis tomorrow at 4:00 P.M. Feeling quite pleased with herself, Josie drove back to Miltonberry to start making lunch.

Press asked Josie to only make another round of sandwiches for lunch and nothing more. "No one has much of an appetite after all this.

Waiting with the others for Tim's grave to be dug up, Meg said, "Maybe Dad got the bodies in their shrouds mixed up and they were buried in the wrong place."

A couple of hours later, John Pete and Joel had finally dug the coffin free. Both men were dripping with perspiration. They placed a rope around it so the sheriff could help them lift it up and place it on the ground next to the grave. By this time, Preston had brought a crowbar and handed it to John Pete to pry open the lid.

"Good Lord, there is no corpse just…what are those…sand bags?" the sheriff said.

"I can't believe it! That was totally dishonest of Clarence," Press said. "I'm sorry, Meg, but he completely lied about this. Why?"

"Why indeed!" said Josie. She couldn't help but think that they should have dug up the grave long ago.

The sheriff turned to Sam and asked him if he had placed the sand bags in the coffin.

"No, the coffin was nailed shut and ready to be buried when we got here."

By this time, Tim's body had been taken to the coroner's office. Two deputies were inspecting the peat for clues inside an area that had been roped off.

The sheriff introduced a detective. "Together, we will interview each of you and will take your testimony separately," he explained. "Mr. and Mrs. Milton, may we use a private room in your house? I would also like to see the stairs where Tim allegedly fell to his death."

"Yes, that'll be no problem," Press said.

The next day, Josie told people that she was going into Spooner to get her hair done and would be back in the late afternoon. Josie disciplined herself to have only one sherry before lunch and none after. When she would normally be taking her nap, she put on a pair of Press' socks that were much too big for her, and then a pair of gym shoes that Press had given her years ago. She grabbed an old coat and scarf out of the coat closet. Josie drove into Earl around 3:00 and parked behind the school house, where her car would be hidden from the road. She waited until 3:45 before she put on the coat and scarf. She removed as much of her lipstick as she could and put her diamond ring in her pocket. Then she remembered that her polished nails might give her away, so she placed her hands in her pockets as she walked over to a bench near the general store. The bench was under a Norway pine. She was somewhat concealed by a branch, yet she had the telephone booth in sight.

A few minutes before 4:00, Meg was in the telephone booth getting coins out of her purse. Josie snuck peaks at her diamond watch and figured that Meg talked on the phone for at least 15 minutes. After Meg left the booth, Josie couldn't see but heard a car start up and go back in the direction in which it came.

Josie considered whether or not she should tell Press all that she had discovered. He will be annoyed with me, she thought, for snooping, not minding my own business. He would definitely not approve of my listening in on a telephone call, so she kept her findings to herself.

A few days later, an article appeared in the *Spooner Advocate*:

Two Graves, One Body = Murder?

By Bob Olson

Thursday, a body was exhumed from an unmarked grave on Preston Milton's cranberry bog outside of Springbrook. The body was expected to be that of an unknown man supposedly found dead in the woods forty-one years ago. Buried in peat, the body was perfectly preserved and was positively identified as Preston Milton's brother, Timothy Zearing Milton. Sheriff Dale Buchman had the body sent to the medical examiner's office in Rice Lake. It appeared that the victim had received a severe blow to his head. The case is being treated as a possible homicide.

For forty years, the Miltons believed Timothy was buried in the grave in front of their house marked with his name. Instead, only sand bags were found there in a flimsy pine coffin. Preston and others had been told that Timothy died from a fall down a stairway in the Milton home, yet no death certificate is on file.

The case is very complicated and involves a deceased Congregational minister, an Ojibwe bank president, the wife of Richard Morris, of the Morris Lumber Company, and her sister, a Massachusetts farm wife.

John Pete Kingfisher, another Ojibwe involved, first came to work for Timothy Milton in 1914. When Timothy died, John Pete continued working for Preston Milton, who assumed ownership of the bog. For forty years, John Pete was convinced that Timothy was not buried in front of the house, as the grave site failed an ancient Ojibwe test. It turned out he was right.

Joel Helmer, the foreman of the cranberry bog and a member of Sarona Friends Meeting, has suggested that interested people, friends and relatives gather at the cranberry bog

*on May 15 at 10:00 A.M. for a memorial meeting to honor the
memory of Timothy Milton.*

A few days later, Josie received a letter from her cousin
MaryAnn. In it, was a clipping from the May 4, 1960 *Chicago
Tribune*:

Penelope Babcock's Society Column

*Josephine Haylock Milton will be receiving guests in her
Springbrook Wisconsin home to celebrate the life of her husband's brother, who died under suspicious circumstances in
1919. The body was recently unearthed from an unmarked
grave on her husband's cranberry bog. Preston Milton became
the owner of the bog when his brother, Timothy, allegedly died
from a fall at the age of 31. There was no death certificate. A
murder investigation is in progress.*

Josie was rather pleased that she had enough notoriety in
Chicago society to warrant an article, but she felt that the article
itself was smug. "Penelope Babcock always did thrive on scandal and gossip! She almost insinuated that you murdered your
brother," she told Press.

A few days later, when Sheriff Buchman received the autopsy
report from the medical examiner's office, he announced that the
case would be treated as a murder.

On May 15, Preston suspended work on the bog to give his
employees the opportunity to attend the memorial gathering for
Tim. Josie noted that many people came from town to support
the Miltons and Helmers. Sheriff Buchman's presence made Josie
a bit nervous, but she understood that he must take advantage
of any opportunity to observe the people involved in a murder
case. Few of the people who came were old enough to actually
remember Tim. Press introduced Josie to Charlie Lewis, a fellow cranberry grower from the Minong area, saying, "Tim told
us how you had given him some good advice when he started
this bog." Josie knew Press was particularly glad that Sam Cloud

came. She could see they were becoming friends.

Josie wrote her cousin MaryAnn:

> *Our two families anticipated a period of quiet reflection with sympathetic friends. Little did we suspect that reporters from three states would seep in as the morning progressed! At one point, I counted ten of them. George Bevin from the* Chicago Tribune *had driven all the way up to Indianhead country, and the sharp investigative reporter, Gustav Swenson came from the Twin Cities. All were taking pictures and trying to interview anyone who lived or worked at Miltonberry.*

Josie had her hair done and dressed carefully for the occasion. She relished the attention of the media. Now that these exciting people were here at Miltonberry, she found herself torn between wanting to talk to them and needing to make sure that the refreshments would be ready on time. She knew better than to reveal information pertinent to the case, but she couldn't resist the opportunity to add to the drama: "Yes, all these years we felt the spirit of 'Uncle Tim' in the house. In the middle of the night, doors would open and shut, the floorboards would creak. We even thought we heard him rocking in his chair."

George Bevin of the *Tribune* asked, "Mrs. Milton, how did you find making the transition from being a Haylock in the whirl of Chicago's high society to the life on a cranberry bog in the North Woods of Wisconsin?"

"Challenging but also refreshing," she answered, with a smile that exposed a minimum of teeth. "If you'll excuse me, I have to tend to things in the kitchen."

After the autopsy, Tim's remains were placed back in the pine box. The coffin was properly buried in its original place—in front of the house, with the same headstone.

As with Em and Joel's wedding eighteen years earlier, people sat in a circle around Tim's headstone. Joel started the Meeting with an announcement: "We ask that no photographs or notes be taken during the hour of quiet. This is a gathering to honor the life of Tim Milton, who died in December of 1919. During the

Meeting, if you are led to say something, please stand and speak loud enough for all to hear you. You will know that the Meeting is over when we shake hands. Following the Meeting you are welcome to go into the Milton's house behind us here, where Preston and Josephine would like to offer you refreshments."

Josie was thankful that it was such a warm day. To have temperatures in the upper seventies was unusual for mid-May. She had worried that people would be too cold to have the meeting outdoors. Joel had told her that it takes a few minutes to "become centered." She wasn't sure what that meant, but she thought it meant to become serious. She became aware of the chorus of insects—crickets, grasshoppers, katydids and mosquitoes. She liked hearing them. Thirty-three years ago she would never have said that.

Em was now a Quaker. Josie noted that she spoke with ease to the gathering, "I have mixed emotions," Em began. "I feel proud to be honoring my father, but I regret that I never had the opportunity to know him. It seems that he accomplished a lot in his short life. I'm particularly grateful that he loved my mother so much, that he realized what a wonderful person she is." Josie saw Meg squirm. Em went on, "He must have been a 'man of vision' because he saw the potential of this bog." She spoke about the *Tales of Elm Grove* that he had hand-written for her when she was just a baby, and how they showed that Tim must have been a kind person. "I know from those stories and drawings he sent that he loved me very much, even though we never had a chance to spend any time together."

Josie noticed that Meg had come out of her meditation and was looking up at the white pine near the bog. Then Josie heard a tapping of a woodpecker. She followed Meg's gaze and saw a woodpecker that was all black. Why was Meg so fascinated, Josie asked herself? Maybe it was the North Woods' equivalent to the raven?

CHAPTER 35

MAY 1961

Sheriff Buchman presented his case to the District Attorney and then to Judge Winston Ward, who said there was probable cause to suspect Sarah Morris and/or her father of murder. Since Clarence was dead, only Sarah was accused. Ward issued the warrant to have the Minneapolis police pick her up. Sarah was kept in the Minneapolis jail while Richard Morris and his attorney, Melvin Howe, fought the extradition hearing. Finally, Sheriff Buchman got Sarah transferred to his jail in Shell Lake. At the initial appearance before Judge Ward, Sarah was formally charged with the murder of her former husband, Timothy Milton. Bail was set at $2,000. Richard easily paid it so Sarah could return to their home in Minneapolis to await trial.

It took a whole year before the case was ready to go to trial. By that time, the *Spooner Advocate* article had been rerun in other newspapers in Wisconsin, Illinois and Minnesota. People everywhere talked about the case. Newspapers played up to the public's desire for gossip. Some wondered how such a lovely-looking woman as Sarah Morris could have murdered her husband. Since the murder happened forty years ago, by the time of the trial, most people involved in the case were in their sixties and were pillars of the community. Outsiders who followed the case did so for the drama—more out of amusement than concern for justice. Everybody at Miltonberry agreed that they couldn't wait for the trial to be over so they could get on with their lives.

Preston was glad that the trial was taking place in the early spring when the bogs didn't need much attention. All the publicity brought about by the murder case had given him the opportunity to inform people far and wide that his bogs were for sale. He very much wanted Emma and Joel to take over the bog at Miltonberry, but for that to be possible, he would have to sell Toto for a good price, and the likelihood of that was remote, just two years after the cranberry scare.

Three weeks before the trial, Press was contacted by a potential buyer from Chicago with the name of Jon Swensen. Jon wrote to Press that he grew up in Superior:

I always have loved fishing and hunting in that area. I've read in the papers about the investigation into your brother's death. I want to send you my sympathies and also tell you that I am interested in your bog called Toto. When I learned it was on the Totogatic River and that it is only forty-some miles from Superior, I started thinking it might be just the kind of investment I've been looking for. I know a lot about the cranberry business, but mostly from the marketing end....

A week later, while Press was showing Jon Swensen around Toto. Jon told him: "That cranberry scare was an eye-opener for many of us at corporate headquarters. We all learned that the growers should be careful when using chemical fertilizers and insecticides, but that was just one lesson. The other lesson was that the public had been conditioned to think of cranberries as simply a holiday dinner condiment. We decided at corporate headquarters that we had to educate the public to think of cranberries as a year-round food. At Ocean Spray Cranberries, we have started to produce a variety of cranberry juices. Other ways of consuming cranberries are on the drawing board. We've launched a major advertising campaign to show how healthful cranberries are. The public will soon know that they are high in vitamin C and good for the urinary tract. Yes, the business should take off in about three years."

Press realized that Jon could afford to be so frank because he knew Press didn't want to be in the business anymore.

"Now's the time to become a grower," Jon said.

In his thoughts, Press completed Jon's sentence—"while I can buy a bog for so little money."

Press walked Jon around the bog. Jon said that he could see its potential for expansion. He offered Preston less than the sale price, but Press thought this could be his only chance to sell, so he accepted Jon's bid.

When Press drove home to Miltonberry, Josie, Joel, John Pete, Em and Meg gathered around the old Chevy to hear the news. Preston could see the relief on all their faces. Cash from the sale would help him stay afloat. Their jobs here at Miltonberry would be secure for at least a few more years.

"Thank goodness Mr. Swensen didn't want to buy Miltonberry," Joel commented.

"I hope you can own Miltonberry some day," Press said to Joel and Em. "That would have made Tim happy. It would help justify what he went through."

~

As Press and Josie walked into the Shell Lake Courthouse, they smelled the fragrance of lilacs. It was a bright, clear, but chilly day, typical of spring. Press felt grateful to have Josie at his side and grateful that throughout this ordeal, their neighbors and acquaintances had been supportive and kind to them.

Almost reading Preston's thoughts Josie said: "I think this investigation and trial are most difficult for Meg. She feels some-what responsible for Tim's death. She doesn't believe Sarah killed Tim. I know that."

"There is nothing any of us can do about this. Once the sher-iff arrived at the bog and saw Tim's body, the death had to be investigated. We cannot control how this trial will come out."

"Look at all the reporters."

As they entered the courtroom, Press and Josie took seats next to Meg, Emma and Joel. They were seated in the first bench behind the prosecutor's table on the left side of the room, near the jury. Press spotted Meg's good friend, Louise. Then he saw Sam and they waved to each other.

"Let me get this straight—Henry Brown is the prosecuting attorney, but who is the lawyer defending Sarah?" Josie asked.

"I think his name is Melvin Howe. I hear he's the Morris family attorney. They have used him for years to fight their battles. He's supposed to be very sharp.

When Sarah left the table for the defense to take the witness stand, Press noticed how slim she was. He figured she must be in her mid-sixties but she looked fifteen years younger. She had on a tailored emerald green dress and a string of pearls. Henry Brown asked her to describe the events leading up to Tim's death.

Sarah: "On Friday, December 26, 1919, Mother, Dad and I caught a train for Minneapolis. Tim rode back to our home on the cranberry bog. He didn't want to go with us because he was in the middle of designing a piece of equipment that would be needed for the next harvest."

Press wondered what equipment she meant. He didn't remember seeing evidence of that. Sarah continued with her testimony:

"Tim really didn't like visiting with our relatives anyway. We returned to Springbrook on Friday, January 1. The plan was that Tim would meet us at the train depot, but he wasn't there. I was put out, and decided to stay at Mom's and Dad's until Tim came and got me, but Dad was not willing to wait. He rode out to our home on the bog to look for Tim. I think Dad was going to tell Tim off. Dad was gone a long time—at least three hours. When he returned he told us that Tim was dead, that he had fallen downstairs. The house was freezing cold, so he must have fallen soon after we left for Minneapolis."

Brown: "Describe how Tim was dressed."

Sarah: "I never saw him after we went to Minneapolis. I've heard how he was dressed from the police report, and it sounds like he had his usual clothes on."

Brown: "Describe his usual clothes."

Sarah: "He usually wore heavy, gray working trousers, a flannel shirt, suspenders, and a sweater."

Brown: "And a pocket watch, did Tim usually carry a pocket watch?"

Sarah: "Yes, he always wore his pocket watch."

Brown: "Describe his sweater."

Sarah: "He usually wore the gray sweater. It was a cardigan.

Brown: "Had he lots of sweaters?"

Sarah: "No, he had a green one for special occasions."

Brown: "How often did he wear that one?"

Sarah: "Maybe once or twice a year. I'm not sure."

Brown: "You slept in separate bedrooms?"

Sarah: "Yes, most of the time, but that is because I am a very light sleeper. We got in the habit of sleeping in separate bedrooms because Tim often had to check the thermometers on the bog in the middle of the night—not during the winter, but at other times of year. I could never get back to sleep, so I started sleeping in the other room."

Brown: "Was there a phone in your house?"

Sarah: "No."

Brown: "So, please go on with your story. You have said in depositions that your father dragged Tim's body to the icehouse. Why didn't you take Tim's body into Hayward or Spooner to a funeral home?"

Sarah: "Dad couldn't see the point of spending the money for them to do what we could do ourselves."

Brown: "Why didn't you get a death certificate?"

Sarah: "Dad couldn't see the point of that either. 'We already know he's dead,' he said."

Brown: "Did you ever see Tim's body before he was buried?"

Sarah: "No, I just couldn't go back to the house at all. I was in a bad state. Dad took care of things."

Brown: "Did your mother, Rose Ellsworth, ever see Tim's body?"

Sarah: "Not to my knowledge."

Brown: "Did you love Tim?"

Sarah: "Some, but not that much."

Brown: "Why not?"

Sarah: "We never fought. It wasn't like that. But looking back on it now, I realized that I was bored. I didn't care much about the bog, and it seemed like it was all that Tim was interested in."

Brown: "There wasn't much passion between you."

Preston noticed a glimmer of a smile from Sarah as she glanced at Richard. He was sitting on a bench behind the table for the defense.

Sarah: "No. There was little passion between us."

Brown turned the line of questioning to Sarah's life before she married Tim, her relationship with her sister, and her aspirations when she was young. Preston was relieved that people spoke loud enough for him to hear.

Brown: "Why did you marry Tim?"

Sarah: "I shouldn't have.... Looking back, I think I was somewhat immature. The marriage was a mistake, but I would never have killed him just for that."

Brown: "Would you have killed him if you knew he loved another woman?"

Sarah (swallowing and answering slowly): "No, certainly not. Murdering anybody is inexcusable."

Brown: "When did you first realize that Tim loved your sister Meg?"

Sarah: "I can't say I ever knew that he loved her, although I realized at Emma and Joel's wedding that probably Emma, Meg's daughter, was Tim's child, because she looks so much like him. That was the first time that I suspected that there had been something between my sister and Tim."

Brown established that Sarah had neglected her parents. That she didn't even go to her father's funeral. "What was the reason?" he asked.

Sarah: "I didn't like my father. He was the cause of all my problems. He manipulated things so I would marry Tim. He held the loan over Tim's head and threatened to call the loan in if Tim didn't do what he wanted. I told him I wanted to get a divorce and he said that would be a disgrace to the family. He wouldn't let Tim and me get free from each other."

Brown: "Did you murder Tim before you left to go to Minneapolis?"

Sarah: "No."

Brown: "Do you think your father killed Tim?"

Sarah: "It's possible. I don't know.

Brown: "Were you afraid of your father?"

Sarah: "Yes, especially after Tim died. He insisted on making all the decisions."

Brown: "Tell the court about Tim's attempt to call off your engagement before you were married back in 1916."

Sarah: "No, he never tried to call it off. He did say to me once that he worried that he had so much work to do on the bog all the time. He worried that he wouldn't have much time to be with me when we were married. I offered to delay the wedding, if that would help, but he said no to that. There was a substantial loan that Mr. Harold Morris, my father's friend, was going to give him once we were married. I don't think Tim wanted to put off getting the loan."

Preston looked at Meg and saw her face tighten. In the morning break he said to Josie, "Sarah's doing her best to make Tim look cold and calculating, as well as to put the blame for the murder on her father."

Josie agreed with him but added, "Sarah may have other reasons."

Press had no idea what Josie meant by that. Before he could ask her to explain, the judge asked everyone to stop talking. Press had noticed that Josie was engrossed in this case. She wasn't drinking as much at home, and she even ventured out on her own around the property. Once he found her all alone inside the warehouse. "Just looking around," was her only explanation. Press scolded himself for letting his mind wander and resumed listening carefully. Sarah was asked about Clarence's relationship to Harold Morris. She told about the hunting lodge. Preston glanced over at Richard and saw not a flicker of emotion on his face.

Brown: "Do you think that Tim wanted to marry you so he would be able to get the loan from Mr. Morris?"

Sarah: "Partially."

Brown: "Do you think Tim loved you, Sarah?"

Sarah: "Now, it appears that he may not have loved me, but I wasn't aware of that at the time."

Brown: "Were you aware that Tim wasn't in love with you at the time of Tim's death?"

Sarah: "Yes, I thought that was probably the case. I can't say that I was hurt by it, because I wasn't really in love with him either."

Brown: "At the time of Tim's death, had you met Richard, your present husband?"

Sarah: "No. I had heard of him, but never met him."

Brown: "Why didn't your father remove Tim's watch so he could give it to you as a memento of Tim?"

Sarah: "I don't know."

Brown: "Did you not want a memento of Tim?"

Sarah: "Dad probably realized that the watch would be nothing more than a reminder of our unhappy marriage. Maybe that is why he left it in Tim's pocket."

Brown: "When did your father first know that Tim loved Meg and not you?

Sarah: "I don't know if he ever knew. I don't think he did know."

Brown: "How do you explain the great effort he went through to make sure Tim's body wasn't seen?"

Sarah: "That's a mystery to me, too."

Brown: "You lied about where Tim was buried?"

Sarah: "No, I didn't lie. I thought Tim was buried in front of the house. My father made the arrangements for the burial."

Brown: "Let's see now, you were willing to follow your father's advice to not get the sheriff, right?"

Sarah: "Yes."

Brown: "You were willing to follow your father's advice to not take Tim's body to a mortuary, right?"

Sarah: "Yes."

Brown: "You were willing to follow your father's advice to not get a death certificate for Tim, right?

Sarah: "Yes."

Brown: "You were willing to follow your father's advice to not be involved with the burial arrangements, right?"

Sarah: "Yes."

Brown: "Mrs. Morris, have you been back to visit the grave where you thought your husband was buried since he died forty-one years ago?"

Sarah: "The only time I went back was for Emma and Joel's

wedding. I don't like to be reminded about how unhappy I was living there."

Brown: "Do you know who Sam Cloud is?"

Sarah: "I had never heard of Sam Cloud until about a year ago, when I learned for the first time that my dad had hired him and his brother to dig the two graves."

～

In the evening after the first day of the trial, Press was enjoying preparing supper. Josie was helping him, and she kept leading the conversation back to the trial and details of Tim's death.

"What I can't understand is why Clarence had two graves dug. I mean, why didn't he just place Tim's body in the pine box and have it buried in front of the house?"

"Um, hmm, I've thought about that…. Are you just about finished making the salad?"

"Yes."

After some thought, Press answered her question, "I think he was afraid that Mom and I would want the grave dug up so we could see Tim's body." Press had already placed the thin slices of tomato on pieces of buttered bread and added strips of bacon. Now he was grating onions into a bowl of shredded cheese—an unpleasant process that made his eyes water. He wanted to finish the job before continuing the conversation. He stirred the mixture before spreading it on top of the bread. "What was it that Susan calls these?"

"Milton pizzas," Josie answered.

"Oh yes." Sprinkling the top with paprika, he said, "They're ready to go in the broiler." Now, Press could concentrate on their conversation. "You know I was put off by Clarence's damn collar. Both Mom and I saw him as someone official. We assumed he was an expert at burials. My God, when I think that we didn't even challenge the absence of a death certificate! I was so concerned with doing what was honorable. It never occurred to me or Mom that Clarence was taking advantage of us."

"Exactly! I have been thinking about Clarence's personality. Do you think he was a psychopath?"

"A what?"

"Oh Preston, you know, the type we read about all the time in our detective magazines. You know…."

Preston interrupted, "Are you ready with the salad? Can I put the 'cheese dreams,' or 'Milton pizzas,' under the broiler?" Preston chuckled to himself. Once again, he noticed Josie only mentioned the detective magazines when they were alone. When she straightened up their bedroom in the morning, she always put them on his side of the bed. Yet when a new one arrived, she was the first to commandeer it.

"From the sounds of it, Clarence loved to be in control. I have never heard one thing about him that suggested that he had empathy for other people. Such people are called psychopaths, I think…you know, they lack guilt or remorse."

"We still don't know for sure that he did murder Tim," Press said. "Tim may have been dead when Clarence arrived at the house. He could have thought the death would look suspicious and he didn't want to chance accusations. It's absolutely certain that he performed a cover-up. He couldn't risk getting a death certificate because then a doctor or the sheriff would have to inspect the body. He knew that other people would think Sarah had a motive and then the whole town would know about Tim and Meg's affair."

"Yes I agree with you there, Press." said Josie, "But I've been thinking a lot about this. I now think that Clarence thought for sure that Sarah had killed Tim, because the gash was on the back of Tim's head. The sheriff never said that the wound matched a fire poker or that any weapon had been used to kill Tim, so that must not have been mentioned in the autopsy report. So the only way Tim could have gotten that gash is by hitting his head when he fell, but because it was on the back of his head, he must have fallen backward from the top of the stairs. In that position it is not likely that one would just fall backward, so he must have been pushed."

"My goodness, Josie, you should be a detective. I am impressed with you."

"Thanks Press. You know, Clarence was in a real pickle," Josie continued. "If you look at it from his point of view, his problem was how to get rid of Tim's body. The ground was frozen solid. He couldn't take it to a funeral director. He couldn't even drop it in the Namekagon..."

"Good God, Josie, you're talking about my brother!"

"Sorry, Press. It's just that I didn't know either Tim or Clarence...but the Namekagon was frozen over, you see."

"Let's eat."

~

The next day, the prosecutor called Louise Ferguson to the witness stand. Louise told the jury that in 1916, she helped her parents tend the general store in Springbrook, which they owned. Louise explained that a month before the wedding, Sarah came into the store and lashed out at her.

Louise: "Sarah actually threatened me if I didn't leave Tim alone. It was so ludicrous because I hardly ever spoke to Tim. He was quiet, not the chatty type. When he came in to shop, he rarely talked to anyone. He was real serious. He didn't hardly look at me, yet Sarah was convinced that I was after her man."

Brown: "Then why do you think Sarah assumed that it was you and not her sister Meg?"

Louise: "Sarah thought looks were everything. Meg was bright, had lots of personality, but she was nowhere near the looker that Sarah was. I think Sarah couldn't conceive of a man preferring Meg to her. Also, because Meg was so trustworthy, she probably couldn't think of her sister loving her fiancé behind her back."

Brown: "Was there a time when you thought Sarah was no longer suspicious of you?"

Louise: "Once they got married Sarah seemed to forget that she ever thought of me as a rival. She became sad and quiet. I was shocked when Meg suddenly left. Meg and I were good friends but she never told me that she was going away. You know a lot of people up here in those days, and still today, get married because they 'have to.' Frankly I was expecting Sarah would be the one to become pregnant before she married. I figured that was why Tim married her, because it didn't seem to me that they were well-suited for each other, but Sarah never got pregnant."

Brown: "When did you first know that Meg and Tim had been lovers?"

Louise: "About a year later, I heard that Meg had a baby in Massachusetts. No one knew if she was married or not, just that she had a baby girl. Even though the Ellsworths never talked about Meg or their granddaughter, somehow the news got out. I started thinking that was why Meg didn't say goodbye. She couldn't explain why she was leaving suddenly without hurting her sister. This got me to thinking that Meg was the person Sarah should have been suspicious of, but then a year later, I heard that Meg married somebody in Massachusetts, so I figured he was the one that got her pregnant. Then, about nine years later, when Em came for the first time to visit her grandparents, she came into the store. I found out that she was Meg's daughter. I could see that she resembled Tim. I asked her when her birthday was, and realized that it was possible that Tim had been Meg's lover, after all."

When Melvin Howe, the defense attorney, had his opportunity to question Louise, he made sure the jury realized that Louise worked for the Miltons and therefore, was bound to be loyal to them.

Preston was Brown's next witness. When asked about Sarah's parents, Press related the Ellsworths' coldness at the time of

Tim's burial. He said that there were several oddities, such as the body already being underground when he and his mother arrived from Chicago. Brown made sure that the jury was aware of Preston's record in the Navy and of the honor he showed by assuming his brother's debts, without the guarantee that he would be considered the legal owner of Miltonberry.

When Howe cross-examined Preston, he asked his questions louder than necessary, perhaps to make Preston seem like an old man. He asked why Tim didn't fight in the war like so many other lumberjacks and farmers from the North Woods had. Preston said that Tim simply had not been called up.

Howe: "Mr. Milton, don't you think that it was reckless of Tim to spend almost all of his inheritance from his father and then have to borrow so much money from Mr. Morris?"

Preston: "This is the plight of all farmers. It takes money to get crops ready before they can produce. It's not a salaried job. Most farmers have to borrow money, at times. You may not know it, but it takes five years before a newly planted cranberry bed can be harvested. You have no income for the first six years, minimum. Mr. Morris understood this and made the interest rate very low. It was only a half-percent. I'd say Tim was lucky, not reckless."

Preston heard comments from the public gallery like, "Ooh… That's wonderful…Imagine that!" Everyone knew that farmers were having a difficult time, what with foreclosures on small family farms and interest rates being so high.

Josie was very disappointed that Mr. Brown didn't call on her. She could think of ever so many things to say. She wondered why Howe had her down as one of his possible witnesses. He had never even spoken to her.

Mr. Brown tried to prepare Josie for being cross-examined by Howe. "He will emphasize your flaws in an effort to downgrade the Miltons."

Press knew what those flaws would be—excessive drinking,

her tendency to exaggerate, her former extravagance and excessive wealth. On the other hand, Press knew Josie was a performer. This type of challenge didn't frighten her.

Just look at her, he thought: beautifully dressed, hair coiffed. Her dress was a bit too low cut for Shell Lake taste, he thought, and she almost tripped stepping up onto the witness stand, but she made up for it by seating herself with exaggerated grace. Her black dress set off her diamond broach as well as her powdered, white skin. She answered Howe's questions with her elbows on the witness box and resting her chin on her crossed hands. This brought all eyes to her diamond and sapphire ring and red fingernails. Press saw her peculiar smile. Her eyes sparkled as she looked Howe right in the eye. By God, she's confident. She is even enjoying this trial. She is making that hard-nosed lawyer ill at ease. The jury loves it, Press noticed. Howe's questioning was beginning to seem pointless. Josie was causing him to appear somewhat ridiculous. After a few minutes, Howe terminated the inquiry and asked Josie to leave the witness box. She probably doesn't want to leave it, Press thought.

Sam Cloud was the next witness. He related the same story Press heard him give in the bank parking lot, only omitting the bit about Al Capone's thugs.

Finally, the prosecuting attorney asked Meg to take the witness stand. She was asked to explain her relationship with Tim.

Meg: "When we realized we were in love, Tim tried to break off his engagement with Sarah. He told Sarah that he loved someone else. Sarah said that he wouldn't be able to get the generous loan from Mr. Morris if he didn't marry her. Tim really needed that loan or else he couldn't continue converting the bog into a cranberry marsh. If he sold the property, he wouldn't recover the money he had already invested, and he would have to give up his dream of being a cranberry grower.

"So we made the painful decision that he would go ahead

with the marriage to Sarah. We hoped that, after a few years, he could divorce Sarah and marry me. When we made that decision we didn't know I was pregnant. I only discovered my pregnancy a month after Sarah and Tim were married.

"Long before I really knew Tim, I was concerned that Sarah was being pushed into marrying him. I told her she would be miserable living on a cranberry bog. You see, Sarah never really enjoyed the outdoors. She always wanted to live in a large city. Furthermore, I later realized that she really didn't know Tim or love him. I am convinced that Dad orchestrated her marriage, thinking that Tim would someday be a wealthy man, and therefore a good husband for her."

Brown: "Who were the people who knew you were pregnant?"

Meg: "Only my mother and Tim knew I was pregnant. Mom helped arrange for me to live with her sister in Massachusetts. Mom knew my pregnancy would infuriate Dad so…. For a long time I couldn't understand why my parents rarely wrote me and when they did, it was just a note. I think my father was enraged because I left home so suddenly. Since Mom had helped me leave without his permission, he wouldn't let her write to me more than once a year. I purposely announced Emma's birth several months after she was actually born—to make it appear that Emma was conceived after I was in Massachusetts. Dad was also angry because I was no longer available to help with both the house and church work. I was absolutely sure that he did not know that Emma's father was Tim.

"Another explanation for why Dad tried to cut me out of the family might be that I was helping another church and not his church. You see, I told Mom and Dad in my letters that I was doing pastoral care work for the Congregational Church in Middlefield. In fact, it was then that I realized just how poor of a minister Dad was, I'm sorry to say.

Virtually all he did was deliver his sermon each Sunday."

Next, it was Mr. Howe's chance to cross-examine Meg.

Howe: "Why did Mr. Morris make the stipulation that Tim had to be married before he would initiate the loan?"

Meg: "I don't know. Maybe he thought Tim would be more likely to carry through with his cranberry business if he were married. Maybe my dad had already put the bug in Mr. Morris' ear that he wanted Tim to marry Sarah? Dad wouldn't have gotten Mr. Morris involved had he not thought Tim would make a good husband for Sarah. He arranged the appointment for Tim to see Mr. Morris about the loan."

Howe: "Did you ever correspond with your sister after she was married to Tim?"

Meg: "It was about a year before Tim died that I received a letter from Sarah telling me how miserable she was married to Tim. I didn't answer her letter or the next one she wrote. Then Sarah started phoning me at my aunt and uncle's. I was still living with them. I told her I couldn't phone her but that we could talk if she phoned me at a time my aunt and uncle were out. We set up a time and we started talking about what she could do. Sarah said that Tim couldn't give her a divorce until he had paid back most of the loan. Tim thought if our father got angry, he could demand that the loan be paid back immediately in full. The loan paper stated that my father had this power."

Howe: "Did Sarah tell your father that she wanted to divorce Tim?"

Meg: "Yes, but Dad thought divorce was sinful and wouldn't allow it."

Howe: "Couldn't Sarah just have divorced Tim anyway. As an adult, she didn't need her father's permission."

Meg: "Yes, but Dad was very forceful and rigid."

Howe: "Did Sarah tell you that her family was going to spend a week in Minneapolis after Christmas?"

Meg: "Yes."

Howe: "Did she tell you that Tim was not going?"

Meg: "Yes."

Preston looked at Josie. He didn't like the direction these questions were taking.

Howe: "Mrs. Lucas, have you seen Tim since you moved to Massachusetts?"

Meg: "Yes, once."

Howe: "When was that? I should remind you that you are under oath."

Meg: "On Saturday, December 27, 1919."

The courtroom exploded with noisy voices. Many in the gallery, like Preston, were stunned. He turned to look at Josie and found, to his surprise, that she was deep in thought. Before he could ask her what she was thinking, the judge rapped his gavel to quiet people down.

Howe: "Mrs. Lucas, why did you not disclose this before?"

Meg: "Maybe I should have, but nobody asked me these questions before."

Howe: "Explain how you came to see Tim on that day."

Meg: "I met Steve Lucas soon after I arrived in Massachusetts, through my pastoral care work. Steve and I became good friends. I told him all about Tim. A month or two before Tim died, Steve asked me to marry him. I told Steve that I wanted to try one more time to get Tim to divorce Sarah. With the family gone to Minneapolis, I thought it would be a good time. I decided to take Emma. I thought he should see his daughter, and maybe that would help to convince him that he needed to be a true father to her. I also went because I wanted to see if my feelings for Tim were still as strong as they had been.

"I took the train with Emma all the way to Springbrook. I saw that the station master was not the old man that I knew. I was glad about that, because I didn't want people to know I was there. We walked to my parents' house to get a horse to ride to Tim's place. Tim was thrilled to see us. He played with Emma for a long time before she needed a nap. We put her down to sleep upstairs on Tim's bed. I shut the door so we wouldn't wake her, and Tim and I went downstairs. He tried to become affectionate, but I told him that we had to talk. We talked and talked but still he said he couldn't divorce Sarah because of the loan. I told him that I was considering marrying Steve Lucas. Emma needed a father. He looked sad but didn't change his mind. Emma was stirring so I went up stairs to fetch her. Tim followed me and before I could open the door to his room, he became passionate. I said no and pushed him away. Unfortunately, he was standing at the head of the stairs with his back to them. I didn't mean to push him downstairs but that is what happened."

Howe: "Was he still alive after the fall?"

Meg: "He might have been. I couldn't tell for sure, but I think he might have been just barely alive. There was blood running from the back of his head. I felt no pulse, but I was never very good at feeling someone's pulse. I had to pull him off the small landing at the base of the stairs, so he could lie flat. You see he had fallen backward and hit his head on the overhang. The overhang was so low that you had to duck your head to get around it. So I pulled him on to the sitting room floor. Thank goodness Em stayed in Tim's bedroom through this. I tried to remain calm so as not to frighten her. I went upstairs and bundled up Em so she couldn't see Tim's body as we went down stairs. We set out for town to try to find a doctor. I found the station master. He said that there was a doctor who was visiting the

Olson family on Spring Lake, but he didn't know his name. To make a long story short, I found the Olson's home. The doctor's name was Dr. Rudy Baldwin and he was willing to ride with me and Emma back to Tim's house. By the time we got back, Tim was definitely dead. Dr. Baldwin filled out a death certificate. He asked me the man's name and I said he was Ryan C. Berr. I told him that he fell down stairs. He filled out a death certificate and asked my name. I said I was Meg Lucas. I'm not sure what exactly he wrote down."

Howe: "It is a crime to give false information."

Meg: "Yes, I know, but I felt it was better than to expose all of this, if it wasn't necessary."

Howe: "Mrs. Lucas, you were willing to have your sister go to trial for killing her husband rather than let it be known that you did it?"

Meg: "I knew there wasn't enough evidence to convict Sarah. Had that not been the case, I would have disclosed what really happened. If it wasn't necessary, I wanted to avoid having my daughter know that her mother killed her father."

Meg started crying.

Judge Ward: "I think we will take an hour recess to have lunch. We will reconvene this trial at 1:30 sharp." He rapped his gavel.

Josie whipped out of the room, saying something very rapidly to Press. He was completely befuddled as to where she was going. He went to their car to get the lunch they had packed. He decided to eat it on a circular bench around a huge elm tree. Press sat down and quietly ate a meatloaf sandwich. A few minutes later, he was aware that a couple had sat down on the bench on the opposite side of the tree. Press laughed to think how Josie would love to hear what they were talking about. He knew that wasn't proper so he concentrated on the view down Fourth Avenue, and the meadows beyond. Then he heard "Richard." Preston froze to listen closely.

"I'm telling you, I'd burn the whole place down this time, if they had pinned anything on you," a man said.

"What do you mean by 'this time?'" replied a woman.

I've heard that woman's voice before. Who is it, Press asked himself?

The man said: "I think you're going to get off…"

Before the man had finished his sentence, Josie had called out from a distance: "Press…Oh, Press, there you are. Why didn't you answer me?" Josie hadn't seen the man and woman on the other side of the tree.

"Sorry, Humpafine, you know I can't hear much of anything these days. Let's go get your sandwich from the car." Press forced himself not to look at the man and woman. By now, he knew who they were, but he didn't want them to know he had heard what they said.

Back in the courtroom, it was apparent that the two lawyers had spoken to the judge during the recess, and they had reached an agreement as to how to proceed with the case.

Judge Ward: "Mrs. Lucas we would like to continue asking you a few questions. Would you please take the witness stand?"

Howe: "After the doctor left, what did you do?"

Meg: "I left Tim as he was on the floor in the sitting room. I gathered our things and left. The fire had burnt down. Six days later, when the family returned, Tim's body would be frozen. There was nothing I could do to help him."

Howe: "You returned to Massachusetts? Did you stay in touch with Sarah?

Meg: "No. I never told her that I had gone to Wisconsin."

Howe: "How do you explain your father going out of his way to bury the body where he thought it would never be found?

Meg: "Sarah is probably the better person to answer that question."

Howe: "Perhaps, but I am asking you Mrs. Lucas."

Meg: "Maybe when Dad found Tim's body he assumed Sarah had killed him before she left for Minneapolis and he wanted to cover up for her."

Howe: "If your father thought that you had killed Tim would he have covered up for you, do you think?"

Meg: "Yes, because he wouldn't want the family's dirty linen exposed."

Mr. Howe asked Meg why her father bothered with a second grave. Meg finished giving her opinion by saying that she thought her father actually believed Tim was murdered.

Howe: "Wasn't Tim murdered?"

Meg: "He was killed accidentally. I don't think that is the same as murder. I loved Tim."

Howe: "Mrs. Lucas, do you have any proof that could verify your story?"

Meg: "No, I guess I don't."

Quick as a flash Josie stood up and said in a loud voice: "I have proof."

Down came the gavel. "Mrs. Milton, this is highly irregular."

"Yes, your honor, but there is no lawyer representing Meg, and I do have proof."

Judge Ward said, "In view of the fact that the case against Sarah Morris will be dropped, would you please step forward to the bench, Mrs. Milton, so I can have a word with you about your 'proof.'"

After a few minutes in consultation with Josie, Judge Ward said to the people in the courtroom: "Please stay in your seats. You may talk to each other while Mr. Brown, Mr. Howe and I check on something. We should be able to resume these proceedings in about 15 minutes."

Back in her seat next to Preston, Josie whispered to him that she had found the death certificate for Tim.

"Where?" asked Press totally bewildered.

"In the Register of Deeds."

"Where's that?"

"Right here, in the court house."

"How did you know that?"

"I had been looking for it before."

When the court came back into session, Judge Ward made the following announcement:

"Although no death certificate had been filed for Timothy
Zearing Milton, it seems there is a death certificate for a
man named Ryan C. Berr, dated December 27, 1919. It is
signed by Rudy Baldwin, MD. It says that the cause of death
is 'fracture of skull due to accidental fall downstairs.'"

The courtroom burst out in cheers. Down came the gavel. When the gallery became silent again, Judge Ward continued:

"In view of Meg Lucas' confession, all charges against Sarah
Morris are dropped. Furthermore, I do not consider that
there is sufficient evidence to warrant charging Meg Lucas
for the murder of Timothy Milton. If the doctor who saw
Tim's body right after he died decided it was an accidental
death, in my opinion, none of us today—42 years later—
can make a more accurate determination. This case is
dismissed."

With a broad smile on his face Press gave Josie a big hug. "Good work, Humpafine." People started lining up to talk to Josie, but they had to wait for Meg to finish expressing her gratitude, in between sobs. Em and Joel were next with hugs for Josie and for Meg.

CHAPTER 36

Back home after the trial, Josie had time to think. She suspected that there was more to Tim's death than the trial summary expressed. She wondered if Sarah and Meg had manipulated the trial. Were they in cahoots from the beginning? These were questions Josie kept asking herself. What troubled her was why Sarah so willingly let herself go on trial. She could have confessed to being in communication with Meg, but she didn't. Josie felt sure that the two sisters had been communicating for years, by how quickly Meg understood the "code" that she should call Sarah from the public phone booth in Earl. Why was that secrecy necessary?

Then it hit Josie.

They must have either planned for Meg to kill Tim or Tim's death had actually occurred as Meg testified, but Sarah knew, and was so happy to be free of the marriage that she kept Meg's secret. Clarence played into their hands by covering it up.

Josie considered whether she should tell the sheriff about her suspicions. It would be impossible to prove that Meg purposely killed Tim. Did Meg have a motive? Meg could be and probably was resentful that Tim repeatedly chose cranberries over being a proper father to Em and a husband to the woman he supposedly loved. Knowing Meg's temperament, Josie did not believe that Meg would have wanted to murder Tim.

Why did Meg not want Em to know who her father was? Perhaps Meg figured that if Em knew, she might also find out that her mother had killed him. Even though it was an accident, it could have been misconstrued. A further reason might be that Meg was ashamed of Tim's character and didn't want Em to learn how weak he was. In choosing not to marry Meg, he chose not to be a father to Em. That would be hurtful to Em.

Meg's pregnancy was the true test of Tim's character. In comparison, Preston was the more honorable of the two brothers. Press had made the same sacrifices for his brother that his brother was not willing to make for the woman he loved and his child.

After hours of deliberation, Josie decided to keep her thoughts to herself. She would not tell the sheriff, or even Press, otherwise his relationship with the Helmers might become strained. Tim was dead. The dirty linen has been exposed and somewhat laundered. Josie thought that each sister got what she wanted—Sarah was living a sophisticated life in a city, and Meg had been able to bring up Em in a healthy environment, far from the source of scandal. Now Meg could live with her daughter's family on the bog which she had always loved.

CHAPTER 37

By the second night after the trial, the Helmer family had absorbed the information that the trial had revealed. The family felt relaxed at last. Em said to her mom, "Aunt Sarah is such a puzzle to me. She must have thought the way Granddad went about things was strange. So must have Grandma. Wouldn't they've been suspicious?"

"We had all learned to go along with whatever my father wanted. Mom and I worked all the time for the church. That's how we stayed in his good graces. Fortunately, we both liked that work. Sarah was Dad's wild card. He was ready to play her whenever there was an advantage. Dad couldn't tolerate having his opinions questioned. Now that I think of it, it's no wonder Sarah wanted to leave for Minneapolis as soon as possible. No wonder she said she wanted to live in a city. She just wanted to get away."

"OK, I can understand that," Em said, "but why would Sarah marry Richard, who as I understand it, was another version of Granddad, only with unlimited power?"

"I don't know. By marrying Richard she was pleasing Dad," Meg proposed. "Dad kowtowed to Harold, Richard's father."

"I watched Richard a lot at the trial," Joel said. "What I noticed surprised me. He seemed to care a lot about Sarah, and she seemed to care for him."

"One thing I can't understand is why Sarah never helped me with either father's or mother's funeral arrangements."

"Perhaps someday you'll be able to ask her about that."

"Wouldn't that be nice, if we could talk frankly to each other again?"

About a week later, Meg and Emma both received letters from Minneapolis.

Dear Meg,

We have both been through a lot. Even though I dreaded the trial, it gave me the opportunity to see and hear you again, and reminded me of what a wonderful person you are. Had I been more mature in 1916, I would have realized that I didn't want to marry Tim, and that my marrying him was a bad idea altogether. If I had known it was you that he loved, would I have acted differently? I don't know. We both played a part in the mess that ensued, and we both have suffered for it. Tim suffered the most. He never got to be with the woman he loved, see his daughter grow up, and as if that wasn't enough, his life was cut short.

I don't know to what to attribute my mistakes. Compared to you, I was lazy. I just wasn't interested in household chores, neighbors or animals. I can't explain why I was different, but I was. Maybe it was because I was pretty. I always got attention and came to expect it. There's a more sinister side of being pretty. You are never sure if people actually like you, or if they just like looking at you. Being loved is much more satisfying than being a showpiece or a doll. I know this now that I have lived with Richard. I truly fell in love with Richard and felt from the beginning the love that he has for me.

After Em's and Joel's wedding, I was mad at you. I felt betrayed. All those phone calls we had before Tim died and you didn't tell me you were the other woman. I am writing to ask us both to try to give each other another chance. We're different, but we are sisters and we can, I believe, become friends again.

Love,

Sarah

~

Dear Emma,

We heard that Preston wants to sell the bog. Somehow it seems that the right thing for me to do is to give you the money that would enable you to buy Miltonberry. Tim would be happy to have the bog stay in the family.

I was so touched that you asked Richard and me to your wedding, after I had ignored you all these years. As you know from the trial, I had a lot to work through—sorrows, disappointments, bitterness, and especially guilt. I am trying to put those things in the past and would like to be a good aunt to you, Joel, and the children.

Blessings to all of you,

Aunt Sarah

Enclosed was a check for $300,000 made out to Emma Helmer.

CHAPTER 38

Now that Preston was 'retired' he could contemplate fishing, building window boxes, and fixing motors in the warehouse at his leisure. He made himself available to Joel whenever his help might be needed. Ever since the trial, he and Sam got together about twice a month. They would go fishing or take long walks. Gradually, Preston learned the ways of the reservation. Sam told wonderful stories that Josie hounded Preston to retell as soon as he got home.

Sam also came to Miltonberry often. He and Preston would spend many hours sitting on a couple of folding chairs on the pagoda that Preston had constructed years ago on the Namekagon, down by the pumphouse. The pagoda was built to offer shade for family picnics and as a platform for the children to dive from into the brown river waters. Press and Sam often sat and chatted while they fished and watched water striders, and dragon and damsel flies. One such day, Sam told Preston his secret: that he was Harold Morris' son.

It took Preston a minute to absorb what Sam had said before his outburst, "My God, that makes you the half-brother of Richard Morris!"

"That's right, but Richard knows nothing."

"I can't think of two people more unalike!"

"The only time I have ever seen Richard was at the trial," Sam said. "I've never even heard him talk. Richard didn't have to testify, you know.... My father thought it best that Richard not find out. He was afraid of how Richard might react."

"Yes, I can imagine.... I don't know Richard either, but if his reputation is anything to go by, I can't say I want to know him," said Press.

"Please don't tell anyone. The only person who knows is my

wife. None of my children know."

Preston was sincere in saying, "Your secret is safe with me...." After thinking for several minutes, he added, "Perhaps I shouldn't say this, but I have some suspicions about Richard—suspicions that I wish I could clear up." Preston proceeded to tell Sam that he thought Richard was instrumental in causing both the warehouse fire and the bursting of Toto's earthen dam on Milton Flowage. He also told Sam about overhearing Richard's conversation with Sarah during the trial lunch break.

Sam listened carefully but really had no information to contribute. That night, Sam stayed for dinner with Josie and Press. The evening sky in late June was still light, so Preston suggested to Sam that they walk down to the bog. When they approached the warehouse, Preston mentioned again the fire that they had there several years before, and his resentment and anger toward Richard.

"You've told me that you are not a religious man, but would you please listen to an old Ojibwe prayer that has always helped me:

> *Oh Great Spirit, whose voice I hear in the winds...*
> *I ask for wisdom and strength,*
> *Not to be superior to my brothers,*
> *but to be able to fight my greatest enemy, myself.*
> *Make me ever ready to come before you*
> *with clean hands and a straight eye,*
> *So as life fades away as a sunset does,*
> *My spirit may come to you without shame.*

~

ABOUT THE AUTHOR

Pamelia Barratt grew up in Chicago and spent summers on her father's cranberry bog in northern Wisconsin. After graduating from Smith College and receiving an advanced degree from Georgetown University, she taught high school chemistry in Washington, D.C. Later, while living in England, she earned a masters degree in Latin American Studies and, with her husband, went on to start a Non-Governmental Organization (NGO) in Bolivia that helps the indigenous Aymara. Recently she has worked as a journalist in San Diego. *Blood: the Color of Cranberries* is her first novel.

Made in the USA